Gold was the stuff of his dreams. Olympic gold medals. Soon he would have his own. His appointment with gold was eight months away, in the hot July days of 1984 at the Olympic Games in Los Angeles. As he ran up the mountain the vision of his gold medals grew until they merged into one gigantic sun that filled the night. The poison of fatigue filtered through his every cell. Yet his mind floated free of it all, floated upward to his golden goal.

Deep in his reverie, Marx did not hear the pounding engine of the truck as it rolled swiftly up toward him. The headlights were turned off. The man in the ski mask was at the wheel, peering intently through the falling snow. When he saw Marx, he aimed the speeding vehicle directly at the kayaker's slowly jogging figure . . .

HAMMERED GOLD

William Oscar Johnson

A STAR BOOK
published by
the Paperback Division of
W. H. ALLEN & Co. Ltd

A Star Book
Published in 1983
by the Paperback Division of
W. H. Allen & Co. Ltd
A Howard and Wyndham Company
44 Hill Street, London W1X 8LB

First published in the United States of America
by Pocket Books, 1982

Reproduced, printed and bound in Great Britain by
Hazell Watson & Viney Ltd, Aylesbury, Bucks

ISBN 0 352 31342 0

PART I

November—December 1983

NOVEMBER 22, 1983
Hintertux, Austria

Snow fell in a vertical curtain through the night. There was no wind, but the snow itself made a soft hissing sound. The steep road through the village was empty except for the stubby figure of the kayaker, Friedl Marx, and the night was serene except for his pounding feet and rasping breath. He jogged heavily through the darkness and the snow.

Friedl Marx had four miles to go on this, his second ten-mile run of the day, four miles more up the mountain road to his training cabin at the 10,000-foot level. As always he wore hiking boots with extra weights strapped to his ankles. A rucksack containing fifteen pounds of weights hung on his aching back. He could not run fast, but it was not speed

3

that he was after. It was endurance, the capacity to move onward through walls of pain.

As he ran Marx examined the specific points of pain in his body to be sure he was dealing himself only the precise portion of punishment necessary to improve his condition and no more. Everything was fine. He found his agony to be routine.

He loped past the Gasthof Munchen, the only tavern in the village. Amber rectangles of light glowed through the gauze of falling snow, and he could make out the shapes of two trucks parked beside the road. He heard muffled laughter and knew that the grooming crews from the ski area were celebrating their night's work with beer and schnapps. Though he did not slow down, he glimpsed a movement outside the gasthof door. He turned his head to see a tall man wearing a long dark overcoat and a black ski mask. The man seemed to be watching Marx. As Friedl jogged by, he heard the man curse noisily as he turned to struggle with the doorlatch. Just another drunken mountain goat, Marx thought scornfully.

He ran on. The drunks in the gasthof were many meters behind him now, a universe away. Darkness was a comfort, and the falling snow formed a protective curtain around him. Snowflakes accumulated in thickening layers on his watch cap, on his sweatsuit, on his rucksack. Each flake added its infinitesimal new burden to his pain and weariness, and Marx loved each one for its tiny contribution to. his dream.

As always during these last terrible uphill miles he began to dream of quite another climb. His mind became fixed on his ascent to a pinnacle where no fear, no shame, no pain, could follow. He was a dull man, unimaginative as a mule in his goals, relentless as a plowhorse in his labors. All romance, all fantasy, had been beaten out of Friedl Marx years earlier by the fat fists of his drunken father. He dealt now only in unmistakable reality. Even his dreams were objective, earthbound, relentlessly simple.

Gold was the stuff of his dreams. Olympic gold medals. Soon he would have his own—one, two, possibly even *three*. His appointment with gold was eight months away, in the hot July days of 1984 at the Olympic Games in Los Angeles. Friedl Marx knew himself and knew the men he would compete against, and he was not worried. He would be the best that day in 1984. It was true that the Russian Michaelov was almost his match, but he was the only kayaker in the world who was close, and Marx could not imagine that even Michaelov would be in such exquisite condition as he. Even now—eight months away from the Olympics—he was hard and fit, as disciplined as a Trappist. At the world championships in October he had entered all three events. He had won two and was second in the third. No one had ever performed so well. It was possible that someday Friedl Marx would be proclaimed the finest athlete ever to perform in his obscure sport.

As he ran up the mountain the vision of his gold medals grew until they merged into one gigantic sun that filled the night. Pain still charged his body. The poison of fatigue filtered through his every cell. Yet his mind floated free of it all, floated upward to his golden goal.

Deep in his revery, Marx did not hear the pounding engine of the truck as it rolled swiftly up toward him. The headlights were turned off. The man in the ski mask was at the wheel, peering intently through the falling snow. When he saw Marx, he aimed the speeding vehicle directly at the kayaker's slowly jogging figure. The front bumper slammed violently into Friedl Marx's back. The impact flung him high in the air. His head was dashed against a tree trunk before he flopped down into the snow.

The truck slid to a stop, backed up, and the man in the ski mask descended from the cab. He moved quickly to

Marx's body. The kayaker's spine had snapped, his skull was crushed. Yet his body continued to twitch grotesquely in its death throes and his powerful heart still pounded furiously. The killer knelt by Marx, calmly placed his fingers on the throbbing jugular and waited while the pulse turned ever more feeble and at last stopped. This took several minutes.

The dead man's sweat was turning to frost on his clothes and in his hair. Snowflakes clung to his clothing. The man in the ski mask lifted the dead man by his sopping armpits. Friedl Marx had been thick-muscled, husky, yet the man dragged his body easily through the snow to the center of the road. The weights in Marx's rucksack clanked when the man let the body fall onto the road.

The killer stood for a moment surveying the scene. The snow was falling so heavily that the track made by dragging Marx's body was covered in minutes. Satisfied, he climbed into the truck and drove away. The headlights were still turned off.

An hour later two drinkers from the Gasthof Munchen weaved their truck up the mountain. When it hit Friedl Marx's body, the truck lurched up in a terrible bump, throwing the two men high off their seats and slamming their heads against the ceiling. Dazed and frightened, they stopped the vehicle and stumbled out into the snowstorm, where they found the dead champion. One tire had made a ghastly track across his back. Assuming they had killed him, they fled.

Around dawn, just after the snow had stopped, a ski patrolman on his way to work found the body lying face down on the road. Six inches of snow lay like a goosedown comforter over Friedl Marx. In the serene gray morning light he seemed merely to have fallen asleep.

Friedl Marx's death was entered in police records as a hit-and-run accident, but the two drunks were stricken with guilt and before noon that day they turned themselves in and confessed.

Marx had been a world champion, but few people, even in his native Austria, paid much attention to kayakers no matter how great they were. He was neither missed nor mourned by the world at large. Naturally the small, far-flung community of Olympic-class kayakers took serious note of his passing, but not one of them mourned Friedl Marx either. Indeed, in the intensely egocentric and predatory world of the athletic elite, his death was more reason for celebration than for grief. New room at the top had magically, blessedly appeared.

The following evening, in his lodge room at the ski area, the killer of Friedl Marx quickly scanned a succinct two-paragraph report of the kayaker's death, which was buried deep in the afternoon paper from Innsbruck. There was no shadow of doubt about the conditions surrounding Marx's demise: it had been officially classified an accident.

The killer dropped the newspaper to the floor and with a light step moved to the telephone. He dialed Lufthansa in Munich and in good German inquired about the schedule of flights to Rio de Janeiro.

NOVEMBER 27, 1983
Chicago

Ordway stood high on the rim of Iceman Stadium. The wind off Lake Michigan gnawed at his face like chewing teeth. Tears brimmed over and flowed down his cheeks. He brushed his eyes and lowered his gaze to the crowd gathered in the stadium below. They stood on the seats, facing up at him, worshipping him like a living idol. There were thousands of them. All gawked up at Joe Ordway, at the famous craggy face and tall figure, at the man they had adored and hurrahed for more than twenty years as the magnificent Joey O.

He toasted them with his cognac-laced coffee, winked, and grinned. They responded with a massive flutter of a thousand arms. The gabble of their excited voices was carried to him by the wind.

The mikes and lights and cameras were in place behind him. The crew had been in the process of setting up their equipment on the stadium rim for most of the morning. Now it was late, after 12:30, and so far they had shot nothing. Ordway glanced at his watch and called sharply to the director, "Look, I *have* to be in the studio in an hour. How the hell can you shoot a whole commercial in an hour?"

The director, a slim, hatchet-faced young man wearing jeans, a cowboy hat, and a sheepskin coat, looked at Ordway coolly. "We have it in hand, old man," he said. "We had to wait for the crowd to gather. Don't worry. You'll have plenty of time to star in a perfect production."

His arch tone irked Ordway, but Joe shrugged and pulled the collar of his wolfskin coat higher around his face. The wind ruffled his hair, which was an abnormally deep chestnut-brown color today, newly dyed to hide the spreading streaks of gray at the sideburns and temples. It made him feel like some foolish old hambone actor trying to look like a young stud again. He had argued, even threatened the people from the advertising agency. But they insisted that the image of Joe Ordway they wanted in this first commercial for the Joey-O candy bar was that of a dashing tough guy who was not aging, not even *middle*-aging. They wanted him to look like the quarterback supreme he had been in his prime. They wanted him to look like the Joe Ordway who might, at any moment, take a big bite of that candy and then lope onto the field with that long, elegant stride of his, chewing his candy bar just as he chewed his famous bit of gum—and *take charge*.

Ordway had argued that he had never dyed his hair for any of his other commercials, nor for the weekly National Football League telecasts for MBC. Who was he supposed to be fooling? He was forty-four years old, going on forty-five in six weeks. You could look it up in the NFL records, in *Who's Who*, in any newspaper morgue in America: born January 13, 1939.

Ordway removed a glove and ran a hand through his hair. It felt like straw. Well, hell, the dye could be washed out. And, as the agency people told him, it wasn't everybody who had a candy bar named after him. It was like being given a Congressional Medal of Honor, even more rare. There was the Baby Ruth and there was the Reggie Bar. Joe Ordway was the only other American sports hero in the twentieth century with enough stature to rate his own candy bar. The agency people told him this enthusiastically. Obviously they expected him to be excited, too, but Ordway was only mildly impressed. His ego had been massaged, inflated, and nicely cared for, for close to twenty-five years now. He had had plaques and medals, trophies, ribbons, photographs, and silver dishes given to him in recognition of his greatness. He had had books written about him, even a bad movie made about him and starring him. He had eaten, drunk and traded jokes with governors, movie stars, astronauts, Congressmen, and every U.S. President in office since 1960. Women threw themselves at him. People recognized him everywhere. His face was better known to Americans than all but a couple of dozen others on earth. He had glowered, grinned, glistened with sweat, from the covers of *Life*, *Time*, *Newsweek*, *People*, ten times on *Sports Illustrated* alone. Joe Ordway had been lionized for close to a quarter century, so a candy bar didn't really make much difference in terms of ego gratification.

Of course, there was the money, but even that scarcely mattered since he had made so much. And there was the slightly more subtle matter of his television image. He no longer played his game, so there was the problem of constantly refurbishing what the flacks and merchandising geniuses at the MBC network called his "immortality factor."

The director strutted about among the TV apparatus like a very young field marshal. He spoke loudly, sarcastically, imperiously, directing many of his remarks to himself as if he were the only one who could comprehend the intricate workings of his complex mind. He ordered a set of flood-lights turned on and Ordway was bathed in blinding white-ness. The crowd below cheered. Joe closed his eyes in pain. The director studied the setup, then said, "Now, the *pièce de résistance.*" He climbed a ladder to peer through a cam-era set high up on a scaffold. The director ordered more lights to splash over the crowd. Another cheer went up.

The director grinned smugly. *"Cinéma vérité.* Art! God-damn art!"

Ordway disliked him enormously. He disliked most of the young men he met in television, particularly those in the "art" of directing commercials.

"Okay, old man," said the director to Joe, "say the em-blem line, Big Joe—'Eat a Joey-O and be full of go.'"

Ordway said glumly, "Eat a Joey-O and be full of goo."

"Very funny. And, ah, you . . . ah, the girl . . . ah . . ."

A very pretty, very blonde, very young model hurried up shuddering with cold. She stood beside Ordway. "Cheryl," she said in a tiny, high voice. "My name is Cheryl."

The director shrugged. "Yeah. So, you stand next to Big Joe, Shirley, and when he says 'Eat a Joey-O,' you take a bite. You can do that, right?"

The model nodded. She hunched her shoulders and shiv-ered. The fur of her coat rose to circle her pink angel face. Ordway looked down at her. He said, "Really cold." Small talk was not his specialty.

The model presented him with a pretty smile that dis-played a sea of small, perfect teeth. "Cold as a nun's twat," she said.

They squinted into the lights. The director looked through the camera and spoke in awe to himself: "God, that's bril-liant." Then to Ordway: "Okay, Big Joe, hold up the candy."

Ordway held it up.

"Speak your piece, Big Joe. Nice and clear."

Ordway said the words loudly: "Eat a Joey-O and be full of go."

"Eat it, Shirley," said the director.

The model bit into the candy with her lovely teeth. Taffy strings pulled from the bar as she lowered it and fell onto her chin. She said, "Oh, shit."

The director cried, "Cut! Goddamnit!"

The model's voice was shrill. "How the hell do you eat one of these fucking things?"

The director was furious. "Goddamnit, Shirley, don't actually bite it. The fucking taffy will string out every time. Suck it. Suck! Think of your last blow job, dear."

The sweet-faced model's eyes widened in anger. She sneered, "Go fuck yourself, asshole."

Ordway turned away from her, sighing. She reminded him of Mimi Manning, the movie actress who had been the worst of his three wives. She, too, had a face like a sexy baby Tinkerbell and she, too, possessed the vocabulary of a street walker.

Ordway absently watched the tiny figures of the players moving around the football field. Footballs flew, some in the long graceful arcs of forward passes, others in sharp-angled peaks against the freezing sky as the punters sent up an assortment of towering spirals.

It seemed so familiar, so comfortable down there. Comfortable? Well, no. On cold Sundays like this, he recalled, he had invariably been down there with his teeth chattering like dice in a cup, shuddering so badly that he could scarcely utter an understandable sentence. His fingers always felt like frozen sausages. His toes were always cold. Ordway saw no heroism in it, not even courage, certainly not immortality. It had simply been his fate, his talent, his blessing—or his curse. He once added up every NFL game he had ever played for the Chicago Icemen. The total was 201—*201!*

A lifetime. He had been told many times that football

games were analogous to war, that nothing short of combat
tested a man like the weekly battles in the National Football
League. When he was very young, Ordway had thought it
might be true.

The director's voice was ragged with irritation. "Let's
try it again, and look, Shirley Sewer-Mouth, keep that stuff
off your chin this time. Suck, don't bite—just like you
learned from Daddy."

"Fuck off!" cried the model.

Ordway said sharply, "Lay off, you two! I have exactly
forty minutes before I have to be at the press box for the
pre-game show."

The director ignored Ordway. He turned to the spectators
carpeted below him and spoke into the amplified bullhorn.
"Okay, folks! Wave the candy bars over your heads and
let's hear it." He began conducting like a cheerleader with
one arm, chanting into the amplifier: "Joey *OH* go-go. Joey
OH go-go . . ."

The multitude picked up the chant in rhythm with him,
rising thunderously in volume. "Joey *OH* go-go. Joey *Oh*
go-go . . ."

Half an hour later Ordway's fifteen-second part in the
commercial had been shot and reshot a dozen times. The
model had accomplished her role with only a few muttered
obscenities between her and the director. Ordway quickly
unfastened his lapel microphone. He would have to fight
his way through the crowd to the MBC press box studio
halfway around the stadium. A flying wedge of eight stadium ushers waited to help get him there on time.

He felt a light touch on his arm. He turned. The baby
face of the model gazed up at him. Her voice was feathery
and sweet.

"Joe, I *never* bite in real life. Only candy bars. Can I
show you?" Her tongue flicked once over her lips.

Ordway said wearily, "Stick to candy bars, Cheryl.
Maybe they'll sweeten up your mouth."

As usual he was nervous to the point of nausea over the upcoming television show. His pre-game jitters were every bit as bad as they had been when he played football here for the Chicago Icemen.

He glanced down at the field. The players were gone. A line of long-legged women was doing a spirited but clumsy kick-dance on the fifty-yard line. They were the Ice Maidens, a combination harem, sorority, and pep squad for the team. They kicked their stockinged legs in a manner that was meant to be as precise as the chorus line at Radio City Music Hall. In fact, it was a very ragged, rather comic facsimile, but it mattered little. Ice Maidens were selected for their sunny smiles and shapely bodies. But the players noticed neither when they trotted grimly through the ranks of Ice Maidens before a game. Ordway remembered what it was like when he ran down that gauntlet of lipsticked grins and voluptuous figures: the Ice Maidens could as well have been the slats in a picket fence for all he had seen— including the Ice Maiden who had been another one of his wives.

He glanced at his watch. Ten minutes to air time. The ushers formed a beefy phalanx in front of him. They descended a flight of stairs into the crowd. They had trouble moving. Ordway shouted, "Let's *go*, damnit!" The ushers bowled into the crowd. There were cries of dismay. The ushers surged ahead, shouldering through human beings like threshers in a field of wheat. Ordway bellowed, "Hurry!" He pushed against the ushers' backs and they began swinging their fists. People responded with anger or fear. Some returned the punches. But then when they saw Ordway's familiar face, they relaxed. They smiled. They cried in delight as they reeled before the force of his escort. "It's Joe! It's Joey Ordway! Go, Joey O!"

Rio de Janeiro

Ernesto Diaz had finished his workout. It did not matter that it was Sunday. He worked out every day at the pool. The medicinal flavor of chlorine in his mouth was as familiar as his own saliva. As always his eyes were like red beads from the effects of the chemical. And as always he was deadly weary through his shoulders, his lower back, and his calves. His left shoulder hurt from an ugly misdive and a bad entry. Yet in his abdomen he felt a comfortable sensation, a general loosening that he knew would soon resolve itself into increasing relaxation throughout his body. The satisfaction he experienced after such a grueling workout was not unlike the easy pleasure that followed sex.

Ernesto moved with lithe strides out of the warm after-

noon sunlight at poolside and into the cool gloom of the
locker room. He slapped his coach on the back and said in
Portuguese, "Is it perfect or not?"

Ernesto's coach was a small bald man with a severe
countenance and, as usual, he spoke harshly. "It falls short
in many places. Your pikes are not symmetrical; you are
floating rather than piercing the air. It is not *close* to perfect."

Diaz knew better. The coach's words were merely a
transparent, stupid attempt to goad him. Ernesto said
sharply, "You know that is not true, you old mule. I was
beautiful today."

The coach turned away. He was a tough disciplinarian
who would rather cut out his tongue than reward his charge
with a compliment. Diaz baited him some more. "You know
that you saw gold medals flashing with every dive today!
You old goat, you know I missed nothing."

The old man raised an eyebrow. "Not the bent knee in
the pike? In *all* pikes? Not the fall that wrenched your
shoulder?"

Diaz grinned and shrugged. "It was a tiny error. I would
be a god if I did not have a slight imperfection. It is only
human."

"You cannot be human and win four gold medals in Los
Angeles. You must be a god."

Diaz flashed in sudden anger. "Goddamnit, can't you
ever talk about what is good as well as the things that are
bad?"

The old man's face was impassive. "You have calisthenics. Do them."

The old man slammed the locker room door. Diaz was
fuming. Who was better than he? Who in the world? Who
had worked harder? Who had taken more punishing blows
from the water in order to perfect the most difficult dives
ever performed? Diaz passed a mirror and glanced casually
at his body. He saw a taut, magnificently contoured figure.

Lithe, muscled shoulders; a tight, broad chest; long, tapering arms; a stomach ridged with muscle; straight, graceful legs . . . a perfect male physique.

No wonder he was a champion. No wonder the girls adored him, fawned over him, took every opportunity to touch his silken skin. No wonder they loved to rub their thighs against his when they sat beside him at the pool. Diaz did not linger before his image in the mirror. He was no narcissist. He needed a physique like that in order to perform his dives, not to perform before himself in a mirror.

Ernesto went to a mat on the locker room floor and began his stretching calisthenics. This involved a total immersion in tedium. It required trancelike concentration to exercise and stretch each separate set of muscles in his body. He went at it with grim resignation, grunting and sighing as much from boredom as from exertion. Forty-five minutes later, his body was glistening with sweat. He was panting hard. Exhausted, he stripped off his bathing suit and entered the shower. The dead weight of fatigue began to wash away as the warm water sluiced over him. By the time he had dried himself with a large, rough towel, his skin glowed and his muscles were loose. His mind was reviving with lovely thoughts about enjoyments that lay far outside the regimen of a world-class diver.

Ernesto felt a familiar restlessness come over him, accompanied by a surge in his groin as he considered the possibilities that awaited him.

Of course, there would be girls waiting in the cafe at the corner. If he went there he would have a cool drink then he would dance. The girls would adore him, for he was the best dancer of all. Ernesto Diaz was only eighteen, to be sure, but he was a young man of such style and dash and magnificent good looks that he was already a hero to all of Rio.

Ernesto dressed carefully and moved quickly into the street, where the traffic of the city rushed by. He had worked

so well today. He had dived so beautifully. Surely he deserved a special reward, something more exciting than the
girls in the cafe. He could go to the house. Why not? He
did not have to pay; it was all free. They loved to give him
the run of the house, his choice of partner—or partners—
at no cost because he was Ernesto Diaz, the beautiful and
manly Ernesto Diaz.

The cafe lay to the right down the brightly lighted avenue,
but Ernesto turned to look to the left for a moment. Carefully
he surveyed the street to see if anyone he knew might be
watching him. When he saw no one he recognized, he
hurried toward the dark neighborhoods to his left.

One person watched him go, a stranger to Ernesto Diaz.
He was tall and wore dark wraparound glasses and a black
skipper's cap. As soon as the diver was out of sight the tall
man hurried to a phone, dialed, waited, then muttered two
words in Portuguese: "Raid it."

Half an hour later Ernesto Diaz was lying nude on a bed
in the back room of a small house in a shabby residential
neighborhood several blocks from Rio's lighted main ave-
nues. Two men were with him. Their naked bodies were
large and hairy and coarse looking. Ernesto was moaning
with pleasure as one of the men rolled his tongue around
and around the diver's erect penis. The other had arranged
himself in a position so that Ernesto could reach his genitals
with his mouth.

For a moment nothing could be heard but the moist
sounds of oral sex and groans of joy. Then the door exploded
open and the tiny room filled with uniformed officers. Two
of them repeatedly fired flashbulbs as the terrified Ernesto
and his desperate companions struggled to untie their unholy
knot. One officer bellowed in righteous rage, "You are all
under arrest for sodomy! For running a house of prostitution!
Animals! You are the foulest brutes on God's earth!"

The police soon enough realized that one of the foul
brutes was none other than the beautiful Olympic diver and

national hero, Ernesto Diaz. They were stunned. They might
have let him slip out the back door, his perversions unre-
corded, but it would have done no good. Nearly every
officer on the police force in Rio was on the payroll of one
of a half dozen sensational journals, each of which paid
them well to leak precisely this kind of lurid information.
Ernesto's indiscretion could never be kept quiet.

In all, two dozen men, customers and prostitutes, were led
to waiting paddy wagons. The tall man stood in the gathering
crowd. His black skipper's hat was pushed back on his
butterscotch blond hair. His dark glasses reflected the spin-
ning dome lights of police cars and the bursting of photog-
raphers' flashbulbs. When he saw Ernesto Diaz come into
view, he grinned. Diaz's face was glistening with tears. His
beautiful eyes bulged in shock and despair.

The tall man stood watching as the police wagons rattled
away into the night. His next destination would be Rome.
He only hoped that his performance there would be as magnificent, as precise, as this one had been.

Chicago

When Ordway arrived in the press box studio, he had a little more than one minute to spare. He hurried past the cameras and was greeted by the voice of Johnny Magnuson, his director, who was watching his arrival on a monitor in the control trailer down in the stadium parking lot. There was relief in the disembodied voice as it emerged from a ceiling speaker: "You're cutting it mighty close, kiddo. That candy better be *real* good, Ordway, because that pipsqueak director of yours has got half the stadium snarled up with his lights and boom mikes. The whole crowd is crazy to get on TV. They probably won't even turn around to watch the game."

Ordway turned to the camera and threw up his hands in

20

resignation. He was too winded to speak and Johnny Mag couldn't have heard him anyway since he wasn't wearing a mike yet. A chuckle sounded from the ceiling. Magnuson said, "I hear the candy tastes like aardvark droppings."

Ordway grinned at the camera. Johnny Mag was one of his favorite people. The director was a tiny, rail-thin old bird, sixty years old, and only slightly larger than the average jockey. His appearance was deceiving, for he was a tough, much admired professional.

"Get up on your stool and try not to let the hangover show." Magnuson paused. "Joe, your face looks ninety, but your hair's nineteen. What the hell did they do to it?"

Ordway grinned sheepishly. A makeup woman came and mopped his perspiring forehead with a towel. She examined his hair as if it were a foreign object. A floor technician reached from behind him and fastened a small microphone around his neck. Now Ordway could speak to Johnny. He said in a winded burst of words, "They say you can't sell candy if you got gray hair."

"You don't even look like yourself. Can't you wash it out?"

"Yeah . . . I didn't have time."

"Okay. So you look nineteen for a day. You got thirty seconds. Get rid of the mink."

Ordway flung his wolfskin jacket on the floor and seated himself on his assigned stool. This placed him, as always, on the right hand of a mountainously fat man with a mane of thick ash-gray hair, white muttonchop sideburns, and a startling pair of huge black eyebrows almost as big as blackbird wings. He had gleaming green eyes and a powdery white complexion. This was T. Miles Cavanagh, known coast-to-coast as the Pope of Sport.

He gazed at Ordway curiously, then spoke in the slow, sepulchral tones that were his trademark. "You're sweating like a stevedore, Joey Boy. Have you been laying Ice Maidens under the stadium again?" Miles Cavanagh chuckled.

It was a quasi-falsetto sound, perilousy close to a giggle.
Then the celebrated bass voice rolled forth again. "It's no
way for an American paragon to act, Joey Boy." He chuckled that near-titter again, then reached over and ruffled
Ordway's dyed hair. "You look more like a ventriloquist's
dummy than ever, Joey Boy."

A floor director was counting off the seconds. " . . .
ten . . . nine . . ."

Ordway took a deep breath. It looked like it would be
a bad day. Cavanagh was plainly in one of his meaner
moods, and Ordway would have to be especially alert. The
dash through the crowd had left him huffing like an old
buffalo.

The floor director said, ". . . four . . . three . . ."

Ginny Graham peeked around the Buddha-like figure of
T. Miles Cavanagh. Her ripe scarlet mouth widened in a
dazzling smile. She waggled her long silver-nailed fingers
in greeting. Ordway smiled back weakly.

The red light on a camera flashed on. Thumping march
music sounded and the voice of a staff announcer in New
York boomed out of the ceiling, "The *NFL Now* is on the
air! Today, coming to you live from venerable Iceman Stadium in Chicago, where the Chicago Icemen meet the Pitts-
burgh Steelers in one of the crucial battles of the year. Here
are your *NFL Now* hosts—T. Miles Cavanagh, the Metro
Broadcasting Company's own Pope of Sport, with Ginny
Graham and the greatest Iceman of them all, Joey O!—Joe
Ordway . . ."

The music rose. Drums thundered. The brass hit a series
of piercing rhythmic shrieks. Ordway's head throbbed. The
music faded. The floor director raised a finger, held it upward for a second, then pointed at Cavanagh.

The Pope of Sport kept his gaze lowered for a long
instant. Then slowly, dramatically, he raised his large head
until his eyes could be seen shining fiercely from under his
grand black brows. He said nothing for another tick of time

that seemed interminable. His pale cheeks were now bright
with two ruddy fever spots. His green eyes were like emeralds. A writer had once described him as looking like a
cross between the Wizard of Oz and Walter Cronkite.

At last Cavanagh spóke. *"This* is Chicago!" He opened
every football telecast with the identical portentous phrasing
that Edward R. Murrow had used to introduce his famed
radio broadcasts from Europe in the late 1930s. (*"This* is
London!"*) He went rumbling on: "This is a day of reckoning
written in the football Doomsday Book from the beginning
of time. This is a day when Thor hurled thunderbolts high
into the ùniverse and they fell to earth here in Iceman Stadium on the cruel winter shore of Lake Michigan . . ."

Joe Ordway tried to concentrate, hoping he would not
miss his cue when—or if—Cavanagh ever gave it.

The Pope blustered on. ". . . the wind today is as vicious
as the 'desperate breezes of death' in Othello. As James
Joyce wrote, 'The day is as cold and mean as broken
glass' . . ."

There are no "desperate breezes of death" in Othello, nor
did Joyce write any such thing. As always Miles Cavanagh
invented such quotations on the spot, convinced that no
sports fan would ever know—or care—whether Shakespeare or Joyce or anyone else had actually said what Cavanagh claimed they said.

His pontificating irked a lot of people. Yet T. Miles
Cavanagh's talent for turning a vapid Sunday football game
into a couple of hours of eyeball-rolling theater had made
him an invaluable asset to the MBC network. In public he
was an unabashed crusader for all sports and all sportsmen.
He could speak of a a field full of football players as if he
were extolling the virtues of a flock of saints. It was an
oddly old-fashioned and worshipful approach to gamès in
the 1980s, the opposite pole from the tell-it-like-it-is school
of broadcasting. It was also totally cynical, for in private,
Cavanagh referred to athletes with blistering and often orig-

inal epithets, calling them "marionettes of avarice, puppets of commerce, toilet-trained apes . . ."

Of course, Ordway did not trust T. Miles Cavanagh. No one did. The man was moody and unpredictable, infected with subterranean angers and anxieties that surfaced in lacerating words. One never knew. . . .

Now, in tones of mock chivalry, Cavanagh introduced Ginny Graham as "our pretty priestess of the gridiron ritual," and she responded with the flirtatious, girlish helplessness that defined her television character. In fact, she was bright, ambitious, and cunning.

"Thank you, T. Miles," said Ginny, exhibiting her sweetest, widest smile. "Days like this make me just *wriggle* with the thought of how lucky we are in America to have this wonderful game. It is a blessing we should count every Sunday."

Cavanagh nodded sagely. "God's gift to America . . . sport." He turned to Ordway now. "And on my right hand, the man known simply as the American Paragon. You have worshipped him for many years . . . I have had the privilege of working next to him for several. . . . Today he is fresh . . . well, perhaps *not* so fresh . . . from a triumphant introductory commercial involving that greatest of all accolades available to American paragons. They have named a candy bar after him! The Joey-O! You look like they worked you pretty hard for that candy bar, Mr. Ordway. Deep lines, pale skin. Does having your own candy bar do that to a man?"

Ordway glanced quickly at Cavanagh. The man was in a treacherous mood, for sure. Ordway kept his voice as light as he could, though he was still slightly breathless. "I had to eat my own candy bar eleven times in eleven takes."

"Honestly now, Joey Boy, what's it taste like?"

Ordway said with a grin, "Sugar and spice and everything nice."

"Not like cognac? I thought maybe a Joey-O would taste like cognac."

Ordway's mind was blank; no clever remark rose to his aid. He said lamely, "No. Not cognac."

Satisfied that he had left a few bruises on Ordway, Cavanagh moved on to the subject at hand. "What do you think will happen this cosmic afternoon, Joey Boy? The Icemen have won eight straight after losing their first four. The Steelers, on the other hand, have lost their last two games. What does it mean, Joey Boy?"

Ordway was furious. He felt the blood pounding in his head, but there was nothing to do. With twenty million people watching, he had to go on pretending that he felt nothing but a powerful fascination for this upcoming football game. He spoke for a minute about the two teams. The floor director signaled him and began a countdown to the next commercial. A large board appeared beneath the camera lens, lettered with the cue to introduce the scheduled sales pitch.

As the count reached four seconds Ordway finished a sentence, but instead of reading from the cue board, he concluded sharply, "Mr. Cavanagh?"

The Pope of Sport did not even have time for a glance at Ordway. There was no way he could avoid doing the lead-in to the commercial. Cavanagh read in his slow pontifical tones, "Here is the food that pooches love, feed them Hy-pro and get a pooch smooch . . ." The picture of a small dog licking a man's face rose on the studio monitor as Cavanagh turned angrily toward Ordway. The spots on his cheeks were flaming now. "You sonofabitch! You *know* I don't do commercial leads! What are you—"

Suddenly a red telephone at the back of the studio began an almost inaudible buzzing. The crew at the cameras froze. Cavanagh's eyes widened. Ginny Graham shifted on her stool. The floor director scrambled over cables to pick up the receiver. He said softly, "Yes, sir?" He paused, then said to Ordway, "He wants you, Joe. Now."

Ordway hopped off his stool and went to the phone. "Yes, sir," he said. He felt very weary.

The voice on the phone was familiar, friendly, mellow with the remnants of a Maryland drawl. "Joe, you know— I *know* you know—that it is in the contract that *you* do *all* the lead-ins to the Hy-pro sells. It was sold that way. It is a matter of contract, Joe."

Ordway sighed. "I know it."

"We sell *you*, Joey, as much as the show. They pay extra for you. *You* are the voice, the style they want. Cavanagh can't get people up for dog food—or anything else. *You* can. You know that. Don't you?"

"I'm sorry, Robin. He just pissed me off."

The voice took on the reprimanding tone of an understanding but unhappy father. "Cavanagh is a child, Joe. A fat-assed child. An arrogant child. A highly intelligent child. But a child. Don't descend to his level."

Ordway could easily visualize the man speaking to him. Robin Booth, the president of the Metro Broadcasting Company, would be in his office at the network building on Sixth Avenue in New York. It was a large, very comfortable room with floor-to-ceiling windows that looked out on the skyscrapers of the competition—CBS's Black Rock and ABC's glass column. Booth would be lounging with his extremely long legs on his desk, leaning back, a model of angles in repose in his black leather Eames chair. His soft white hair would be a bit unruly, his glasses raised above his smooth, high forehead, his shirtsleeves rolled halfway up to reveal bony wrists and sinewy forearms covered with silvery fur. His lightly freckled complexion would be noticeably radiant due to the exercise of power that this phone call symbolized. Ordway liked Robin Booth, liked his direct, down-to-earth approach to problems and people, his common sense, his general air of relaxation and calm amid the frenzied environment of commercial television. Booth was Ordway's mentor and good friend. Their association went back more than twenty years. Of course, this call on the dread red telephone amounted to a public put-down: the network president never called except to issue a reprimand. But Ordway knew it was justified.

Ordway said, "Don't worry, Robin, I'll sell the goddamn dog food." He hung up. The show was on the air again, and he raised himself carefully onto his stool beside Cavanagh. The Pope turned to Ordway as if he had been sitting there all the time and said, "Joey Boy, Bradshaw seems to go on, season after season, despite the vagaries of age and the debilitation of physique. Why is this? No man is immune to old age. You succumbed. You grew old and inept. Why not Bradshaw? Is it that he doesn't drink—unlike so many of you? Is it his abstemiousness? Or is it his born-again Christianity among so many heathens?"

Ordway felt a flush climbing into his cheeks once more, but he held his temper. "He's thirty-six, and thirty-six is not exactly the age for the wheelchair, Miles. I'll be forty-five in January and I actually carried my own suitcase through an airport last week."

Cavanagh grinned wolfishly. "But may I point out that you threw no touchdown passes last week."

Ordway laughed. "Never even touched a football, Miles . . ." Suddenly things were moving more smoothly. He felt in charge now. The lethargy and fatigue of the hangover had lifted. He felt stronger, able to handle Cavanagh's rips and ripostes. Ordway said easily, "No touchdown passes, but I stayed up till after eleven o'clock at night a couple of times and I even skipped my warm milk." Ordway did not leave an opening for Cavanagh to reply. He was relaxed and casual, yet he spoke in crisp, authoritative sentences. He finished his dissertation on the life expectancy of quarterbacks, did a brief analysis of the strengths and weaknesses of the two teams, then told a humorous anecdote

about an Icemen–Steelers game in 1971. He finished it
precisely at the moment the floor director raised his fingers
and began the count to the next commercial. As effortlessly
and naturally as he had ever dropped back to throw a pass,
Joe Ordway read the commercial lead-in: "Winter weakens
your battery. Take the sputter out of winter. Use a Full-of-Life
battery . . ."

DECEMBER 11, 1983
Rome

The church was clammy and dark, its stones so steeped in the chill of the Roman December that they spread waves of cold air. Enzo Pavone knelt at the base of the image of the Virgin and said the first fifty of the three hundred Hail Marys he had vowed he would recite each day until the Olympic Games. He tried to keep his mind on various religious visions he knew he should be contemplating at such times, but even as he murmured on . . . *Hail Mary, full of grace* . . . his attention kept returning to the pulled tendon at the back of his left thigh. As he knelt in the cold of the church at the Piazza del Pozzo, he could feel no actual pain although he thought perhaps he could sense some stiffness. Or possibly it was his imagination . . . *Pray for us sinners now and at the hour of our death* . . . He tried to bring his mind back to visions of angels or of the Virgin herself . . . *Hail Mary, full of grace* . . . It was very difficult to concentrate.

Possibly the dankness of the church itself was causing the tendon to stiffen. But he could not stay away from the church no matter how it might affect his injury. There was no other way to assure God's guarantee that the gold medal in the 1500 meters would be his in Los Angeles. Anyway, he knew that the injury was not serious. It would clear up in a few days. He knew his body well, especially his celebrated legs. . . . Yet there *was* just that flicker of pain when he extended his stride, just enough to cause him to double his daily quota of Hail Marys this week . . . *Hail Mary, full of grace* . . .

Enzo Pavone finished and rose to his feet. With lithe, quick strides he moved to the front door and stepped into the piazza. His spirits rose immediately.

The rush of Roman traffic was muffled, far away across the piazza. The pace of the city was as frantic as ever, but where Enzo stood life moved at an even, easy gait. Two nuns strolled by. Some children played hopscotch. A few old people moved in the stately, patient pace of the aged.

Enzo breathed gratefully of the wintry air. It was, for once, a clear day and he exulted in it. His sweatsuit was light and he shivered, but he knew that in a few moments he would be well into his preparatory calisthenics. Perspiration would be flowing; his blood would be pumping quickly to warm his muscles, his bones, his very soul. Soon he would be moving with the easy grace of an antelope on his ten-mile morning run through the streets of Rome.

He felt the lovely surge of anticipation that always swept over him before he ran. He didn't like to admit it, but running actually seemed to reward him with a spiritual peace that his religion never quite attained. This knowledge worried Enzo, but it was true—he had come to love his running more than his God.

Enzo relaxed in the tranquility of the Piazza del Pozzo. Sweetness and gentleness seemed to permeate the place. It was a small square where few tourists came. Thus none of the hawkers and hucksters who infested Rome's larger piazzas ever appeared. As was his habit following early Mass and his first quota of Hail Marys, Enzo Pavone moved to a place beneath a plane tree. A few yards away two old men played chess as they did every morning. Enzo nodded and smiled at them; they ignored him as they did every morning. He began his warm-up calisthenics.

The nuns were new to the square and they watched him, smiling beatifically. They had seen Enzo Pavone kneeling earlier at the Virgin's feet inside the old church. Plainly he was a good Catholic athlete, a devout man who so loved his religion that he trained in the very shadow of his church.

Enzo began to sweat. The chill of the stones left his bones and a fine, familiar feeling began to spread through his system. It was something more than physical, this buoyant sensation. It reflected Enzo's pride in his position at the top of his sport. It reflected the joy he felt over the world record he had held for more than a year. It reflected the splendor of being an athlete, of being an Italian, of being a Catholic, of being the best middle-distance runner in the world. . . .

Suddenly the chess players looked up as if some clock had struck a special moment. Beyond the piazza, walking quickly on the cobblestones past the row of trees, came three men. Two were short, with rough features and wide shoulders. The third strode along in the middle and was tall, with a head of thick gray hair and the aquiline features of a Roman aristocrat. He wore an expensive dark suit, gleaming handmade shoes, a rich silk tie.

One of the chess players looked at his pocket watch and said to the other, "As punctual as Il Duce's trains."

The other nodded, his eyes fixed on the imposing central figure. "If his automobiles were as dependable as his religious habits, we would all be better off."

The man was Victorio del Pozzo, the minister of industry in the cabinet. He was also the owner of a dozen automobile factories throughout Italy. The two men with him were bodyguards. They had originally been hired to protect him against the demented hordes of political terrorists that had held Italy under siege during the violent years of the late 1970s. Time and again, fanatics had struck, kidnapping or killing leading politicians and industrialists. There had been a lull in these attacks lately; two years of relative peace had passed.

Each Sunday at this hour Victorio del Pozzo stopped at the obscure church in the square named for his family. He was a man of rigid habit, and even during the worst of the terrorism he had insisted on visiting his church on schedule. He had then been accompanied by as many as a dozen bodyguards—del Pozzo's Brigade they were called. But the force had been reduced as the danger decreased.

Enzo was so accustomed to these visits that he did not look up from his calisthenics as Victorio del Pozzo and his guards marched past. Suddenly he heard a hoarse cry of alarm. At the same instant the tranquil square exploded with the nerve-shattering sound of automatic weapons fire. A nun shrieked. Enzo saw four men kneeling low on the piazza behind del Pozzo and his guards. All were firing their chattering weapons at a level no more than two feet above the ground, aimed squarely at the legs of the cabinet minister and his guards. After two bursts of bullets the trio lay squirming and screaming on the ground. Their legs were shattered, spewing blood over the piazza stones.

Enzo Pavone was paralyzed with shock. He did not think to run. Suddenly his own legs caved in beneath him. He had a terrifying impression of heavy swift blows, as if cement blocks had been hurled with enormous force at his legs. But he felt no pain as he fell. Enzo saw nothing clearly, but he had the fleeting impression that one of the gunmen had turned quite deliberately away from the squirming bodies of Victorio del Pozzo and his guards and taken careful aim at him.

That night the newspapers of Rome were splashed with black headlines that told of the atrocity. There were photographs of the carnage and reprints of a hand-scrawled letter in which members of a hitherto unknown right-wing organization claimed credit for the shootings of the Minister of Industry. Most of Rome's front pages were dominated by this news, but all of them also prominently displayed stories reporting the fate of Enzo Pavone, the world-record holder for the 1500-meter run.

He had been gunned down accidentally in the attack, the papers said, an innocent bystander in this latest bit of politically inspired savagery. His legs were pulverized by the bullets; one knee had literally exploded. Amazingly enough, no one else in the square had been hit—not even two old men playing chess at Pavone's side.

Enzo Pavone would not die nor would the other three men, but all would be crippled permanently. It was a terrible fate for all of the victims, the papers said; but for the great runner, Enzo Pavone, the horror and the irony of the event was by far the worst—an athlete with no politics in his soul whatsoever, ruined in the capricious crossfire of a fanatic political attack.

New York

Robin Booth watched the telecast of the MBC weekly NFL game as it appeared on a huge television screen set into his office wall. As the telecast unfolded he watched uncomfortably as Miles Cavanagh sniped and snapped at his partners on air. Booth sighed. He had always known that Cavanagh was a foolish, vindictive man, as vain and thin-skinned as any ego-driven actor who ever walked a stage. After all, Cavanagh had been Booth's own creation. The man had been an all-night disc jockey at a 50,000-watt radio station in Tucson in the late 1950s. His deep, flamboyant voice, his stentorian way of introducing with grandiose language even the most foolish music of that foolish era, had appealed to Booth when he heard him one night on a car radio. Within two weeks T. Miles Cavanagh had been hired as the lead news commentator at the TV station in Baltimore where Booth, then barely into his twenties, was news director.

The two of them had risen almost in tandem. Booth went from Baltimore to the CBS network in New York, where at twenty-eight he became the number one producer for news, then a vice-president. He rose no higher at CBS so he moved to MBC. T. Miles Cavanagh had followed Booth to CBS, then to MBC, where he became a superstar whose face and voice and style were so well known that he was mimicked by nightclub comics from Las Vegas to the Catskills.

But now the time had come, Booth knew, to rid the MBC network of Miles Cavanagh. Publicly the man was a joke on himself. Privately he was as unpredictable as a scorpion. Booth had already begun to construct a plan that would lead to Cavanagh's demise. It required a certain subtlety, for as things stood now, any of the other three networks would sign Cavanagh if he were to quit MBC. Thus, Booth would have to destroy the man in such a way that he would no longer have any value as a public figure to anyone. Cavanagh's reputation would have to be so totally ruined that he would become a pariah.

As was his habit, Booth had made sure, many years earlier, that he knew exactly the point at which Cavanagh was weakest, that he knew precisely which thread to pull to unravel the fabric of his life. To Robin Booth, knowing a man's weakness was in many ways more important than knowing his strength.

Booth watched the screen as Joe Ordway spun an airy anecdote. The ex-quarterback was a dream personality for television. His delivery was casual, graceful, infinitely believable. Unlike Cavanagh, who had had to invent a public role for himself, Ordway was as natural as rainwater. He had required none of the intense coaching usually needed to lighten the lumber-tongued speech of neophyte athlete-announcers. From the start he radiated a magic that could not be learned.

It was their longtime friendship that had prompted Ordway to sign with Booth at MBC when he had retired from football six years earlier. The deal had been particularly appealing to Booth, for, like Miles Cavanagh, Joe Ordway, the American Paragon, also possessed a very valuable flaw, which Robin Booth had discovered early in their association.

Now the picture on Booth's screen showed a close-up of Ginny Graham. Her teeth gleamed as her crimson lips spread in a smile. Her carefully studied girlish charm wafted like a fragrance through Booth's office. He studied her face, a very beautiful face, and he fondly considered the things she liked to do with that lovely red mouth.

He placed his feet on his desk, sipped at a cup of black coffee, and settled back. A sense of well-being, something close to euphoria, enveloped him as he watched the lips of Ginny Graham. Then a buzzer sounded on his squawk box and Booth started as if he'd heard a shot. Quickly he removed his feet from the desk and snapped his long body to attention in the chair. Involuntarily he nipped up his loosened necktie before he flipped the switch. "Yes, sir?"

The voice was harsh and loud. "Let's get started."

Booth cleared his throat. "Started?" He had not expected A. J. Knox to be in his office on Sunday. It was not unprecedented but it was distinctly ominous.

"Come on up," said the chairman of the board. The squawk box went dead.

Booth stood up, tucked in his shirttails, rolled down his sleeves, and swung his blue blazer from the back of his chair to his shoulders. He shot his cuffs and straightened his tie once more.

Booth was not really frightened of A. J. Knox. But the chairman was a crusty and unpredictable old man, given to swift and arbitrary reversals of opinion and direction. He was particularly ruthless in his dealings with top executives. The one thing that Robin Booth feared most at this stage of his life was that A. J. might suddenly and capriciously decide to fire him.

It was the loss of neither money nor prestige that Booth feared. Booth had a dream. It was an unlikely dream for a man of his position and personality, perhaps an impossible dream. Though he was a shrewd, even cunning businessman, Robin Booth was also a sophisticate, a cultured man of refined tastes, an intellectual. And what he dreamed of doing was changing the very character of American commercial television. He wanted to revolutionize programming. He wanted to improve its quality to the point where it would add a new richness, perhaps even a touch of inspiration, to the lives of the American masses rather than insult them with the mindless fare they were habitually served.

If his colleagues had known of his dreams, they would have laughed in scorn and disbelief. He was forty-eight and his climb had been tenacious, unswerving, ferocious—even compared to the jungle predators of network television. At heart, he knew himself to be a dyed-in-the-wool idealist. But if Robin Booth was all that, he was also a pragmatist, and he knew that he had to solve the problems at hand before he could change the system. And he had not, so far, been able to raise MBC into the top position among networks. He had not yet had enough time. He knew that, and he had assumed A. J. Knox knew it, too.

A. J. Knox was eighty-two years old, but he was as tough and spry and vital as a man twenty-five years younger. His spine was straight, his stomach flat, his handshake dry and strong. He had the shoulders of a blacksmith. He had been born poor in Chicago, the son of a drunken bricklayer. He had sold newspapers on the streets, worked his way through college, became an engineer, and made a million dollars before he was thirty. He had bought the fledgling

MBC network in 1932 and was said to be worth two hundred million dollars now.

There was still an enormous supply of vigor in the old man, although sometimes it flowed with an unsteady current. His voice was strong and rich at times, even booming, but at other times it would weaken and fade, sounding as if it were coming across a great open distance. His glasses were thick; his vision had long been bad. Yet he could be as fierce as an old vulture when he was angry. His fists were like knobbed stones when he pounded his desk top. He had girlfriends even now at eighty-two, and as he confided to his cronies, "I still like to have my ashes hauled three or four times a week." His phenomenal physical condition was probably due to his youthful obsession with odd and extremely demanding sports.

His best event was the heel-toe walk, a horrifyingly painful sport that A. J. described with relish as "the closest a man can come to feeling the pangs of childbirth." He had also been, in his early twenties, the American All-Around champion. This was an agonizing competition in which each contestant was forced to perform ten separate events, all in a single afternoon, with no more than five minutes between each event. A. J. Knox was twenty-two when he won the United States All-Around title, and he was canonized on the spot by sportswriters who labeled him the Champion of Champions.

So it was with a dry throat and a sense of danger that Booth entered the sanctum of the Champion of Champions on this Sunday afternoon. He saw that the television set was turned off. "You don't want to watch the game, A. J.?"

"Hell, no. All those damned football games look the same to me. All that phony violence, armored up like some kind of gladiators. They're a bunch of overgrown children, banging on each other like yeggs in a street fight. Hyenas. Damned uncivilized."

Knox's sympathies had always lain with the solitary

mountain climber. "I'd rather watch *The Dating Game* than this football crap. It's insidious stuff, teaches violence, teaches mechanical obedience, teaches corporation thinking. It's a lot of crap," he grunted.

Booth said, "It's a lot of crap that makes a lot of money."

"Right. That doesn't mean I have to have it in the same room with me. Leave it off. It's your part of this goddamned operation and don't tell me any more about it other than how much it costs and how much it makes."

Booth was in basic agreement with the old man. His own interest in sports was largely a matter of corporate profit and competitive success. He found the majestic spectacles of American games neither intellectually compelling nor esthetically moving. Booth saw in the Super Bowl, the World Series, the Indianapolis 500, the Masters, only slightly differing ways for men to waste time and energy.

To the old man Booth said lightly, "There *is* a certain sameness to football games."

"Sameness! I'd rather watch an eagle flying in circles for an hour, same circles, same eagle, than watch an hour of this mechanized mayhem."

Booth sat down on a tweed-covered couch across a large Persian rug from the chairman's desk. An El Greco crucifixion hung on the paneled wall behind the chairman and the burning eyes of Jesus seemed fixed on Booth. He felt a flicker of déjà vu, something ominous revisited. Robin Booth had been president of the network for almost four years—forty-four months to be precise. He was handed the job at a similar Sunday afternoon affair in this very office in April 1980. The couch, the rug, the painting, the jade figures on Knox's desk—all had been the same. Only the cast of characters was different. In addition to Booth and Knox there had been Bill Sweeney, who was then the network president; Adam Milton, then executive vice-president for programming; Robert R. Smith, then executive vice-president for public relations.

The old man had sat in the same place. He had addressed the gathering in tones of pain. Sadness shone from his gray eyes. "Why in hell aren't you men helping? Why aren't you behind me? Why have you turned on me?"

The then-president, Sweeney, spoke in his expansive salesman's bass. "You know, A. J., we have all pledged to do anything . . . *anything* . . . for you and the network."

The chairman picked up a sheaf of computer readouts. "These are Saturday's overnight ratings. You have seen them?" All nodded. "You know that we are in *fourth* place again this week? We did not even rise to the level of the pap they're serving at NBC."

All nodded and Sweeney said, "It was the movie, A. J. We . . ."

The chairman waved his bony old hands. "How did this happen, you mush heads? Why are you doing this to me?" His rage and anguish filled the room as if a terrible wind had torn through the walls. He stood, his arms stretched out. His body seemed as filled with suffering as the one in the painting behind him.

Sweeney, the president, stuttered, "The movie w-wasn't what, w-what . . . we expected, ah . . ."

Milton of programming said, "It was two hours down the drain. . . . We took a chance . . ."

And Smith of public relations murmured in his silky way, "A. J., A. J., there was just nothing to be done. ABC had the Brighton Kids and CBS had High Plateau . . ."

The chairman snapped, "I know what was on against the movie, you rubber heads. I know what beat it. It's the same thing that beats it *every* Saturday! What I don't know is *why* you scheduled it."

Smith of PR said, "Maybe it was a mistake, maybe . . ."

"Maybe!" The chairman's roar was like an elephant's trumpet in that room. *"Maybe!"* The old man glared at

Smith. He pointed a long finger at him as if he were about to fire a rifle. When he spoke, his voice was soft and strangely distant.

"Get out," he said. "Please get out of here."

A. J. turned to Sweeney. "You, too." Then to Milton. "You, too."

Booth did not cringe. If the old man were to include him in the bloodbath, so be it. He would accept it stoically, with dignity. But he was not particularly worried that this would happen to him today. For one thing, he had had a most impressive run as vice-president of sports and news at the network. He was his own man and his career was in no way connected with the careers of the other three men. He had kept it that way on purpose, knowing Knox's tendency toward overkill in dismissing executives. More to the point, he had written the board chairman a confidential memorandum no more than a week earlier, suggesting that the use of movies on Saturday nights had come to have a progressively negative effect on MBC's overall standing in the ratings. Booth had done a bit of arithmetic and discovered that the network would have bettered its standings by a point or two each week if it had managed to finish better than fourth on Saturday night. He had suggested starting a news-magazine show in those critical hours.

Knox had not even acknowledged the memo, yet Booth could see before him now the carnage that it had triggered.

Sweeney said pleadingly, "But, A. J. Why? We're making money. We've never had more profits piling up. Why?"

The old man was quivering with anger. "Profits? Anybody can make a profit in this business. There's so damned much money out there waiting to buy time we could sell commercials if every day was forty-eight hours long. Profits? Shit! An orangutan could make profits on a television network. What I want are *ratings!* We've been third for five years, fourth before that. I started this business when I was thirty years old. I have owned it for fifty-two years and goddamnit, I know when I've got fools running it for me. You're out. All three of you."

Sweeney looked up sharply. A vein pumped visibly in the middle of his forehead. His eyes were bright. "Three?" He looked at Booth. "There are four of us here."

The old man sat down, clasped his hands together on his desk top, and said, "There are three of *you*. And there is one of him. He stays. He's the president. You three are out."

Everyone assumed, of course, that Booth somehow had engineered the massacre, and he let them believe that. The fact was, Booth had had no clue that the old man was about to perform such a massive execution. He was not even pleased to be pushed into the top spot so quickly. He would have preferred that it happen after the old man had retired or died. A. J. Knox's capriciousness and quick temper were legend. Being president of MBC under his chairmanship was to occupy an exposed and dangerous position.

Booth had gotten along well enough with the old man for these past forty-four months. But now he could feel the icy winds of A. J.'s impatience beginning to whip about his ankles. MBC was still third in the ratings on an annual basis, although the network had climbed into second place for a month or two at a time. It was a significant improvement on the past, yet the old man was growing more and more testy. Fortunately Booth still held one ace that should be good for at least another eight months of tenure: the 1984 Olympics in Los Angeles. He had bought the rights to the Games in the spring of 1979. It was an enormous project and an enormous gamble. No one else at the network knew as much as Booth did about the technical and economic operation of those three weeks of telecasts. He had manipulated things so that he alone controlled the essential reins of command for all Olympic operations—from commercial contracts to construction of the broadcasting facilities in Los Angeles. He had carefully channeled all the details through himself, creating an operational labyrinth so complex that only he fully understood it. It was his insurance.

Now the old man said, "Is there any hope at all, for Christ's sake, that this network will be number one?"

Booth said flatly, "Not this year, A. J. No hope at all."

"Okay. I know that. What about next year?"

"You know about that, too. We *could* do it. It all depends on the summer . . ."

"The Olympics."

"The Olympics. If we get the ratings there, we should be able to promote the fall programs, build up expectations, get people in the habit of watching us during prime time. We will have a damned good shot at moving up."

ABC had done exactly that a few years before and the strategy succeeded so well that it had become textbook television theory. ABC had attracted enormous audiences for its telecasts of the 1976 Winter and Summer Olympics. It had then saturated the Games coverage with endless plugs for other ABC prime-time programs. The combination of millions of viewers suddenly growing accustomed to tuning into ABC for the first time, plus the hard-sell promotion of programs many viewers had never heard of before, had worked to put ABC into first place for the first time in years. NBC had hoped to accomplish something similar with enormous prime-time coverage of the Summer Games in Moscow in 1980. It might have succeeded, too, except for the United States boycott of the Moscow Games.

"You paid three hundred fifteen million bucks for it," said the chairman. "It damned well better give some return. Everyone thought then and still thinks you're crazy. Or, more to the point, that *I'm* crazy."

Booth sighed. "It is a gamble, but you know damned well we figured it was worth it."

"I just wonder if we had to go so high. Three hundred fifteen million dollars. Christ, Robin, that was sixty-five million dollars higher than anyone else."

"We didn't have anything going for us except money at that point. ABC had done all those Olympics before. They had the horses, everyone was familiar with them. Sure, the Olympic committee knew me. They knew I was tough, that I had the NFL, some baseball, the college football programs. But they wouldn't have let us have it unless we hit them with a high dollar. The Olympics is the crown jewel, A. J."

The old man shook his head. "It's nothing but politics in short pants and sneakers. I hate to be a party to it. But goddamnit, we have to make something out of it now." He paused. "Look, Robin, I'm telling you right now, either this network is flying high—number one or close to it—by this time next year or your name is mush." He looked at Booth closely. "I like you, you know that. I like the way you think, the way you talk. You've got a lot of style and you're a pragmatist. But you have to deliver something more than you have so far, see? I want MBC up there—and you have one year to do it."

When Booth returned to his office, he turned on the television. The heavy face of Miles Cavanagh loomed huge on the wall before him. Booth grimaced in distaste and turned off the sound as the man began to speak. Getting rid of him was all-important. Cavanagh had to be forced out by the start of the Olympic Games in July. It might take some time, but he was certain that he knew how he could best guarantee the ruination of the Pope of Sport.

PART II

February 1984

FEBRUARY 9, 1984
St. Petersburg, Florida

She introduced herself to Ordway during the taping of one of those god-awful celebrity superstar competitions that he detested so much. She was tall, with short, curly, dark brown hair. Lively blue eyes gazed out at him with engaging frankness. Her voice was warm and lilting. "Mr. Ordway, I'm Maggie O'Rourke. We haven't met, but Robin Booth said I should just walk up and say hello."

Usually Ordway was attentive to pretty women, but he looked at her bleakly. He wanted to go home. He had just finished a segment acting the jocular play-by-play commentator for a particularly cretinous competition in which two television actresses ran fifty yards while bumping balloons aloft with their chests. There had been much giggling and jiggling from the actresses, accompanied by heavily suggestive humor and much show of festivity among the bystanders. He stared in cold silence at the woman and her smile dimmed.

She spoke more tentatively, "I wanted to interview you about—"

"Are you with a paper or what?" Ordway interrupted. "Interviews are supposed to be cleared through PR."

Her face clouded. "No. I'm writing an article. I . . . talked to—"

"Look, I'm sorry," he said sharply. "I can't sit down and talk with you right now. I'm very busy."

Now her voice turned sharp, too. "Yes. I just watched you being *very* busy with a *very* important sports event. Which pair of boobs won?"

He scowled at her. "What the hell kind of crack is that?" Ordway had come to befriend a few select journalists, but very few, and his instinctive reaction to all others was to go on the defensive.

Maggie O'Rourke tried to keep her temper. "That crack was just to get your attention. I tried to tell you that I talked to Robin Booth about this last week. He also told me just this morning that he had mentioned it to you."

It dawned on Ordway. "Oh, God, I forgot about it. Yes, he mentioned it."

He and Booth had had lunch a week earlier during which they discussed many things, and some time in the course of the meal, Ordway now recalled, Booth had asked him, "Do you know the name Margaret Anne O'Rourke?"

Ordway replied absently, "She's some kind of a writer."

"Some kind of a writer, all right. She's a tremendous novelist, a brilliant essayist, and a hell of a journalist. I've known her for years."

"Okay. So?"

"She's doing an article on the state of the American hero.

It's going to be a book eventually. She asked me if you'd be willing to, as she put it, 'sit for a hero's portrait.'"

"Hero's portrait? What the hell does that mean?"

"Maggie has this theory that heroes today aren't anything like what they used to be. No military types, no Boy Scout lifesavers, not many firemen-save-my-child types. She says heroes are now mainly addendums to technology or public relations. Like astronauts. Or television personalities. Or rock stars. Or sports superstars. Which, of course, is where you come in."

Ordway had stated bluntly his reluctance to get involved in such a project, but Booth had been persistent. "Do it, Joe. She's a smart woman. You might learn something about yourself. Also, it will be good for you, good promotional stuff, to be part of something classy like a Maggie O'Rourke essay."

"She might just cut me up and leave me for dead," Ordway said. "I never scored very high with English majors."

Booth had reassured him—and then the discussion had slipped Ordway's mind. Now he said to Maggie O'Rourke, "I'm sorry I was rude. Robin did mention you. We'll get together. I promise."

"When?"

"I can't do a damned thing until tonight. I'll call you, okay?"

Her smile widened. "Wonderful!"

Ordway made himself another cup of cognac-coffee and went listlessly back to work. The show was called *Galactic Celebrity Games*. It was a two-hour prime-time program that MBC broadcast every six weeks. It involved two teams of show business personalities competing in a series of mindless relay races. Each contest was fraught with suggestive byplay and witless wisecracks. The silliness of its format was beyond description, yet it consistently drew high ratings.

Now there was only one more of these shows on his contract and Ordway was grimly determined not to renew. Today, however, he had to do it.

Maggie O'Rourke looked on with a small curious smile while Ordway began to tape the opening segment. The script included an interview with a "team captain," a notoriously lewd nightclub comedian named Lyle Bluff. Ordway's first line was to ask the man what his team's "strategy" would be. Bluff smirked and said, "First we get Monique's chest in the balloon race. That's first. That's also second and third and fourth and . . ."

Ordway smiled woodenly and read his lines. "That's your whole strategy? Monique's chest?"

The comedian put on a serious face, pulled his baseball cap down to his nose, and said, "Well, I've been thinking about that, about 'strategy,' I mean. And I can't tell what I'm going to do because I don't know what the word *means*. . . ."

These lines were met with deserved silence by the few bystanders allowed on the set during the shooting. A storm of yuks and guffaws would be dubbed in later in New York. After the interview with Lyle Bluff, Ordway turned to the other team captain, Red Holt, an aging western movie star. Ordway asked him about his "strategy" and Holt said, "We'll just head 'em off at the pash, I mean pass." His seamed face broke in a wide, floppy grin. He winked, belched, and said, "Sheeit."

Ordway struggled through the taping, an ordeal that took ten hours. When it was over he was drained of all strength and most of his self-respect. He had not seen Maggie O'Rourke for hours and he sighed with relief. Maybe she was so disgusted that she would now leave him alone.

At the hotel he found a note under his door. "Joe: I could not stand to watch a decent man suffer such indignities a moment longer. You were noble, but helpless. I eagerly await your call. M. O'Rourke."

She sounded friendly, thought Ordway, but he did not feel friendly, not in the least. As always after a day's immersion in *Galactic Celebrity,* he felt soiled and unfit for human company. He decided that he would call her and cancel out.

Before he could do that, his phone rang. The producer of the *Galactic Celebrity Games,* a particularly officious young man, was on the line saying that the whole crew and the contestants were expecting Joe at a big "fun" cocktail party and dinner within the hour. Ordway was, of course, the major attraction, the producer said. "They all want to get to know you a lot better, Joe. Especially Monique." The producer's leer almost hissed through the phone.

Quickly Joe replied that, no, damnit, he wouldn't be able to come because he had this longstanding dinner date with this Maggie O'Rourke, the writer. Robin Booth had insisted on it and there was no way out, no way at all. When Ordway phoned Maggie O'Rourke, he said, "First drinks, then dinner. And I promise no balloon-bouncing races."

She laughed. "I'm really looking forward to it. Seven in the bar?"

When she entered the bar, he noticed how attractive she was—genuinely attractive, too—not like the girls on the set. Her blue eyes were sparkling, but he also could see a slight air of coolness, a tightness about her. When she reached the table, she was frowning. "Look, Joe, I've been thinking about this and I'm sorry you feel that you're being forced to do this. You don't have to, you know. Robin Booth made it sound as if you were enthusiastic about the project."

Ordway could not hide his surprise. "He did?"

She spoke gently, but her disappointment was clear. "He didn't tell me the truth, did he? You weren't even a little bit interested in doing this with me, were you?"

Ordway frowned and sipped at his drink. What could he say? She was looking at him with a quizzical smile. He

knew she had to be in her late thirties at least. Undoubtedly
she was the most elegant woman he'd spent time with in
ages. She wore a burgundy wool dress and a string of pearls;
her legs were long and slim but seemed poised for flight.
He decided to tell her the truth.

"You're right. Robin lied. First of all, I don't want to
be made into a hero. I'm a retired quarterback who makes
a living sometimes doing that dreck you saw me doing
today. Second, I really don't like doing interviews with
writers because I almost always find that they hear me say
things that I just don't remember saying. Third, I have a
feeling that you and I probably don't even speak the same
language—"

She quickly interjected, "What language do you speak
that I don't speak?"

"Well, I read one of your books once and I didn't understand much of what it was about. So I guess that's one
language I *don't* speak."

Her eyebrows shot up. "You did read one of my books?
Which one?"

"The one about a women's college."

"Organized Lives."

"I guess so. I barely remember it at all except there was
some kinky sex. Fairly raunchy stuff at the time. That's
why I read it, I suppose."

She smiled and said, "It was, ah, ahead of its time a
little. It was my first."

He shrugged. "As for the language I do speak—I can
remember every touchdown pass I ever threw, the yardline,
the position of the receiver, the position of the officials, my
blockers. If I try, I can remember every player on the field."

She leaned forward, genuinely interested. "Can you
really? That's the way it is with great chess masters. They
can tell you every move of every piece they ever made from
the first game they ever played."

He was baffled. "You think I'm like a chess master? That's about the *last* thing I'd compare myself to. . . ."

She laughed lightly. "No, no, no—you're not like a chess master, not at all. They are the world's craziest people. I lived with one for a little while—" She stopped, embarrassed.

He filled the silence. "Well, I've never even met a chess master, let alone lived with one." He paused, then turned and smiled at her. "But then I've never met a woman who is a *tremendous* novelist, *brilliant* essayist, and *one hell of a* journalist till now either." He emphasized each adjective with a stentorian flourish. She looked at him, puzzled. He explained, "That's what Robin called you. 'Tremendous, brilliant, one hell of a'—all that."

She smiled. "He always does tend to overstate things, but thank him for me anyway."

"Okay. Now tell me exactly what it is you want to do. I'm against it right now. Convince me." He settled back, confident that she would not be able to change his mind.

She leaned forward, almost touching him. "Well, I will want to talk to you a lot—maybe thirty-five or forty hours of interviews, plus conversations with people who have known you, players and parents and coaches and girlfriends. And wives . . . are you married?"

"Not now. I was. Three times."

She said almost to herself, "Three times? Fascinating." It was as if she had come upon something unexpected but extremely interesting in a laboratory experiment.

She went on, her voice intensifying as her enthusiasm grew. "The idea is to produce the profile of a modern American hero. Mostly I want to do that through your own sensations and your own observations. Just what *your* perceptions of heroism are, how you value the rewards of heroism in the United States. Money, fame, and, of course, sex . . ."

"Of course sex?" said Ordway. "What do you mean, *of course sex?*"

"Well, you see, I think sex is a prize, like a medal, a decoration for today's heroes, Joe. I'm talking about it in a clinical fashion, not personal. I mean that sex is a very significant element in the psychological, physiological, and sociological definition of an American hero—especially a sports hero. Do you see?"

"Yes, ma'am."

"The point is, I want to find out what it means to *you* to be a hero under modern conditions. My theme is that real heroism in the 1980s is basically extinct. What we have instead is a kind of manufactured product that is divorced from genuine human values. Heroes are a product of technical achievement and corporate organization more than of simple human bravery displayed in the face of something daunting. For example, war heroes simply don't exist now. They were snuffed out for good by Vietnam. Do you see what I mean? The heroes of the sixties—the crusaders for civil rights, the kids fighting the Establishment, the war— are no longer current. The causes aren't sharply defined anymore. Good guys and bad guys aren't that easy to delineate."

She paused and smiled. "I'm just filling you in quickly here. It's much more complex. One of my main themes is that heroes don't sacrifice anything anymore. Mainly they just reap rewards—money, sex, celebrity. That's because we end up with heroes who are created by machines, by business, by the media. Astronauts and test pilots are nothing but functions of machines. TV manufactures heroes all the time—politicians sometimes, rock stars, talk show types. They aren't real, of course, they just *seem* heroic. And sports heroes—also totally unreal, artificial, *packaged.*"

Ordway was frowning and she quickly placed a hand on

his arm. "No, no, it isn't meant to be negative, Joe. I'm not accusing *you* of being artificial. It's just that your existence as a hero today in the 1980s is dependent on artificial means. Do you see? And I have dozens of questions. Do you need this status of being a hero? What obligations do you feel because of it? Oh, there are lots of questions. . . . Could you function *without* celebrity?" She paused. "That's what I want to write about." She stopped. Her eyes shone with excitement.

Ordway looked at her warily. He had no idea what his answers to such questions might be; they had never occurred to him. But suddenly he was more than a little curious. Of late he had felt confused by the turmoil in his life. He seemed to exist in a whirlwind, always traveling, always in a state of high tension and incipient fatigue. He knew he was drinking too much.

He looked at her. She was obviously a very lively, very intelligent woman. She wasn't a naive kid, she wouldn't be shocked by his stories, and her energy, her enthusiasm, her brightness, were contagious.

He said impulsively, "Okay, let's try it. Who knows— I might learn something, too. But here I've promised to reveal my deepest secrets to you, and I don't even know whether to call you Miss òr Mrs. or Ms. or what?"

"I've been Mrs. a couple of times but I am now Miss O'Rourke again. Maggie, to you. And I've already been calling you Joe. Is that okay?"

He said with a straight face, "No, I'd prefer it if you'd call me by my given name. Luther."

"Luther?" Her eyes widened.

"Luther. The name is Luther Joseph Ordway. Mother was a true believer."

"A Lutheran! People see you as this dashing, romantic hero with a thousand women's scalps on your belt—and here you are, nothing but a fallen-away Lutheran."

"Worse than that. A fallen-away *Missouri Synod* Lutheran from Blooming Prairie, Nebraska. Not exactly the home of famous men."

"Until you came along."

"Yes. Until I came along."

"Tell me about Blooming Prairie."

Ordway plunged right in. "It didn't ever bloom very much. Winters were fierce as hell. Snowbanks plowed up along the roads were higher than car roofs. Summers were scorching. Even the dirt seemed to get bleached in the heat. We had to drive twenty-five miles to the nearest town with a movie theater . . ."

Ordway paused, suddenly aware that he was comfortably launched in what would be a very long narrative. He chuckled and said to Maggie, "My God, do you realize that I am already well on the way to telling you my whole life story?"

Her smile was radiant. "That's exactly what you're supposed to do. Don't stop."

"I've never told my life story before. I didn't know it would be so enjoyable—especially on an empty stomach. Let's eat before I starve us to death with reminiscences."

Joe was pleased when, as they left the cocktail lounge bound for a restaurant, Maggie slipped her hand through his arm.

Munich

Horst Grunwald leaned against the wall and flexed the thick muscles of his back, stretching the powerful lumbar slabs along his spine, feeling the good pull through his wide shoulders. He stood at the back of the ballroom because that was the place he preferred whenever there was a public function. He did not care for the limelight; he did not seek the attention of others' eyes.

Indeed, even tonight—the last party winding up Fasching carnival week in Munich—he had refused to wear one of the wildly lavish costumes that so many of his teammates wore. Willi Dortmund, the hammer thrower, had come to the ball dressed as a rooster. Johann Neureuther, the shot-putter, came as a milkmaid. And Anton Bogner, the second-

best discus thrower in West Germany, was dressed as an
Apache dancer. Horst Grunwald wore his usual turtleneck
under his baggy loden jacket and corduroy trousers. His
only bow to the carnival masquerade was to wear a long
rubber nose with a black mustache attached to a pair of
artificial black-rimmed glasses.

Horst lifted the mustache so he could sip at his stein of
beer as he watched the swirling mass of guests at the ball.
There were perhaps five hundred people. Many of them
were athletes like himself, since this gala affair was spon-
sored by the local sports club. But there were also many
local celebrities—dignitaries from the city government,
clergymen, businessmen, as well as faculty members from
the university. At any other time of year it would have been
a docile, even dull gathering. But in the week of Fasching,
that traditional carnival time preceding the forty days of
Lent, all of Germany went wild. People seemed to abandon
their usual personalities. They became strangers and lunatics
in the frenetic celebration.

As Horst watched the revellers he saw many bizarre
incidents. A stodgy, straitlaced coach from his own sports
club did a very dirty bump-and-grind. A fat and ordinarily
pompous city councilor performed a jig so strenuous that
his face had turned red as a radish. One of the most pre-
tentious members of the university faculty, an expert on the
works of Spinoza, was dressed in a loose Greek toga and
giggled crazily as he repeatedly lifted his skirt to show that
he wore only a jockstrap beneath the garment.

Horst Grunwald chuckled merrily at such sights. He was
an uncomplicated young man, dedicated to throwing the
classic round plate, the discus. He held the world's record,
and he was the one member of the West German team
considered to have a real chance to bring back a gold medal
from the Olympics. He was a graceful giant of a man,
standing more than six feet five inches tall, weighing 265
pounds, and had the physique of a gargantuan Greek statue.

His shoulders were as broad as many doorways. His chest was fifty-four inches around while his waist was a waspish thirty-two. He was a magnificent sight to behold yet he was modest to a fault. He always wore loose and rather shabby clothing. In winter he pulled a stocking cap down over his ears in a way that made him look slow-minded.

But that was Horst's way. He was a man of sports and he cared nothing about other things. He preferred to perform with a minimum of public accolades or rewards.

Now Dortmund appeared at his side. The hammer thrower, a man as massive as Horst himself, looked absurd with his rubber rooster's comb flapping over his forehead. Dortmund grinned loosely. His eyes were glistening, his cheeks aglow from the schnapps he had consumed. "Horst, old man, we will have a little surprise for you in a few minutes. Are you ready?"

Grunwald grinned amiably. "You will surprise me by laying an egg?"

"Not that, no, not that. Just wait here, my friend. Do not go anywhere." Dortmund giggled and vanished in the crowd. Suddenly Horst felt a powerful hand on each of his arms. He turned to see the shotputter, Neureuther, on one side and his fellow discus thrower, Bogner, on the other. Each was grinning foolishly, expectantly, at Horst. Neureuther handed him a tumbler full of schnapps. "Drink this, Horst, old friend. You will need it for what is to come."

Horst felt a stab of anxiety in his chest. Good God! They were going to name him King of the Carnival! He struggled instinctively, trying to break away. What a thing to do to him! What an embarrassment. How could they pull this sneak tactic on him, spoil his Fasching by turning him into a fool?

He said breathlessly, "I am to be King?"

Neureuther shouted in glee, "Your Majesty! Drink to yourself!"

Horst paused, considering the possibility of a charge to

the exit. No, he could not. There was no choice. It was
meant to be an honor. There was no way he could escape.
To prepare himself for the coronation, Horst Grunwald
drained the tumbler of schnapps in a single draught and held
out the empty glass for another.

He was on his third drink when he heard the booming
voice of Willi Dortmund introducing him on the stage. Horst
drained the schnapps and headed through the crowd. He
was staggering slightly from the alcohol, but instead of
feeling easier about the spectacle to come, he felt an increasing sense of foreboding.

Traditionally, as King of the Carnival, he was to be
subjected to a series of weird and mildly insulting shenani-
gans, all calculated to leave the drunken gathering howling
with laughter. So he was not surprised when they stripped
off his shirt and painted his splendid bare chest with the five
Olympic rings. Or when they threw a tattered cape made
of torn sweatshirts and dirty sweat socks over his grand
shoulders. A crown, entirely too small and cut from a coffee
can, was planted on his large noble head, and around his
neck they hung a bicycle chain from which dangled a toilet
seat painted a glistening gold as a comic symbol of the
triumph he would experience in Los Angeles.

They led him to his throne in the center of the dance
floor. The crowd began to prance and weave around him
in an intoxicated parody of loyal subjects paying homage
to royalty. Horst sat straight and tall, his great shoulders
squared, his spine stiff. The bizarre kaleidoscope of masked
and drunken people swirled around him faster and faster.
He continued to drink tumblers of schnapps and tried to
smile and catch the humor that seemed so contagious to all
around him.

But he could not. His face grew progressively more slack
and sickly as he became drunker.

Against a wall at the back of the room stood a well-
dressed man wearing the rubber mask of a mountain troll.

His eyes glittered through the eye holes and he kept them fixed on the increasingly melancholy figure of Horst Grunwald. The troll man's right hand remained in the pocket of his blue blazer and occasionally he moved his fingers about to feel the five small hexagonal pieces of steel he had there.

Shortly after midnight, though the party had not yet reached full crescendo, Horst Grunwald decided he could take no more. Without a word he suddenly rose from his throne and moved unsteadily through the crowd. At the edge of the dance floor he threw off the foolish costume of the king and put on his own clothes again. Automatically he replaced the mustached false nose and black-rimmed glasses on his face. Then he stumbled out of the hall onto the street. After a short search he found his car. He squeezed his bulk into the Volkswagen Beetle for the drive home.

Horst was too drunk to notice that a tall man wearing a troll's mask climbed into a Mercedes Benz and followed him down the street and out onto the deserted autobahn. Horst drove as if in a haze, speeding up to 120 kph on the broad sweep of the highway. He scarcely noticed when the Mercedes pulled up at his left side. When it did not pass him, he looked over blearily and saw that the driver wore a mask. Suddenly a blinding spotlight hit him like an explosion. His eyeballs felt as seared as if burned by a blowtorch. Instinctively he yanked his steering wheel to the right. Immediately the right front end of his little car dropped as the wheel flew off. The axle hit the autobahn surface with a shriek and a spray of sparks. The car tumbled into a series of end-over-end somersaults that went on for more than a hundred feet along the highway surface.

The Mercedes stopped briefly by the silent, crumpled remains of Horst Grunwald's car. The searing spotlight illuminated the driver's window. It revealed in its glare the bloody face of the dead discus thrower. He was still wearing the false nose and outsized glasses. Satisfied, the troll man slowly drove away.

A mile down the road he stopped the Mercedes, removed the rubber mask, and flung it over the embankment. Then he reached in his blazer pocket and took out the five hexagonal pieces of steel. He rattled them together like dice in the palm of his large hand, then flung them—the five nuts he had removed from Horst Grunwald's right front wheelhub—far away into the night.

St. Petersburg, Florida

Ordway didn't quite know why, but the first story of his life that he chose to tell Maggie O'Rourke was the one about Jim Thorpe. He could have started anywhere, but somehow that episode seemed to rise to the surface immediately.

It had happened in the summer of 1950, when Joe was eleven. His mother had died that past winter. His grieving father bought a used Nash not long afterward and announced to Joey that the two of them were going traveling to California in hopes that new scenery and new faces would help them shake the grief and gloom of their loss. At the time Joey had never been more than a hundred miles away from the hamlet of Blooming Prairie.

"California was like going to the moon," said Ordway.

"Compared to Blooming Prairie, *everywhere* seemed romantic and mysterious. The highway was a little local road
with almost no traffic. Trains went through sometimes, but
they never stopped. The depot had been locked up and
abandoned about the time I was born. To my way of thinking, California was the Garden of Eden. And besides the
trip itself, my father kept saying that once we got out there,
he had a really *big* surprise for me."

Ordway's father, Rollie, had been the opposite of his
dour, religious mother, a bluff and hardy man, big-shoul-
dered and broad-chested with a seamed face that split constantly in a grin as big and pearly as a quarter moon. He
was a born optimist despite the fact that he'd been raised
in desperate poverty and had never succeeded at anything
he'd tried.

When Luther Joseph Ordway was born in the depths of
the winter of 1939, Rollie promised himself and anyone
who would listen that his son's days would be grandly
different from his own pinched boyhood. To Rollie, sports
represented the big difference—the big *American* difference—between being deprived and being well off. To him,
sports symbolized the one most precious thing he had never
enjoyed as a child: freedom—freedom to spend time or
energy or thought or dreams on something besides bleak,
crushing, eternal hard *work*.

"You have to realize," said Ordway to Maggie O'Rourke,
"that my father wasn't really a sports *fan*. He hardly even
knew the rules of most games. When he threw a ball, he
was awkward and clumsy, like a girl, because he had never
learned how as a kid. But he liked the way sports worked.
He liked the clean definitions of who won and who lost,
the fact that rules were unmistakable, and that men could
become legends. Most of all, he loved stories about how
sports had given some born-dead-broke guy a chance to
develop into someone great, someone heroic, I guess you'd

say. That's where Jim Thorpe came in—the Great American Success story."

His father's smile beamed for hours every day during the trip to California, but on this particular afternoon it seemed brighter than ever. He was driving the Nash along a narrow highway outside Los Angeles. Palm trees and low flowering bushes lined the road. The rich land of the valley was carpeted green with crops on both sides of the road. A sign indicated that they were about to enter the town of Lomita. Rollie Ordway's wide grin erupted into an excited chuckle. "This is the place, Joey! *This* is the place! You'll never forget this day. I guarantee it!"

Joe was desperate in his pleas for his father to reveal his splendid secret, but he refused. "This is going to be bigger than any birthday, Joey. Bigger than Christmas!"

They stopped at a gas station. The attendant came to the car window, but Rollie Ordway got out and insisted that they talk quietly several yards away. When he returned to the car, his smile was slightly dimmed. "I can't believe he doesn't know how to find the place," he said.

They made four more stops at gas stations, then another at a small, ramshackle grocery store. This time, when Rollie Ordway came out, he was beaming again. "I know how to find him," he declared.

"Find *who?*" Joe was almost beside himself with curiosity.

His father's grin widened. "Okay. We're going to visit the man who has been named the greatest athlete of the first fifty years of the twentieth century. They elected him that officially, you know, Joey. The sportswriters. He lives here in this town. You know who he is?"

Ordway was almost dizzy with excitement. His voice was barely audible. "Jim Thorpe? We're going to visit *Jim Thorpe?*"

"You bet your boots!" His father's voice boomed with

pride. "He lives right down this road. The greatest athlete who ever played any game! *Every* game!"

Joey had been hearing about Jim Thorpe from his father since he was a baby. The magnificent Indian athlete, born dirt-poor and sickly in a shanty in Oklahoma, had grown up to excel at every sport he ever played—an Olympic gold medalist in the decathlon; a rugged, swift halfback; a slugging outfielder; a man who had become a legend before he was thirty. No athlete alive—or dead—could match the versatility and excellence of Jim Thorpe. Joey had been shown dozens of pictures of the great man over the years. He was tall, lean, with wide shoulders and a deep chest, long muscular legs, the noble, classic features of Indian royalty. Rollie Ordway had spun homilies for hours about how Jim Thorpe was living, breathing proof of how sports can ennoble and enrich even the poorest lives.

The town of Lomita lay behind them. They were in the country again, and Rollie Ordway turned the Nash off the concrete highway onto a gravel road. They drove by a few squalid shacks and trailers.

"They said his name is on a mailbox," said Rollie Ordway. "Keep an eye out for it once we get past this rundown stuff."

The road became rougher, more twisting. The dwellings showed no signs of improving. Then Joey saw a rusted mailbox perched on a spindly post. Almost illegible, but unmistakably scrawled on the side, was the single word, "THROPE."

"Dad," he said, "could that be it?"

"'Thrope'? That's not it. It's *Thorpe!*"

Beyond the mailbox was a decrepit house trailer. It sat on the rusted rims of its wheels. The sides of the trailer were peeling. A screen door hung by one hinge at the entrance. A cement block served as both step and front porch. The yard was littered with rubbish, tin cans, tires.

Rollie Ordway drove past, on up the road until it came to an end at a dried creekbed. Sadly he turned around and said to Joey, "Maybe we better check that fellow Thrope."

Joey was beginning to experience a terrible sinking sensation. He said, "Let's not stop, Dad. I doubt that it's his house anyway."

"I'm sure you're right, Joey, but I'll just ask whoever it is if they know where Jim lives. They might be some kind of illiterate relatives or something."

Flies buzzed in and out the open door of the trailer and there was no sound inside. Rollie Ordway banged on the side of the trailer. "Hello! Anyone there?"

There was silence inside. Joey's father stepped up on the concrete block and stuck his head around the side of the door. "Hi, there!" he shouted. "Hey! Wake up, can you? I'm trying to find Jim Thorpe. Can you help?"

Joey heard a deep sighing sound, then soft incoherent murmuring. He heard a thump on the floor of the trailer, the sounds of movement. His father stepped back off the concrete block. "Sorry to wake you, sir," he said. "Sorry, but we really have come a long way to see Jim Thorpe. Can you help?"

The open doorway filled now with the figure of a very fat, drunken man. His skin was coppery and his hair was black. His face was bloated and shiny, his nose was swollen, and his eyes were puffed and bloodshot. Down the front of his soiled workshirt were stains that may have been vomit. His fly was unbuttoned, his trousers were too long, and the frayed, filthy cuffs covered his feet. The man swayed in the doorway. He braced himself with one hand on the frame and reached down with the other hand to scratch his crotch. He seemed oblivious to the man and the boy standing before him.

Joey's father went on explaining, trying to maintain his friendly smile, talking brightly. "We saw the name Thrope

on the box, and we thought you might know where Jim
Thorpe can be found. We thought you might be a relative,
sir."

The man's terrible red eyes seemed to focus on them for
the first time. He opened his mouth and produced a tremendous belch. He brushed one hand through his still jet-
black hair. He licked his cracked lips with a tongue that
seemed dry as sand. Then he spoke. His voice was thin and
the words were slurred. "You want see me? You got money?
Coshts moola t'shee Jim Thorpe."

He held out a hand. The fingers were stained deep yellow
from nicotine; the palm was scarred with a deep cut that
was infected. The hand shook as if it were a leaf in a violent
wind. Joey stared in horror at the man. Rollie Ordway's
smile had vanished now and he could only gulp,
"No . . . no . . . but, no . . . no."

Desperately Rollie Ordway dug into his pocket. He
pulled out a wrinkled dollar bill. Without taking his eyes
from the ravaged face, he placed it in the shaking hand.
Then he took Joey's arm in a tight, painful grip and hurried
him to the Nash. They left without looking back. After a
silence of perhaps ten minutes they reached the main highway. Rollie Ordway turned to his boy and said, "That wasn't
Jim Thorpe, Joey. That was not Jim Thorpe by any stretch
of the imagination. You don't believe it was, do you?"

Joey said no, he didn't believe it was. But he knew in
his sinking heart that it was Jim Thorpe for sure. He shuddered as if he had been hit by a blast of winter wind. His
father looked at him in concern, then put his large, gentle
hand on the boy's head and ruffled his hair. "That wasn't
Jim Thorpe, Joey. That was just some crazy drunk suffering
from DT's and delusions of grandeur."

Of course, two years later the last doubt was laid to rest
when the great athlete died and all the obituaries began by
saying that he had died alone and penniless in a broken-
down house trailer on the outskirts of Lomita, California.

When Joe finished, Maggie O'Rourke's eyes shone with sympathy.

"What a shock."

He nodded slowly. "It was like seeing a ghost. I had nightmares about it, but you know in some ways it bothered me more as an adult than it did when I was a kid. In fact, that vision of Jim Thorpe haunted me most when I started getting too old to play."

"Did it really?"

"Jim Thorpe really *was* the greatest athlete this country ever produced. It doesn't take a neurotic imagination to understand how fragile an athletic career is. Some guy once said that every professional athlete dies twice—the first time when his body dies because he's too old to play anymore, the second for real."

"Did you actually feel as if you were *dying* when you had to quit playing?"

"Worse, in a way. Real death can be sudden. This was like having an incurable disease that kills you very slowly. For years my reflexes were so good that I never even had to think about what I had to do. I could pass, run, move where I wanted—all of it without a conscious thought. Then it started. I couldn't get out of the way of a tackler. I couldn't quite connect on a pass with a guy who was wide open. The fatigue after a game took two days to clear up, then three days, then all week. It was an entire aging process condensed into maybe three years. I changed from a tough, quick young man into the equivalent of a feeble old codger. I had to quit. I couldn't believe it."

"But you'd played sixteen years in Chicago. Wasn't that enough?"

"No. There had never been a time in my adult life when my idea of myself didn't depend on sports, mainly football. It was who I was. Sixteen years of it *wasn't* enough because football was all there *was* to identify me—not just to the public but to *myself*."

"And you saw yourself as another Jim Thorpe when you had to quit? A derelict thrown on the rubbish heap?"

"Not really, but the memory of that poor stinking old bum in the broken-down trailer haunted me." He looked at Maggie in grim surprise. "In fact, believe it or not, now that I think about it—it still does."

"You're not *really* worried you might still end up a drunk like that? You've made several million dollars, haven't you?"

"A couple anyway."

"So you aren't anywhere near being destitute and discarded like Jim Thorpe was. In fact, you're more famous and richer now than you were when you were actually playing, right?"

Ordway frowned. "I guess that's true. But sometimes after a day like this, playing sideshow barker to the freaks in the carnival, I feel a little like old Jim Thorpe must have felt. Ah, kind of empty, you know . . . misused . . ."

"Violated?"

"Probably that's too strong." He did not raise his eyes from his glass for a moment, then he looked up at her and rose from his chair. He sighed. "It's just a case of being depressed by some of the people in this business."

Yet as he followed Maggie out of the restaurant, Ordway was pleasantly surprised to find that he felt far less depressed after this day of taping the *Galactic Celebrity Games* than he ever had before. In fact, as he watched her stride in front of him, her hips swaying, he found that for some reason he was feeling *very* damned good.

FEBRUARY 14, 1984
Munich

Ivan Bulov paused for a moment to listen to the sounds of the golden-haired girl performing her post-coital ablutions in the bathroom. Then he returned to the newspapers. As he had known they would, the stories of Horst Grunwald's death had at first appeared everywhere on Page 1, a series of stunned, tear-soaked reports of the accidental death of this modest young German hero. Two days after he died there had been editorials—heavy, melancholy tributes and grand teeth-gnashing over the black irony that a man of such youth, such courage, such promise, had been cut down. Three days after he died the papers covered his funeral. Now, four days later, the outcry and the weeping was over,

71

and though he scrutinized every column of every paper in Munich, Bulov could no longer find any reference at all to the death of Horst Grunwald.

Of course, that meant that there was no suspicion over the cause of the accident. The missing nuts from the wheel-hub had not been noticed, and Bulov had once again performed to perfection. He moved to a mirror so he could gaze at himself. The mirror was on the bathroom door, and as he admired his image he could hear the golden-haired girl behind the door. She was humming happily—of course.

Bulov gazed at himself. Of course, he had satisfied the girl in bed. That was a result he never doubted, something he simply took as one of his many natural gifts. The endless success of his strange and lethal missions around the world was something else again. He was functioning with an efficiency and—yes—with a flair that were truly amazing. It was particularly astonishing when Ivan Bulov recalled that he had come to this calling out of quite another kind of career: hockey.

Not just any hockey player, of course. Ivan Bulov had been a great one, a hero known all over the Soviet Union for sixteen years. Hockey had been his life, utterly consuming. *For sixteen years!* It seemed absurd to think that he had committed himself so thoroughly and for so long to a mere game. Yet he had always known that his motives for playing well had sprung from something more basic than mere public adulation. He realized very early that hockey had been his means to guaranteed survival. As long as he played the game well, he was assured a life free of fear. True, he had been given what material luxuries the Soviet Union had to offer—his own apartment, a car, food tickets, widespread travel, fluency in several languages, but in Russia survival without fear is the most priceless luxury, and hockey stardom had been Bulov's protective armor, his insurance against fear. But, of course, he could not play forever. And now? Exactly what was he now?

K-1 called him an "executor of high policy." Considering the bloodshed and brutality of these missions, the cold bureaucratic impersonality of the term gave Bulov a certain comfort. Yet he could not see himself merely as a bureaucrat, not even a bureaucrat who executed high policy. He had been a sportsman too long. He needed a dash of romance, a bit of swashbuckle. Bulov had read doggedly through a couple of Ian Fleming's novels in English and liked to identify himself with suave, luxury-loving James Bond—another "executor of high policy," in his way.

In some ways Bulov saw himself as a very believable impersonation of Bond. He was tall, six feet three inches, and although his neck was perhaps thicker, his chest more bull-like, his shoulders brawnier than the more slender 007, Bulov's waist was small, his hips narrow, his legs long. His hair was thick and long. His handshake was strong and manly, his fists hard and quick. These things fit the image of James Bond nicely. But then there was the unfortunate matter of Ivan Bulov's face. It was true that he possessed a firm chin with a deep cleft, good ears set close to his head, and lips that were full and sensual. But his eyes were set a bit too close together, and they glittered out of deep recesses made by heavy Slavic cheekbones and a low, bold brow. And one could scarcely ignore the hockey scars—the ubiquitous crisscross tattings from sewings on some three dozen cuts, the dent on the left bridge of the nose, the clump beneath the right eye. And worst of all was the smile. Bulov's teeth had taken much punishment in his years on the ice. They had been broken, cracked, blackened, loosened, and extracted. Repairs were sufficient for utilitarian purposes—that is, the teeth chewed and bit nicely. But cosmetically they were unmistakably a product of Soviet dentistry, and when Bulov smiled, the array of metals—steel, gold, old silver, new lead—grinned out of his mouth like a ring of melted typewriter teeth.

His reverie was interrupted by a sharp knock on the door

from the corridor. Bulov spoke in French to the girl in the
bathroom, telling her to stay where she was. He put on his
dressing gown of rich brown velvet and strode with athletic
grace to the door. Expansively he threw it open. Bulov
knew he had nothing to fear at this moment—not from the
KGB, not from the German police, not from any other
source of unexpected revenge or secret betrayal.

Nevertheless, he was startled when he saw the small,
fidgety figure of Ludwig Scheibl standing in the corridor.
The familiar cherubic face was wreathed in a smile. The
spongy brown curls were arranged like a halo around the
balding pate. The rimless glasses shone as if reflecting the
pure light of innocence. Bulov knew they were part of
Scheibl's masquerade, as was his dark gray double-breasted
suit, which also generated a distinct, though totally erro-
neous, impression of good faith and honest business habits.

Scheibl bobbed his head rapidly twice, then drew himself
up to his full height almost a foot below Bulov and announced in German, "I've just come from Moscow."

Bulov replied sharply in Russian, "You have always just
come from Moscow, Herr Scheibl. Someday they will keep
you there and the world will be rid of another rodent."

This little man from Liechtenstein was never welcome
in Bulov's presence. For all his cherubic grins and beams
of innocence, Ludwig Scheibl remained engulfed in shadows. He called himself a sports impresario, dealing in everything from television rights to athletic shoe promotions. He
moved with a suspicious ease between East and West.
Everything he did *seemed* totally self-oriented and, therefore, *seemed* insignificant. Yet one had to suspect the worst,
for it was an unavoidable element of Scheibl's sleazy mys-
tique that he *might* be anything.

Scheibl's smile widened, but behind the glasses his eyes
remained cold, untouched by the expression on his mouth.
He spoke now in Russian. "Herr Bulov, I was surprised to

learn you were in Munich in February. It is an evil season. Raw, cold, wet."

"I travel where I must as a representative of Soviet sports." No one outside the Kremlin knew that Bulov was in Munich. How did Scheibl know?

Scheibl's smile grew speculative. "And to whom are you representing Soviet sports in Munich? May I guess?"

"You know, Scheibl, as well as I, that the International Wrestling Federation is meeting in Munich in three days. You know I attend all such international conferences."

"Yes. The wrestling I have forgotten."

Bulov shook his head. "You forget nothing. What is it you want?"

"I have been wondering how you are, Herr Bulov, that is all. So I ask, how are you?"

Bulov cursed and began to close the door. Scheibl quickly put up one small hand to hold it open. "In fact, Herr Bulov, I have a message for you from Moscow. It came indirectly, but I am told that you will understand the meaning. It is from Fraulein Natasha Penska, the former famous figure skater. She sends you her love." Scheibl paused, watching Bulov's expression.

Bulov managed to keep his face stony. It was seven years—more—since he had heard her name spoken. He had last seen her after the 1976 Winter Olympics, here in this very city of Munich. Bulov had blocked her out of his thoughts ever since. Now, against his will, he began to remember again the details of Natasha—her enormous brown eyes and the pale, oval face; her long, perfect legs; her sensuous hands; the gossamer body that turned so dense, so demanding during sex . . .

And much against his will he recalled the last night they had lain together, tense and trembling in the shabby hotel room here in Munich. He remembered the knock on the door. He remembered—oh, God, he had wiped it out so thoroughly for so long—how could he remember it so clearly now? He remembered the banging on the door in the early morning darkness, the figures filling the little room, the arc of the truncheon, her scream . . .

Bulov blinked and pulled himself back from that ancient nightmare. "*Who* sent the message, Ludwig? Who the hell told you such a disgusting thing to say?"

"Disgusting? To receive the love of a beautiful young skater—ah, sorry, a beautiful young *former* skater."

Bulov eyed Scheibl. Did he know the truth? Bulov's survivor's brain worked cautiously, trying to calculate the logic in this unsettling situation.

Of course, the message must have come from K-1. It could *only* have come from him. No one else knew. No one save Natasha herself, and she was in no position to send messages of any kind. Scheibl's message had to be a cold threat from K-1. But why? And why *now*? And why use Ludwig Scheibl?

Bulov's brain began to swim. There were so many questions. Certainly K-1 woud not trust someone like Scheibl with the truth about Natasha—would he?

Or was Scheibl, too, an agent of the KGB?

Or was he something even more important?

Could Ludwig Scheibl—this insect, this *germ*—could he be the mysterious "Gamesman" that K-1 had referred to in the summer of 1980 just before Bulov's missions began? Bulov could not bring himself to believe that. The smarmy Liechtensteiner was too unreliable, too mixed up in too many shady affairs. He might even be an employee of American intelligence. Or British. Or Chinese . . . or . . . or . . .

Bulov recovered his aplomb. All this speculation led into a trackless swamp, and he would have to find his way out later. He spoke in as brisk and controlled a voice as he could muster: "Thank you for the message. It is unexpected."

He turned to close the door, but again Ludwig Scheibl put one hand against it. In his other hand he held a four-day-old *Morgen Post*, which carried the story about Horst Grunwald on Page 1. He raised the paper to Bulov's eyes. "A tragedy, is it not?"

"Tragedy?" Bulov fought to keep his voice flat. "Yes, of course."

"Yes, of course. The death of a champion at the peak of his life, it is a tragedy certainly. No Olympics for this champion. No gold medals. A tragedy."

Scheibl went on casually, conversationally. "But then it is a tragedy for the whole of Eastern Europe, this coming Olympics. What athlete would attend the Games of the hated Americans?"

Bulov's mind was racing deeper into the swamp. What was this little bastard up to?

"Revenge deserves revenge." Scheibl smiled innocently. "An eye for an eye. An Olympics for an Olympics."

Bulov was exhausted by the anxiety generated from the man's smiling presence. "What is it you want, Scheibl? You have delivered the message from whomever it came, and now you wish to *chat?* I have company I prefer over yours in my room."

Scheibl cocked his head in a way that made his glasses gleam brightly. "Aha, yes. It is a certain French skier, then?"

Again Bulov was shaken. He had thought the affair with the golden-haired girl was a secret only the two of them shared. He managed to speak quietly: "Skier? She is a woman. That is all that is necessary."

Scheibl shrugged. "All women are not equal. This one, I suspect, is a rather splendid specimen."

Bulov replied coldly, "I have no interest in your judgment of women. Good-bye."

Scheibl said, "I shall see you at the wrestling meetings."

Bulov sneered, showing two rows of clenched metal. "I shall avoid you, Herr Scheibl—at all costs and at all locations."

Scheibl shrugged. "Perhaps you will be able to avoid me. Perhaps not."

He turned and walked quickly down the corridor, looking back once over his shoulder to see if Bulov had remained at the door.

Bulov sighed. He would never be able to avoid Scheibl— his role as promoter, producer, agent, impresario, and middleman in almost every international sport made their meetings inevitable. Ivan Bulov's official position as the Soviet government's diplomatic athlete-emissary to the International Olympic Committee, as well as a dozen worldwide sports federations, would always place him in the same vicinity as Scheibl. For Bulov, Ludwig Scheibl was as ubiquitous as air.

Bulov closed the door softly and glanced at his wristwatch. It was 7:30 P.M. Suddenly it struck him—as sharp and painful as a punch in the stomach: *this watch had been a gift from Natasha Penska!* She had bought it for him in Innsbruck in 1976. Until now, Bulov had been able to look at the watch dozens of times a day for all those years without thinking once of Natasha. But now her face rose before him. He saw the high color in her cheeks, lips moist and smiling, hair tousled as it was during sex. He shuddered as if he were confronting a ghost. She was probably not a ghost, for she was not dead, though he knew it would be better if she were. A wave of grief and guilt hit him so suddenly that he had to sit down on the bed. Blood pulsed through his head. He breathed shallowly, quickly. His stomach churned. He fought to regain control. Natasha was long gone. Ludwig Scheibl knew nothing. He was merely a bit player used by K-1 for . . . for . . . what? Bulov could not follow the labyrinth that was K-1's mind. What was he supposed to do now?

He stood up and began again to examine his reflection in the full-length mirror on the bathroom door. Suddenly the mirror swung away and the golden-haired girl stood before him. She had put on her makeup but not her clothing. Bulov's gaze swept up and down her tall, naked body. She moved to him, embraced him, then gently backed him to the chair until he sat down once more.

She stood before him. Her belly and pubic hair were level with his face. For a moment she was motionless, her thighs together. Bulov gazed at her curly golden triangle. Slowly she moved one long leg to the side, wider, wider, until she was standing with her feet almost a yard apart. She took Bulov's hand and used his fingers to caress the moist crevice between her legs.

Her voice was gentle, coaxing, and she spoke in French. "Come to bed, my animal love. Come and love me once more."

Bulov watched in fascination as she moved his fingers slowly back and forth, deeper between her legs. He leaned forward and kissed her belly. She dropped his hand and lay on the bed, her legs spread wide, her knees high to present him an open gate to sex.

Bulov rose and removed his robe slowly and untied the string of his pajama trousers, letting them down very slowly.

"You are teasing me," she said. "Stripteasing me."

"Yes," he said.

He could not resist a sidelong glance at himself in the looking glass. As he met his own eyes he saw that he was grinning openly, lasciviously, showing all that ugly metal. He closed his mouth quickly, but when he looked back at the golden-haired skier, he saw that she was not watching his face or his mouth or anything else above his waist.

Her eyes were narrowed and hungry. Her breasts were rising and falling. He was erect now and as he moved toward her he allowed himself to smile broadly in open lust and anticipation. He knew that she, like hundreds of other women before her, would never remove her eyes from what she was watching.

Bulov moved onto her, then into her. He began the slow, rhythmic rising and falling of his hips over hers, and she joined him in the rhythm. He moved his hands tenderly beneath her buttocks. His fingers were thick, the knuckles popped and knobbed, but they were gentle as he held her closer to him in the ebb and rising flow of sex. She sighed.

Then the pretty face of Natasha burst into his mind again. He saw the arc of the truncheon again and, again, Natasha's mouth flown open, taut and stretched, and again that unearthly screech sounded in his mind.

Bulov's sure, tender strokes became uneven. The rhythm of his lovemaking faltered. He felt himself begin to soften. The skier groaned and then cursed. Bulov could do nothing. He was limp. His lust, robust and exhilarating, had been replaced by fear—heavy, gray, deadening.

FEBRUARY 23, 1984
New York

Robin Booth spoke harshly into his phone. "Cancel the commercial, and cancel it *now!* It's offensive as all hell, and I don't want MBC associated with it."

He put down the receiver and turned to Ginny Graham. "Those damned sexist jeans ads again. They make it seem as if any woman who wears them is ready to flop in the street for the next pimp who comes along in a black hat."

She smiled and said, "There's a difference between sex-*ist* and sex-*y*, darlin'. I'm not sure but what you are seeing things that aren't there."

He said briskly, "Goddamnit, I think they're demeaning to women, and one hell of a lot of women seem to agree." He picked up a fistful of papers from his desk. "We've got mail on those things piling up, a hundred letters an hour."

She shrugged. "As you know, I'm not always exactly in tune with the pissers-and-moaners in that ERA crowd." She crossed her legs, long and shapely in sheer hose. "Also as you know, I don't ever wear pants just in case some pimp in a black hat does come along." She flashed her bright smile and said in an exaggerated sultry siren's voice, "Want me to show you, baby doll?"

Booth gazed thoughtfully at her. She had been his lover for three years, an exciting, voracious, yet high-spirited and humorous woman. It was an affair in which neither of them crowded the other in terms of permanent commitment or constant presence. They simply met and made love or ate dinner or spent a weekend or a week together and then went their separate ways. Both of them spent occasional nights with other partners, and nothing was made of it—although it was their habit to speak openly and in detail about any unusual aberrations they may have encountered in the beds of others.

It was, to Booth's way of thinking, a perfect relation- ship—cool, civilized, satisfying. Booth genuinely liked Ginny, and she was very good at her work—though the flighty and flirtatious personality she displayed in her sports telecasts routinely drew angry and insulting mail from "the raised-consciousness crowd," as she called them.

His grin widened and he said, "Show me."

She laughed out loud, a hearty, delighted sound. She rose and lifted her skirt to her waist. "See? I lied. It's February for God's sake!"

He felt a brief sensation of arousal as he looked at her long legs and womanly hips. Then his mind switched gears. "Tonight, my dear, tonight. I've got lunch with A. J. and the board to get the stockholders' meeting presentation set up."

She dropped her skirt and spoke in a serious voice as if

the preceding moments of sex and flirtation had never occurred. "Robin, what are you going to do about Miles?"

Booth hesitated. He had purposely not mentioned to Ginny his displeasure with Cavanagh. And, certainly, he had said nothing about his determination to bring the man down. He replied casually, "What do you mean—'do about Miles'?"

"He's gotten to be almost impossible. Being on the air with that backbiting bastard is like having a gila monster in your bed. I don't think the man is sane."

Booth raised his eyebrows skeptically. "Oh, come on, Ginny. He might be a little more intense than usual. But nothing like that comes across on the tube. He seems the same old lovable, overblown character we want him to be. I think you're too close to him, Ginny. You can't judge how he comes across on the air."

She frowned. "Joe is going crazy with him. He's tense, all coiled up inside whenever he's in front of the camera with Miles. Can't you see that?"

"It certainly didn't show in the telecasts." Booth kept his voice smooth and even. "You've just been too close to the whole thing, Ginny. The season ended six weeks ago. You're just remembering the worst things. Relax. Forget about Miles."

Her eyes narrowed and she spoke crisply. "Robin, I think you ought to consider firing him. He's dragging everything down into his own mean-minded little ego."

This was exactly Booth's conclusion. "Ginny, dear, Miles Cavanagh has a contract with MBC that is unbreakable except by acts of God. He is locked into this network tighter than A. J. himself. There is no way to get rid of him. And frankly I don't want to get rid of him. For every piece of hate mail we get about Miles there's a counterpoint from someone who says he couldn't imagine an NFL game without Miles. He's a folk figure."

"Okay," she said, "I'll drop it. We've got seven months before it all starts again."

When she left the office, Booth began to skim through his mail. He came across a small beige envelope with the initials "M. O'R." on the back. Booth tore it open and read it quickly.

Maggie O'Rourke's note was for the most part a graceful thank-you for his help in setting up the meeting with Joe Ordway. There was a postscript sentence, however, that moved Booth to thoughtful reminiscence: "After all the years since Breadloaf, I hate to ask, but I have to—whatever happened to *Childhoods?*"

The sentence jogged a memory so buried beneath the work and ongoing success of the last couple of decades, that for Booth to bring it back was like trying to retrieve a very small rock from the bottom of a very deep pool.

The time was August 1963. He and Maggie O'Rourke and her first husband were among visiting members of the faculty at the Breadloaf Writers' Conference in Vermont. She was fresh from the widespread critical success of her first novel. Her husband was a well-known poet. Booth was already celebrated—nearly to the point of having a cult—for the subtlety and depth of his television documentary work. He had been invited to Breadloaf as one of the first non-literary types to lecture there, and this was considered a coup of enormous worth.

At the time Booth was in his late twenties, a certifiable wunderkind so full of ideas and ideals, and blessed by a creative force of such energy and originality, that almost anyone who came in contact with him was turned into a convert.

In those days Booth had felt as if he could—and certainly would—make his mark in history in television documentaries. He had already produced several prize-winning pieces, including a tough and controversial film on the life and ideas of J. Robert Oppenheimer, the nuclear physicist;

another on the great contralto Marian Anderson, another on the conditions in Montgomery, Alabama, five years after the original bus boycott in 1956. His range of subject matter was amazing: he had also done widely admired documentaries on such disparate personalities as the octogenarian cellist Pablo Casals, the bombastic Illinois Senator Everett M. Dirksen, and the rookie quarterback for the Chicago Icemen—none other than the 22-year-old Joe Ordway himself.

All of this work had brought Robin Booth accolades and awards to a degree unprecedented for someone so young, and he did not respond to it with entirely unmitigated modesty. There was a natural arrogance in Booth anyway, an assumption of superiority that sprang from his birthright as a member of an aristocratic and artistic family from the Eastern Shore of Maryland. One ancestor had signed the Declaration of Independence. The name Booth came from the same aberrant tree that produced the famous family of actors—the Shakespearean genius Edwin Booth as well as the mad assassin of Lincoln, John Wilkes Booth. Robin Booth had finished Harvard at twenty in 1954. He ignored the family tobacco business and plunged instead into the whirling new world of television news, beginning as news director at a Baltimore station. From there his star ascended at a terrifying rate and by the summer of 1963 he was the top news documentary producer at CBS.

He and Maggie O'Rourke had met at Breadloaf during the first faculty reception. Her husband was an effete and moody man who spent much of his time taking long walks in the woods, so Booth and Maggie ended up together a lot. His interest in literature was as intense as hers. They developed a growing mutual admiration for each other's ideas. At one point Booth told her about his major pet project that he hoped to accomplish sometime in the next few years.

"It's very large and complex, and *very* delicate," he told her. "I can't hope to get started on it until I've gotten myself some real power at the network. I call it *Childhoods*. I want it to be a series of one hundred episodes. Each an hour, at least, maybe two hours. The idea is to utilize the Freudian view of infancy and childhood to define real people who, as adults, have become movers and shakers, celebrities, role models. What I want is for these people to dissect their childhood on TV. They would sit and talk about nothing but that—their childhoods. We would restrict them to what they remember up to their tenth birthdays. We'd have them reconstruct the toys they played with, the sense of what the sky looked like as babies, what their cribs felt like, their fears of the dark, what nightmares and dreams they had."

She had responded enthusiastically, but after the month at Breadloaf, Booth had plunged again into his frenetic schedule at CBS. He started a series of reports for the nightly news about the volatile civil rights situation in the South that fall. From there he had been swept on down the tumultuous mainstream of current events in America. He headed network coverage of the political conventions, as well as presidential campaigns. Coverage of the space shots of the middle 1960s also came under his charge, then the increasing American immersion in the swamp of Vietnam.

He became more and more involved in the frantic day-to-day production mechanics, did less of the creative on-location work. He rose in the news hierarchy, but when A. J. Knox at MBC approached him, he was ecstatic. Knox offered Robin Booth a vice-presidency that included not only news, but sports, too. Knox's network had wallowed in fourth place for so long that many people considered Booth a fool to jump from the opulence and prestige of the top network into the shabby environs of MBC. But it was just that challenge that fascinated him.

At first he was best known for the way he beefed up MBC sports programming, adding an almost infinite number of novel and exciting techniques for brightening up the ongoing repetitiveness of game telecasts. But he also developed and expanded original ways of covering the news, including the earliest weekly "magazine format" documentary in prime time. MBC's ratings for the most critical area of its scheduling—prime-time entertainment programs—remained mired in third or fourth place, but Robin Booth's success in his own tightly controlled empires of news and sports made him a shining knight in the eyes of A. J. Knox.

In the years that followed August '63 at Breadloaf, Booth and Maggie O'Rourke saw each other occasionally at New York cocktail parties. She had never again brought up Booth's discarded dream of *Childhoods*. But it was always clear to him that she harbored a certain disappointment in the ultimate direction of his career.

He skimmed Maggie's note again. *Childhoods!* Yes, well, it had been an interesting concept dreamed up in the mind of an idealistic young man, but he had found far grander visions to deal with in the ensuing years.

He glanced at his watch. One P.M. It would be ten A.M. in Tijuana. He dialed quickly, listened for a moment until a voice answered in Spanish. Booth spoke slowly in English: "Cavanagh will be there next week, after the Champions' Open at Pebble Beach. I want you to watch him every minute he's in Tijuana. You know what to expect? You know when to blow the whistle?"

Booth listened, then said, "Exactly." He put down the receiver with a grimace of distaste. Not everything he dealt with these days came under the heading of "grand vision." Not by any means.

Moscow

In the hours before the sub-zero February dawn, Moscow's streets were empty, its windows dark. It was as if the citizens had fled. Such was the menacing atmosphere of winter in Russia that men hid from it by sleeping whenever they could.

But not K-1. He ignored such things as weather, seasons, time. To him one season was like another and day was like night. His office, on the innermost corridor of the Kremlin, had heavily draped windows, thick carpets, acoustical walls, a constant temperature of sixty-five degrees. His apartment was there. He rarely left. He believed that he thought more lucidly, operated more efficiently, if he did not deal in diurnal or climatic change. He wanted his quarters—indeed, his life—to be like an incubator, clean, totally functional, touched by a minimum of external influence, including the passage of time.

He turned to his work. He began to read again the folder concerning the next mission in Operation *Igry*. It was a thick file of densely written reports. After a few minutes K-1 shook his head in admiration. The intelligence was brilliant, the detail superb. It was every bit as good as the material on Friedl Marx, Ernesto Diaz, Enzo Pavone, Horst Grunwald—and the eighteen others who had gone before. As usual, background detail on the four most recent victims in the *Igry* conspiracy had been accurate down to the most subtle items. For the Austrian kayaker, the night running on the isolated mountain road, the nightly drinkers at the Gasthof Munchen, the trucks . . . for the Italian runner, the Piazza del Pozzo, the church, the weekly visit of the finance minister . . . for the Brazilian diver the homosexual brothel . . . for the German discus thrower the drunken celebration of the Fasching king. Not a particle had been lacking and not a scrap had been in error. A few bits of the intelligence had come from K-1's own agents. But the single greatest source had been the one called the Gamesman. Indeed, the initial suggestion to dispose of the unknown champion Friedl Marx had come from this source, and in retrospect K-1 had to admit that since Marx was so obscure, he and his own agents would probably never have thought of killing him. Diaz, Pavone, and Grunwald were more obvious choices, of course. The next target for *Igry* was an even more obvious victim, a glittering celebrity. Because she was so famous, her case would have to be handled with extreme subtlety. Murder would be too sensational. It would sound an alarm, raise too many questions. But once again the solution was here in the Gamesman's plan.

Kiki Ankeny, the newest darling of the gymnastic world, a feisty doll now seventeen years old, would be the next victim. She had risen like a Yugoslavian angel out of the world corps of tiny, lithe girl acrobats to win the overall world championship in September 1983. With saucer-round brown eyes set in a pretty oval face, buttercup-blonde hair, and a dazzling smile, Kiki Ankeny was certain to be the next Olympic heroine. She would be adored in 1984 as Nadia Comaneci was in 1976 and Olga Korbut in 1972. But she was not like those two. Kiki displayed neither the dour fatalism of Comaneci nor the melancholy anxiety of Korbut. She was outwardly a sunbeam, a flower, a delight.

K-1 skimmed again the details of the gymnast's rise to stardom, then settled back to re-examine the paragraphs that held the key to her demise: "Even though she seems superficially to be totally happy, at ease, and healthy, Kiki A. has a weird, almost psychotic attachment to her brother. Their mother is dead. Their father is an ignorant, abusive farmer who was kinder to his cattle than to his children. The brother is a year younger than Kiki A., an angelic young man, almost as beautiful as she is. Kiki A. idolizes him. It is quite likely sexually based. They seem inordinately physical and very sensual together. He rubs her muscles before she performs. She allows no one else to do so. Whenever she is next to him she makes certain they are touching— hips, shoulders, fingers—there is almost always contact. She is very calm when she is near him, as if deeply satisfied. They have always been inseparable. One or two people in Grotz, the small town in the interior where they grew up, say they have had an incestuous affair."

The report went on about the brother, describing his penchant for rock music, his liking for drugs, his odd asexuality with everyone except his sister. "He is always at hand for her performances, always very serious, very beautiful, very possessive—though often starry-eyed and nearly incoherent from the dope. Once when he was not there, she wept and became quite rigid with alarm. She could not go

on without him. When he appeared they both wept, then
she performed brilliantly. Kiki A. has a fragile psyche. She
is far less resilient and self-confident than her sunny appearance implies. She depends on her brother as if he were
a father, yet dotes on him as a mother would a child . . ."

As K-1 began to consider the myriad possibilities in the
case, he found that his mind was functioning with a lucidity
and an efficiency that bordered on the supernatural. It was
a familiar sensation to K-1 and he presumed it meant that
the dark hours of morning were upon Moscow. Though he
had banned all timepieces from his environment, he knew
that certain habits of his work were related to a time of day.
Whenever he looked back over the hours of a particularly
impressive decision-making period, he found that most often
they had occurred between two and five A.M.

Indeed, two weeks before in this same black hour before
dawn, K-1 had dealt quite brilliantly with the incipient problems of Ivan Bulov's ego. As was his custom with all men
in his network, K-1 knew Bulov's every neurosis, every
turning of his simple athlete's mind. He knew Bulov's grand
capacity for self-congratulation and he knew that once Ivan
Bulov fell into one of his orgies of self-admiration, he could
begin to assume too much power for himself. And then he
would become guilty of the most dangerous attitude a man
in K-1's network could have—an assumption of independence. That would not do, particularly not in an operation so sensitive and far-flung as the vast conspiracy known
to only a few in the Kremlin as *Igry*—the Russian word for
"games."

The operation required a tight noose around the neck of
every agent in the field—Bulov's most of all. K-1 disliked
having one individual responsible for so large a segment of
an operation as Bulov was for *Igry*. But given the ex-hockey
player's easy movement through the international sports
establishment, and given his proven capacity for cold-

blooded pragmatism, there was really no other choice. The
man could be a machine, the best K-1 had ever seen for
sheer, detached amoral performance. But it was fear that
kept Bulov toeing the line; he had to feel anxious, threatened. Then and only then was he at his best.

K-1 had sent the Liechtensteiner, Ludwig Scheibl, to
Bulov with the message that he knew would shock Bulov
out of his predictable attitude of self-congratulation and into
one of fear and abject obedience. As far as he knew, Bulov
had obeyed orders perfectly in every detail of each of the
missions he had performed. But K-1 wanted no deviation
from this pattern. Nothing freelance, nothing extempora-
neous. The use of Scheibl as the messenger would create
terrible questions in Bulov's mind. The constant sight of
the little Liechtensteiner at international sports events
would, from now on, serve as a sharp Pavlovian reminder
to Bulov that he was probably under surveillance—if not
by Scheibl, by *someone*. And he would never forget that
he was on a tight, treacherous leash from K-1 in Moscow
and that one quick yank could prove fatal.

K-1 smiled wanly as he considered his efficiency in this
affair. But he did not congratulate himself. He was a bureaucrat, a Spartan, and, above all, a master of survival.
For work well done he rewarded himself with more work.
This not only pleased him, it also protected him. The
stronger his command over each harsh killing detail of his
work, the better his chances to continue living. The mere
fact that he had survived for so many years—almost
twenty—at the top of the Soviet system of secret police and
intelligence was symbol enough of his success. Yet success
itself could be dangerous. The best of them all, the evil and
efficient Lavrentia Beria, the Soviet policeman supreme,
had succumbed after eighteen years at K-1 because he had
become *too* good at his work, *too* efficient at collecting
secrets and using them to ruin his enemies. Beria had fright-

ened others in the Politburo and, of course, they were forced to kill him to insure their own survival.

K-1 had long ago determined that his own empire would always remain ostentatiously subservient to the powers of the Kremlin. To that end he was very reticent about his successes. Though inwardly he was enormously pleased with himself, outwardly he was self-effacing, almost obsequious.

He returned to the problem of Kiki Ankeny. He realized almost immediately that the key to her demise lay in her relationship with her brother. A fatal accident, an overdose of dope, even outright assassination of the boy, were possibilities. K-1 puzzled over the solution for a time. Then, in another more general piece of intelligence, he came across an interesting fact: The next major international competition in gymnastics was to be held in Ankara, Turkey, two weeks hence.

K-1 raised his eyebrows. Ankara? He allowed himself a thin smile. The brother was heavily involved with drugs, and Turkey's official policy toward any incoming traveler involved in the use or import of dope was cruel and inevitable. That was the answer: Turkish customs would be alerted. The brother would be carrying drugs in his luggage. . . . Immediate arrest. Sentenced to a Turkish jail. The boy would not be seen again for *years!* It was a fate more effective than death in this case; Kiki Ankeny would be mired in a continuous state of anxiety, loneliness, ongoing grief. K-1 would arrange for photographs to be sent to her at regular intervals showing the constant physical deterioration of her beloved brother in his Turkish prison cell. . . .

He began to dictate into a tape recorder. Slowly, carefully, he detailed the times, places, possible methods for planting drugs in the brother's luggage. He called for personnel dossiers on his own men in Turkey. He called for a special file on individual Turkish customs officials and began an analysis of the mechanics, the bribes, the blackmail that would be necessary to arrange this particular series of events.

Hours passed. Dawn came. There was no sense of morning breaking over the city, only a creeping cold translucence. K-1 was unaware of even this subtle change outside. He was at work, safe and unapproachable in his timeless chamber.

PART III

March 1984

MARCH 10, 1984
Carmel, California

MBC had rented an enormous Tudor mansion for its
executive and broadcast staffs for the Champions' Open at
Pebble Beach. It stared down majestically at the boiling surf
and rocks of the Pacific Coast. The standard crew of some
two hundred technicians, cameramen, and production executives was in residence, along with the ten on-air performers. Miles Cavanagh was the anchor, and Joe Ordway
was doing the so-called color work, which consisted mainly
of feature stories peripheral to tournament play. The other
announcers were the usual golf-tournament mix — a couple
of British writers with Colonel Blimp accents, three ex-
athletes, a silver-haired former golfer with a buttery southern
drawl, a former football linebacker and an ex-jockey and

97

three standard-brand professional sportscasters, inter-
changeable men with slightly better voices and slightly
larger vocabularies than the ex-athletes.

During the final two days of the tournament, Saturday
and Sunday, this MBC broadcast "team" would be strate-
gically arranged over the last ten holes of the golf course.
Everyone would be busy on these two final days, but the
first two days of the tournament involved little more than
technical preparations and a lot of parties. Thus, when
Maggie O'Rourke had phoned Ordway the week before to
ask when they might continue their interviews, he suggested
she meet him in California.

He reserved a room for her at the MBC house and arranged for a network limousine to pick her up at the airport
in San Francisco and drive her directly to the house. When
she arrived in the late afternoon, she blinked at the imposing
mansion and said "Good lord, this is some kind of natural
habitat you inhabit, Joe. Wow!"

He grinned at her exuberance and guided her into the
spacious living room, where some of the MBC crowd was
having cocktails. Eventually the two of them took their
drinks to the terrace overlooking the ocean. It was chilly,
but the setting sun warmed them a little.

Maggie said, "It's like something out of a California
Great Gatsby. The chauffeured limousine, this incredible
house, this party of well-dressed strangers without a host.
There's something otherworldly about it, Joe."

He shrugged. "This is pretty much the way it is at all the
big events the networks broadcast—the Derby, the Masters,
Wimbledon . . . we always live at some grandiose place.
It's partly for public relations, a place to entertain. Robin
Booth would probably have a revolt on his hands if we
didn't do it this way. Everyone's so used to it, it's expected."

"Is Robin around?"

"He hates these things."

A slim, pallid man in a blue blazer appeared between

them. "Joey, old man. How's it go? Need another drink?"

Ordway looked down at him. The man's eyes were a touch glassy. Joe said, "Maggie, this is Al Breck, public relations. Al, Margaret Anne O'Rourke, the writer."

"A writer? Who you with, baby?"

"I'm with, ah, Alfred Knopf, you might say," Maggie said with a grin.

"Oh, you *came* with a writer?" He jabbed Ordway playfully in the arm. "Hey, Joe, she comes with Alfred what's-his-name and you move right in? What kind of an act is that?" He finished his drink and said, "Want one, you two?" They said no. "Okay, how about Alfred then, Maggie, you want me to fix him up? Point him out to me."

Maggie said apologetically, "No, I meant Alfred Knopf, the publishing house. It was a confusing answer."

The public relations man said vaguely, "I get it, I get it." He left.

"What an odd conversation," Maggie said, laughing.

They picked two more drinks off a tray offered by a white-jacketed waiter, then moved indoors to a corner of the living room not far from a large stone fireplace where a fire was crackling. Maggie gazed at the crowd, her eyes shining with interest. "Some of the faces look familiar."

"Some of the big-name golfers are here. Maybe you know some of them."

Ordway was about to mention his growing hunger pangs when he saw the massive form of T. Miles Cavanagh moving through the crowd. The Pope of Sport carried a tumbler filled with clear liquid, no ice. Ordway knew it was straight vodka, a signal that Cavanagh was in a dark and petulant mood. He took Maggie's arm and began to steer her out of Cavanagh's path, but clearly they had been his target from the beginning.

"Aha, Joey Boy, and what are you doing in the company of this paragon of feminine literature?" He bowed in Maggie's direction, a slow and dignified move that contained a certain elegance despite the man's bulk. "I feel I am in the presence of literary royalty."

Ordway said quickly, "Maggie, this is T. Miles Cavanagh."

Cavanagh's face darkened in a scowl. Before Maggie could respond he said in a heavy voice, "When aristocracy meets, Joey Boy, you needn't supply obtrusive and unnecessary introductions. Miss O'Rourke is as familiar with my work and my name as I am with hers."

Maggie was quiet for a moment, then spoke very clearly: "I don't know how familiar either of us is with the other, Mr. Cavanagh, but when you use the term 'feminine literature' it sounds like something written on the side of a tampon box. That isn't exactly what I have had in mind all these years."

Cavanagh sipped his drink. Fever spots brightened in his cheeks. "Your talent for barbed repartee is impressive. You seem capable of a veritable storm of sharp retorts." He slurred his words slightly. He turned to Ordway. "I assume this has not gone over your head. Miss O'Rourke has just scored a very impressive point on me, Joey Boy." He took a large swallow of vodka. "She is a most worthy opponent. She has turned the very first words I have uttered into a scoring situation for herself. I'm explaining this to you, Joey Boy, because it is a very complex and subtle game, this contest of wit and wills in the course of cocktail party put-downs."

Maggie said brightly, "Mr. Cavanagh, I'm sorry I spoiled your good time with a couple of careless words. But I really don't consider that I write 'feminine literature' and, I'm sorry to say, I'm not sure I know who you are at all."

Ordway said quickly, "Miles and I work together, Maggie." He knew that Cavanagh was very drunk, even more dangerous than he had seemed at first. He took Maggie's arm and began to move away.

Cavanagh wanted the last word. He said, "I accept your

apology, Miss O'Rourke. But allow me to apologize to you, in advance, for the various nuisances, pestilences, and unspeakable gaffes that my colleague is certain to commit in your presence. He is a former professional athlete, a man of no taste, no wit, and the manners of a baboon. If you see him during the course of the evening taking a pee in a champagne bucket, forgive him. He was born and bred a jock and his habits are as ingrained and unchangeable as those of a skunk or a weasel. Forgive him, just forgive him . . ."

Maggie took a breath to speak out. Ordway gripped her arm tightly and steered her out of Cavanagh's presence. He said quietly, "Ignore him. He just gets worse the more you try to put him down."

She was outraged. "That poison-fanged son of a bitch! Where does he get off acting like some kind of pharaoh? Who does he think he is?"

Ordway shrugged. "He didn't used to put down so much booze. He was always pretty mean and unpredictable. Now he's almost beyond control."

She grabbed Ordway's hand sympathetically.

"Let's go," he said, pulling her along. "I've got a quiet little restaurant picked out and we can talk there."

Maggie flashed her glistening smile at him and said, "Okay, but please don't ever put me in that man's presence again."

"I promise."

Prague

Stella Kvisto rose in the grayness of dawn. She rolled her head around and around, loosening the taut muscles of her shoulders, feeling the tensions in her strong neck begin to vanish. She yawned, a grand animal sound that was loud enough so that her husband, Paavo, shifted irritably in the hotel bed. She looked at him with a faint smile on her long, angular face. He looked like an angel there, his eyes closed in beatific sleep, his dark curly hair framing his smooth white forehead, his full lips relaxed and beautiful. A cherub, a sexy cherub.

She stifled another mammoth yawn so she would not disturb him further. Stella Kvisto could scarcely believe her luck. Paavo Kvisto, her husband, her lover, her partner for life! It was still hard to believe, even now more than three years after they had been married. She was tempted to wake him on the spot, to reach under the thin blanket, to slip her wide, square hand into the waistband of his pajamas, to reach the limp penis and, there, to begin the things he liked. Ah, God, she loved to think of it. She would feel him grow hard and she would not be able to wait, she would have to have him inside her. She would lie on her back, as always, her eyes closed, her fists clenched in the excitement of it. And Paavo would slip that lovely shaft of his into her and . . .

But, no, for God's sake! There was no time to do this today. The competition was this very afternoon. This was no time to think of sex. She took her eyes off Paavo and began a brisk set of calisthenics, bending and twisting from the waist, touching her large palms flat upon the floor, feeling the stretch in her broad back, the pull through her wide hips. As the calisthenics became more vigorous, Stella began to grunt and pant. She began to sweat. She moaned and puffed . . .

His voice came like a spurt of acid from the bed. "Stella, you are bellowing like a fucking hippopotamus. Go outside and let me sleep."

She turned to him, distraught that she had been so stupid as to forget the noises she made when she worked out. "Oh, God, darling," she said, "I'm so sorry. I forgot, I—"

"Just go! Do it in the parking lot. Do it in the stadium. Go!" His eyes remained closed.

Stella gazed at him, her gray eyes wide. She was panting from the exertion of her exercise, but now she also felt the familiar rising desire for sex. "Paavo?" He seemed to be sleeping again but she was certain he was not. "Darling?"

He wrinkled his nose in distaste and said, "No."

"No? How do you mean 'no'? I have asked you nothing."

"I do not feel like fucking you, Stella. I have no desire. I am sober."

She swallowed. God, she loved that man. His prettiness, his manliness, his desire for her. His desire? No, that was finished long ago. But, still he was here, he was with her. When Paavo Kvisto had married her, no one in their village in Finland could believe that such a peacock, a man so sharp and so clever, would ever tie himself to Stella Haakon. She was as tall as most men. She had the hips and behind of a draft horse, the flat chest of a boy, the shoulders of a blacksmith. Her face, well, that was strong and handsome—too angular perhaps, but still possessed of stunning gray eyes like the eyes of a fine Persian cat, with fine lashes, high cheekbones, fine full lips. . . . She had had no real suitors in her life until Paavo Kvisto. She had been in bed a couple of times with men from the Finnish national team— rough, quick episodes. Her first coach, a middle-aged dictator with the character and appetites of a billy goat, had bedded her several times when she was still a docile teenager. She had always hated it.

But Paavo Kvisto had wooed her and loved her. They had made love often at first. They joked that it was part of her training, that her excellence in throwing the javelin was enhanced through her excellence in servicing the "javelin" that Paavo possessed. Stella recalled those times with fiery excitement. Paavo had rescued her from a lifetime of feeling freakish, overly big, and overly muscular, a woman who was different from other women in that she was an athlete— a superb athlete, world-record holder in the javelin throw, Olympic heroine-to-be for certain. Paavo had revealed for her the sensations of being a woman, of sex and tenderness. Her bigness did not matter in bed with him; indeed, he praised her grand and womanly hips, joyously licked the stiff, red nipples that rose like strawberries on her flat breasts.

In her memory these things seemed to have happened an hour ago, but it had been months ago, maybe a year ago. Oh, they had made love more recently—just last week, in fact, but it happened only when Paavo was drunk. And it was always so quick, such a short, almost desperate tussle—the hurried humping, the quick spurt, the rolling away, his instantaneous sleep while she lay there churning and tense, sad and confused.

Stella left the hotel and went to the stadium to complete her calisthenics, half an hour of strenuous reaching and stretching. Then she slowly jogged four miles and returned to the hotel for breakfast. She found it difficult to eat; the tension over the upcoming competition was beginning to grow in her like a tumor.

She returned to the hotel room. It was nearly noon. She dressed for the competition. Paavo seemed asleep. She touched his shoulder. "Darling, I am leaving for the stadium. The javelin throws begin at two. I will see you?"

He opened one eye and said gruffly, "You never see me even if I am there."

She sighed. "I know. I am always so deep in my throwing trance. I will try and remember to look for you today."

"Don't bother."

She returned to the stadium, and for the next hour and a half she loosened up more, slowly working her muscles, her shoulders, her all-important right arm, into a state of relaxed strength. Her mind became more and more condensed, her thoughts slowly turning in on themselves until there was a single focus—the javelin.

She began to pantomime the three long steps, the hop and the throw. Again and again she concentrated on this all-important action, the momentum that would coil her body into its maximum strength, then the swift and perfect spring-like action as she flung the spear into the sky. The beauty of it, the joy, the soaring sensation of her own perfection . . .

Now someone was tapping on her arm. Tap-tap-tap . . . it took a while to break into her shell of concentration. At last her mind loosened from its tight focus and she said irritably, "What is it?"

A voice, the voice of her coach, spoke loudly. "Stella, Stella, your husband, this man from the Olympic committee says Paavo is terribly ill in his room. He is crying for you. In the room, Stella. Do you hear me?"

Her attention snapped onto those words. "Paavo . . . ill . . . crying . . ." She let out a small scream of alarm. She had the impression that another man also spoke to her. He stood next to her coach. He had a Russian accent, an oddly glinting mouth. Apparently he had brought the message.

She sprinted to the hotel, through the lobby, and climbed the stairs three at a time. At the door to her room she paused in confusion. She had no key! Then she realized a key was in the lock. She turned it and burst through the door. The room was brightly lighted, the television set was on, the crackle of gunshots sounded from the screen. Her breath came in hoarse gasps, her nostrils were flared with the exertion, and her eyes bulged with fear of what she would find in the room . . .

It took several seconds before she realized that what she was seeing on the bed was not the limp and pallid figure of a sick husband. Quite the contrary. The sick husband was lying face downward, nude, and his alabaster buttocks were pumping up and down in fierce and wanton action. He lay between the widely spread legs of a woman, a blonde, a small and pretty blonde whose heavily mascaraed blue eyes gazed in fright and surprise at the large huffing figure of Stella Kvisto.

Later, Stella could remember no thoughts, no reflections, no plans that preceded her next action. She grabbed Paavo by his curly black hair and yanked him like a doll off the woman.

He fell back immediately, his head gushing blood, and Stella stood in shock, holding in her hand the hair and the ragged piece of scalp she had ripped from his skull.

Paavo began to whimper in pain. The blood from his

head poured over the blonde. She tried to push Paavo off, to free herself, but Stella moved like a lioness onto the bed, grabbed her throat, and, with a very small twist, broke the woman's larynx.

There was more mayhem done that afternoon. Paavo's jaw was broken and the room was reduced to wreckage. When the police arrived, Stella had left. She had run out of the hotel lobby, muttering quietly to herself. People reported that her eyes were wide and blank, as if she were in a trance. A few minutes later she appeared on the field at the stadium. The competition began. Stella had taken her first throw and was leading her nearest contender, a brawny Russian woman, by a full nine feet — when a police sergeant quietly informed the chief judge of the competition that, no, they could not wait until Fraulein Kvisto had completed her throws. They had to take her into custody immediately. She had killed a woman . . .

Carmel, California

Maggie sipped her wine, then said, "Remember I told you that one of the elements of this profile about you is going to deal with sex? As a reward, as a totem, as a way that people identify with—and exploit—their heroes, especially sports heroes? Should we, ah, begin with this?"

He said with a chuckle, "*Penthouse* interviews Joe Ordway? Okay, why not. First I'll order us each a cognac—just to loosen tongues a little more, if you don't mind."

The waitress brought the drinks, and Maggie turned on a small tape recorder she had in her purse and said, "Shall we begin with the beginning—the first time?"

Ordway hesitated. The *first* time? Good God, he wondered if he could even remember. There had been a lifetime of women since then—uncountable one-night stands with most every type of female imaginable, from cocktail waitresses who knocked on his hotel door at four in the morning to Junior League wives who gave him their engraved cards with four-letter suggestions to country club matrons who groped him on the eighteenth green—virginal cheerleaders and predatory celebrities and teenaged groupies . . .

He said, "Her name was Darlene Hanson . . ."

He had been a freshman in high school, but already he was six feet tall, long-legged and graceful, the starting quarterback for the Blooming Prairie Gophers. Darlene had been a senior at Blooming Prairie High School, a cheerleader, and a Sunday school teacher at the Missouri Synod Lutheran Church. She was pretty with a round face, bright brown eyes, and dark brown hair worn short and curly. She had a sweet disposition and an angelic smile. In the fashion of the day, she emphasized her breasts with tight sweaters and her fine hips and firm behind with tube skirts. These were attributes that had not yet attracted the full attention of Joe Ordway, fourteen.

On this particular Saturday in September he and Darlene Hanson had volunteered to count and sort hymnals in a small storeroom in the basement of the church.

As they stood before the bookshelves Darlene Hanson turned to him and fixed him with brown eyes that glistened like a gypsy's and said in a soft voice, "Joey, what do you want to do now?"

Surprised, he turned to her. Her lips, shiny with deep crimson lipstick, were slightly parted. Her breathing was quick and audible.

"I don't know. What do you want to do?" he said.

She took a deep breath and moved so that her breasts touched his chest. She said, "This is what I want to do."

She placed one hand behind his neck and gently pulled his face down toward her. They kissed. He felt the pleasant, slightly slippery surface of her lipstick and tasted its flavor.

He waited, his eyes open, his gaze fixed on the shelves of hymnals behind her.

She opened her mouth and moved her tongue across his lips. She pressed closer; her pelvis rose against his. He felt himself growing harder against her. He moved his own tongue tentatively over her lips. She stepped back. "I'm going steady with Bob Steel," she said breathlessly.

"I know that." Joe was surprised to find that he was panting too.

"You're only a freshman."

"Yes."

"I'm a senior."

"Yes."

She paused and said, "What are you—fifteen or sixteen?"

"Fourteen."

"God." She rolled her brown eyes at the ceiling. "I suppose you've never gone all the way."

"What?"

"Have you gone all the way?"

"All the way where?"

She giggled. She put a hand gently against his cheek and said, "You're so innocent, aren't you?"

Until that moment, Joe Ordway had considered innocence a virtue, but he said gruffly, "No, I'm not."

She gazed at him, breathing rapidly. She came closer again and kissed him. He stood still, his hands on her hips, an erection growing in his trousers. A moment later she stepped back and gave his cheek a sisterly pat. "See you around," she said. She left the storeroom. After a moment of utter confusion, Joe did too.

The football season began the following Friday night. Joe Ordway started his first game at quarterback. He scored one touchdown and threw a pass for another, and the Blooming Prairie Gophers won the game. Eight weeks later he passed for three touchdowns and the Gophers completed their first unbeaten season in thirty years. The crowd went mad with joy. They carried Joey off the field on their shoulders. Darlene Hanson saw him at the dance after the game and said coolly, "Going to count hymnals?" He said he didn't know. The following afternoon he went to the church storeroom. She was there. They kissed immediately. She placed his hands on her breasts. He squeezed them, rubbed them. She moaned with pleasure. So did he.

Darlene Hanson guided his hands under her skirt. She hooked his thumbs into her panty tops and guided them downward until they lay at her feet. She directed his fingers into her moist vagina. They lay on the floor. She manipulated his stiff penis into her, but then she gave a little shriek that frightened him as he penetrated her. They undulated on the floor until Ordway suddenly felt himself erupting with an orgasm. She was startled and seemed about to push him away, then she relaxed, closed her eyes, pumped against him furiously a few times, and gasped wildly. When he rose he was frightened to find blood smeared over their bare legs. She calmed him, explaining that she had never gone all the way before either. She kept her eyes downcast. She said, "Joey, you won't tell anyone?"

He said, "No, no, I wouldn't think of doing that."

"I'm going steady with Bob Steel."

"Yes."

"And you're a freshman, Joe, and I'm a senior. You understand that."

Every Saturday afternoon through the winter and spring they "counted hymnals." Their affair did not exist outside the church basement. They saw each other alone nowhere else. That June, two weeks after graduation, Darlene Hanson married Bob Steel, a rough-edged but friendly farm boy with no interest in athletics. Five months later she had a baby.

Maggie O'Rourke gulped. "Yours?"

Ordway shrugged and grinned sheepishly. "It never oc-

curred to me until five years later that it might be. I don't
know, but it probably was."

She gazed at him somberly. "There's a sort of primitive
ritual here, I think. If you can touch a deity, someone
imbued with supernatural powers, the powers might rub off
on you. It's a myth as old as the human race. Maybe something like that affects sex in sports. Touch and love the
athlete, and his vitality will revitalize you. Love an athlete
and tap the mystical resources that make him great. . . ."

Ordway frowned. "'Mystical resources'?"

"It's a form of mutual exploitation. A woman gets self-
gratification and possibly some mystical self-improvement
at the same time she is rewarding the hero with his well-
earned prize."

"Maybe that's what it was with Coach Bruhl's wife."
Ordway hesitated.

"Tell me about that."

Ordway could easily recall the ludicrous figure of Coach
Arnie Bruhl, but he had to reach deep into his memory to
recall his wife—what *was* her name? Dora, yes, Dora
Bruhl. Her face remained dim, but the coach came to mind
immediately—his blunt and pallid features, the thick
glasses he wore to correct his myopia, his thinning blond
hair, his paunch. He walked with a swagger of his shoulders
and at each step he bounced up on the balls of his feet so
that the whistle around his neck constantly danced on his
chest and belly.

Arnie Bruhl was a bully. He had made all of them, at
one time or another, weep from anger or shame or frustra-
tion. He was a martinet and an egomaniac, with a streak
of cruelty that under other circumstances might have made
him a fine hand-to-hand combat soldier. Whatever his strong
points, or weak, the Blooming Prairie Gophers set records
under Coach Bruhl that hadn't been matched in the state of
Nebraska—a winning streak in football had stretched to
thirty-six games when Joe Ordway graduated.

Yes, Ordway could remember Coach Bruhl clearly. Dora Bruhl was something else. Now, as he concentrated, he finally remembered a tall, gentle woman with a vaguely pretty face and a bright though enigmatic smile. Like the coach, she had to be forty or more. She wore glasses, though her eyes were a splendid blue and her hair was deep brown. She had no children and she did nothing all day but keep house for Coach Bruhl, who would not allow her to take a job.

One May afternoon in 1956, about a week before Joe Ordway was to graduate, Dora Bruhl telephoned his home and asked if he might come to her house and help move furniture. He had thought it odd, for Coach Bruhl made it a point never to fraternize with his players, but he immediately rode his bicycle to the Bruhl home.

Dora answered his knock and with her wide smile invited him in. The house was so still that Joey could hear a fly buzzing in the kitchen. He said, "Coach is gone?"

She said, "Yes, he's out of town."

He paused, then said, "Where's the, ah, furniture?"

She said, "It's that couch, Joey. Sit on it, please."

Puzzled, he obeyed. She knelt in front of him and he recalled that her glasses flashed in the sunlight as she removed them. To his astonishment she unbuckled his belt. He began to protest but she spoke gently, quietly, seductively. "Don't move, baby, please, baby, please, baby."

With her fingertips she massaged his penis through his trousers. It grew beneath her touch. She unbuttoned his fly and slipped his trousers and briefs down his legs. His naked member stood before his own surprised eyes, and he watched as if in a dream as she stroked it with her hand, very slowly. Then she placed it in her mouth. At first slowly, then more rapidly, she ducked her head up and down, up and down. Perhaps it took no more than a minute. Joey never knew. But it seemed an hour, a day, a lifetime. Then he burst deep in her throat. She continued for a time after-

ward to hold him in her mouth. Then she looked up at him.
She smiled again, that enigmatic smile. Her face was flushed
and radiant. She said, "You're the football captain, Joey.
I have done this for every football captain since we first
came to Blooming Prairie fifteen years ago. I guess none
of them has ever told anyone. I hope you liked it, dear, I
truly hope you did."

He could only say softly, "Yes. I liked it." At the door
he said, "Thank you, Mrs. Bruhl."

As she let him out into the warm May sunshine she said,
"All the football captains liked it, Joey."

Ordway turned to look at Maggie. He grinned shyly.
"If she meant it as a reward, I never felt better rewarded
in my life. And until this moment I've never told anyone
at all."

Maggie said nothing for a moment. Then she swallowed
the last dregs of her cognac. "Maybe she was collecting
something owed to *her*, Joe. Something dramatic, something to offset her own emptiness. She might have gotten
more of a reward out of it than you did—more than you
could ever imagine." They left the restaurant in silence and
drove back to the MBC house.

MARCH 20, 1984
New York

Ordway, Magnuson, Ginny Graham, and Booth sat on a banquette at Lutèce. The occasion was a lunch they had scheduled, canceled, and scheduled again and again since late January. They had intended it originally to celebrate the end of the NFL season. Magnuson raised his cocktail and said, "Well, here's to the last kickoff. Frankly, I've totally forgotten how wonderful it felt to get it all over with."

Ginny Graham produced a dazzling smile and placed a long-fingered hand on Booth's wrist. He seemed to wince. She raised an eyebrow. His face was glum and he had said nothing since they sat down several minutes before. She looked at him curiously, then turned to talk to Ordway and

Magnuson and said brightly, "I don't know what's worse for you two in the NFL meatgrinder, but if I had to do one more interview with one more slob of a defensive end, I think I'd take poison. Did any of you ever have your nipple tweaked by a three-hundred-twenty-pound football player? Can you imagine what that feels like?"

Magnuson chuckled. "I imagine it feels a lot like you just got your tit caught in the proverbial wringer."

Ginny laughed huskily. "Your poetic sensitivity is beyond belief, you lovable twerp." She lay her head on his narrow shoulder and rolled her eyes sexily.

Booth's face turned even more grim and he kept his eyes cast down. Then Ordway realized the table had been set only for four. He said to Booth, "Isn't the Pope coming to the party?"

Booth sighed. "I've been trying to think of a reasonable way to break the news. But there's no approach to it except head-on." He took a deep breath. His voice was low and somber. "Miles was arrested last night in a motel room in Tijuana. He is charged with sodomy and criminal assault on a minor. The victim was a boy, eleven years old. Miles picked the kid up on the street and offered him money to come to his room. The kid must have figured he could take Miles' money and still get away without getting hurt. He'd probably done it dozens of times before. But Miles had been drinking a lot and he apparently went crazy when the kid tried to fleece him. He punched the boy around and knocked him out. The kid was unconscious when Miles began to bugger him. The cops found him in the act when they broke into the room."

Ordway gasped. "Is this on the level?"

Johnny Mag took a quick gulp of his drink. "I don't believe it."

Ginny Graham spoke crisply with a curt nod of her head. "It figures. There always were funny vibrations around

Miles. That giggle. That mean streak. Maybe you had to be a woman to sense how weird he was . . ."

Booth went on, "Miles had had some trouble like this before. A long time ago. I knew about it but it seemed to be a temporary aberration."

Magnuson asked, "How did the cops happen to raid that hotel at that exact time? Christ, in Tijuana buggering little boys is practically part of the guided tours. He wasn't set up, was he?"

"No, no. Someone apparently was with the kid, a partner who followed him to protect him if something like this happened. He heard Miles beating him up and called the cops."

"It wasn't in the papers. Does anyone else know?" asked Ordway.

"So far it's been hushed up," Booth said. "There's no way to keep it quiet for long, though. The cops in Tijuana will sell anything and this kind of a story is worth some dough."

"Is the poor guy still in jail down there?" Ordway asked. He disliked Cavanagh intensely, yet he felt sorry for him.

"The kind of creeps they got in jails down there would kill him for his socks" said Johnny Mag with a grimace.

"They practically did," said Booth. His face was very sad. "We sent Ed Moore from PR in Burbank as soon as we heard. But he couldn't get down there until eight this morning. He had to throw around a lot of money to get Miles out. Ed brought him back to the Beverly Hills Hotel. Miles was a mess. He couldn't stop crying. He had been beaten really badly. It seems the jail guards had put him in the drunk tank with a bunch of real hard-assed Mexicans and let them know what Miles had done to the kid. He was in there just five minutes but they pounded him to a pulp."

"Poor Miles." Ordway shook his head sadly. "What does this do to his career? To his life?"

Booth said, "He's finished, of course. We can't keep him up there on a pedestal with this on his record. We can't do a thing for him. It'll come out in a few hours."

Magnuson said softly, "What will the poor bastard do?"

Booth shrugged. "He's made a lot of money."

"He'll never live this down," Ordway said. "All his life people will see him and they'll recognize him and . . . why, Christ, the man will never even be safe."

Ginny Graham said sharply, "He should have thought of that before he started banging little boys. That slimy bastard! God! It makes my skin crawl."

They ate lunch quickly and left the restaurant in gloomy silence. As they emerged from the elevator in the MBC building Booth said to Ordway, "Come with me, Joe. It's important."

Booth's office was bright in the afternoon sun, and things there seemed a bit less horrifying to Ordway. Booth swung his suit jacket over the back of his chair. He loosened his tie and called his secretary through the intercom: "I'm out, Jane. No interruptions."

Booth poured two glasses of Scotch. He took a deep draught from his, then spoke quickly. The brisk, efficient tone of his voice was an abrupt departure from his demeanor at lunch. "I don't know if you've the inclination to think about what's coming next, Joe, but life goes on, and everyone will know about Miles damned soon." He held up a piece of memo paper. "This is from PR. The papers are beginning to get onto it. So we're going to break it ourselves on the network news tonight." He shook his head in irritation. "The son of a bitch sure gave us a madman's swan song, didn't he?"

Ordway began to rise from his chair. "Look, you've got too much on your mind, Robin. I'll come see you in the morning."

"No!" Booth's voice crackled with authority. "There's

nothing as important now as what I have to say to you."
He swallowed another mouthful of Scotch. "Joe, I've decided that you are going to take over Miles' anchor spots for us. You're going to be the main man—for *everything* at MBC Sports. All the NFL shows and *Sports Week Magazine*." He paused dramatically. "And the Olympics."

Ordway was not prepared for this. The anchorman at the Olympics would be the most significant job in televised sports. He shook his head in disbelief. "Robin, I don't have the stuff to do a whole Olympics. I can't come on like the Pope."

Booth spoke sternly. "You aren't going to be the Pope! You've got one hell of a lot more going for you than Miles did. He had to invent that character he played on TV. He had to crank himself up to play that role just like some old ham playing Lear in a tent show. You, Joe, don't have to pretend one damn thing! You are genuine. You couldn't make a misstep in this business if you tried."

Ordway frowned. It still didn't make sense. "It seems to me it's like trying to turn Don Meredith into Walter Cronkite.

"You are to be yourself—not Cavanagh, not Cronkite. You've got a credibility rating in this country that's better than Cronkite's ever was. Whatever you say—and however you say it—*people believe you, Joe.*"

"Okay, okay." He was still confused, stunned.

Booth smiled and raised his glass. "I've been planning to put you in this job almost since the day I first met you. I could see that you had the quality the first time I ever saw you."

Booth's eyes glowed. Ordway felt the man's energy occupy the room as if it were a powerful source of light. He had been like that the first time Ordway met him, a man driven by his own enthusiasm, intent on making things happen as he wanted them to.

They had met for the first time in the summer of 1961, just as Ordway was about to begin his first season in the National Football League. He had been an All-American quarterback at the University of Michigan. His team won the Rose Bowl. Ordway won the Heisman Trophy. He was picked as the number one draft choice in the entire NFL. And he went to the Chicago Icemen, a team that had long been the doormat of the league. Chicago's other team, the Bears, had been known for decades as the Monsters of the Midway, but the Icemen were long called the Midgets of Lake Michigan, and Joe Ordway was hailed as a prospect so great that he might lead even the hapless Icemen to peaks of success. He was then twenty-two.

It was a windless, scorching summer day in the Wisconsin north woods when Ordway and Booth met. Ordway had just reported to the training camp of the Icemen, a bleak, mosquito-swarming cluster of frame buildings that had once been a tuberculosis sanitarium. Though he had no particular desire or need for it, Ordway had expected something of a reception from the team management when he arrived. At least a couple of the team's coaches or executives, maybe a TV crew, possibly even a band.

Instead his bus had been met by a sad and almost totally uncommunicative little gnome named Lou something, a janitor at the camp. When Ordway got off the bus, Lou was waiting sullenly at the wheel of a rusty pickup truck. He honked the horn once to indicate he was Joe's transportation to camp.

After a rattling ride over back roads, the janitor stopped the truck by an ordinary-looking, shingle building and pointed wordlessly to a window on the third floor. He did not offer to help Joe carry his suitcase and his duffel bag, and Ordway was soaked with sweat by the time he had climbed the three flights to his room. He was alone. He slumped on the bed. The room was hot and stuffy. He felt like weeping. He lay down and dozed off. When he awoke, he saw Robin Booth standing over his bed. He thought he was dreaming.

From Ordway's reclining position, Booth looked enormously tall, even taller than the six feet five inches he actually stood. He spoke rapidly. "Joe Ordway, I am Robin Booth of CBS News. I have a favor to ask. I hope you'll say yes."

Ordway swung his legs off the bed and sat up to confront this apparition. His mind was fuzzy from his fitful nap in the heat. "Who did you say you are?"

"Booth. Robin Booth. CBS News. Look, I'll make it simple. We want to do a documentary about you. About your first year in professional football. We're going to call it *Rookie,* just *Rookie.* The point is, Joe, you're starting in pro football at just the point where it's going to explode. I *know* it is. It's going to be more popular than baseball, I promise you. We want this film to show the genesis of all that—of both you as a new pro and pro football as the new national pastime."

Ordway was tempted to say yes on the spot, but he had a natural caution, and neither was he new to fame and the demands of the media. He said, "Hold on. I'm just another new guy here. They sure aren't treating me like a star. I don't think the team management would go for this."

Booth said, "Management already has gone for it. They feel it'd be fantastic public relations for the Icemen. And for you."

Ordway shook his head. "I'm going to have too much on my mind—learning the plays, getting in shape. I haven't got time to be some kind of an actor."

"You don't need to be an actor, Joe. You won't even know we're filming you most of the time. We're using hidden cameras, concealed mikes. This is *cinéma vérité* for TV, Joe. It's never been done like this."

Ordway resisted. "It would wreck my concentration. It could do a lot of damage to my standing with the other players, the old-timers particularly. They'd resent the hell out of me. Besides, we'll be on television every Sunday. That's enough TV for me."

Booth narrowed his eyes and looked closely at Ordway as if taking a new subtle measurement of the young quarterback. At last he said softly, "Joe, we've been filming you since you arrived. Every step, every frown. We had cameras at the bus stop—concealed, of course. We arranged it so the janitor met you alone. The owners' original idea was to organize a big welcome—Ice Maidens, cheerleaders, bands. I convinced management that to do this right, you should arrive by yourself, melancholy, nervous, lonely, like all rookies. You aren't a conquering hero—yet. We followed you in the heat with your luggage, up the stairs. We even have shots of you here in the room."

Ordway couldn't decide whether to be outraged or flattered. "What is this? Some kind of joke? I was on camera all that time?"

"I've never seen a man more born to the public eye." Booth's face was flushed with excitement, his eyes shone. "Joe! Joe! We are going to make a historic film! This is the beginning of a fantastic life for you!"

Of course, Joe finally gave in and the hour-long documentary was shown in prime time at the end of his first year in the NFL. The timing could not have been better. Plainly, he was fated to be one of pro football's most captivating heroes. Young as he was, he had led the league in passing, including twenty-five touchdown passes. The Icemen finished with an 8–4 record, their best in sixteen years. After just one season Ordway had already taken on the size of a legend for fans across the country. The nickname Joey O was his and no one else's.

Robin Booth's documentary was immediately declared a classic. Amazingly enough, except for a one-minute introductory montage of film snippets that displayed Ordway in action, *Rookie* never showed another moment of actual game action. Instead Booth had focused tightly on Ordway's face during locker room orations, at moments of tension and excitement on the sidelines, during the intense hours of practice when he was mastering the tricks of his trade. The film was incisive, sensitive, brilliantly insightful. This was all the more surprising in that Robin Booth not only knew nothing about the mechanics of football, he also considered most men who took the game seriously to be practically beneath contempt.

Now Booth spoke with his typical brand of pulsating enthusiasm: "Joe, you've had one hell of a career so far, but the best is *ahead!* From the '84 Olympics on, people will follow you to hell and back. You will be able to do no wrong."

Ordway took a deep breath. He knew he really had no choice. "Robin, I'm glad you want me to do it. I know I can."

Booth grinned. "Damned *right!*" He poured two more drinks. "We've got four months. That's plenty of time to get you prepared right down to the last millimeter. And I don't mean prepared just for the events. Anyone can memorize who won the pole vault in 1956. That jockstrap stuff will be a snap. That's just the tip of the iceberg. Where I want to excel is by being able to talk about the human, the sociological, the psychological, the political elements involved."

"Jesus, Robin, I don't know if I—"

Booth interrupted. "Joe, these Games might very well be explosive as all hell. There could be terrorist atrocities, boycotts, walkouts, all sorts of political chicanery. This is 1984, remember. The world is damned close to chaos. We can't overlook any possibility. I mean, what if the Russians decide to enter the Olympics?"

"The Russians? There's no chance of that, is there?"

"Probably not. I keep in constant touch with the Russian desk in the State Department. No hint at all that they've given an inch. They're reacting to our 1980 boycott with their own boycott. I don't think they'll change, but they might, and that's exactly my point, Joe. We have to be prepared for *everything!*"

"God, I feel like I ought to go into some kind of isolation booth with nothing but historians and political scientists and—"

Booth held up a hand. "Joe, I promise—you will be supplied with the most intricate, thorough, sophisticated background available in the *world* for these Games. We are going to make history! This will be classic! Revolutionary! From now on everything ever done in TV news or sports is going to be compared with what we are going to do in Los Angeles next summer! And the Olympics is just the beginning! The network will be on top or close to it if we get the kind of ratings I suspect we'll get. And then there is no limit. We will put such quality, such creativity, such goddamn *inspirational* stuff on that miserable little tube, that—well, goddamnit, the world will never be the same again!"

Booth's breath came quickly now and his face was flushed with the splendor of his dream. He paused, inhaled deeply, and was about to continue when the squawk box buzzed. He pushed the switch and said irritably, "What is it?"

His secretary's voice was choked and blurry. "I . . . I . . . "

"Damnit, Jane. I said not to bother me at *all*—"

She began to sob. "Mr. Booth, Mr. Booth. Please listen. They just called from Los Angeles. They have found Miles Cavanagh's body in his hotel room. He . . . he killed himself, Mr. Booth . . . slashed his throat with a broken vodka bottle . . . "

She broke down. Ordway and Booth stared at each other. The office was silent except for the strangled sounds of the secretary's sobs coming from the squawk box.

MARCH 21, 1984
New York

Maggie O'Rourke awoke and gazed blankly at the sunny ceiling of her bedroom. She began to stretch lazily, then she suddenly realized she was not alone. Startled, she rolled onto her side and saw the shape of a man, a tall man, next to her. There was an instant of panic. Who *was* that? She hadn't been in bed with anyone she didn't know for years . . . or anyone at *all* for a couple of months. Skeptically she looked at the man's head. Brown hair with some gray, a thick neck, wide muscular shoulders—well, it was Joe Ordway, wasn't it? And now that she had her wits back, she recalled that it had been a fine, rousing night, too.

There had been no hint in the way the previous evening began that it would come to this. Ordway had phoned her from the MBC Building shortly after six o'clock. He had sounded a little drunk and very tense. "Still want to interview your favorite hero?" he asked. "You ought to hear about my latest step on the stairway to stardom."

The harsh sound of his voice troubled her. She had said to him, "Has something gone wrong? We can postpone this for another time. Tomorrow, the weekend, whenever."

His voice was rough. "I have to be in Los Angeles on the weekend. I have to be in Stockholm next week. Let's do it . . ." He seemed to falter, then he spoke in a surprisingly flat and weary tone. "Something terrible has happened, Maggie. I'd like to talk about it with you."

When he arrived his eyes were bloodshot and the fumes of Scotch clung to him like cheap shaving lotion. But he seemed to be in control and relatively calm. He told her the story of Miles Cavanagh's arrest and subsequent suicide. He told her of his own promotion to the MBC Sports anchor position. He told her of his uneasiness, his obscure sense of guilt over the juxtaposition of events.

"I just can't feel good about any of this. It's a hell of a job. Robin Booth is going to use the Olympics as a springboard for a whole new kind of programming. You should hear him talk. He's like an evangelist. But, God, for me to get this chance only because poor old Miles has been caught like that and then cuts his throat . . . I should feel great, but I'm so damned depressed . . ."

"I don't blame you," she said. "It's a shock. But 'poor old Miles'? I thought you detested the man. Look Joe, it's all an unlucky, unhappy coincidence. But you didn't *cause* it. Maybe you feel guilty because you really did dislike Cavanagh—a lot. In fact, you probably would have been delighted to see him brought down. But now that it's happened, you feel subconsciously that your dislike for him might have *caused* it. Which, of course, is not true."

He said, "I hated the son of a bitch most of the time."

"How could you stand it? Six years with a man like that?"

He shrugged. "Apparently we were a hell of a team on air. People liked the contrast between us. Robin Booth always said there was a compelling chemistry between us."

"Does everyone know what happened to Cavanagh? I'd have thought it would be all over town by now."

"The network is going to break the story on the *Seven O'Clock News*. There have been hints about it on the AP wire and it will be in the morning papers anyway. Robin decided we should do it first."

She turned on the television set. "The news is on in five minutes. I'll make us a drink."

The MBC *Seven O'Clock News* led with the story. Martin Door, the anchorman, read a straightforward lead: "T. Miles Cavanagh, one of the most famous and admired men in American television, died by his own hand this afternoon in Beverly Hills, California. The suicide followed by less than sixteen hours his arrest in Tijuana, Mexico, on a morals charge. He was fifty-eight years old, a fixture with MBC Sports since 1966. Police in Tijuana gave few details of the incident that led to Cavanagh's arrest, saying only that he had been found in a motel room with a male minor, that he had been disorderly during a night's stay in a jail cell. He had been released on bail . . ."

Martin Door looked up. His eyes were sad. "Miles Cavanagh was much loved by his colleagues here at MBC. He was admired for his mind as well as his great knowledge of sports. A closer friend of his than any of us was Joe Ordway, who sat next to Miles during countless memorable telecasts over the years. Here he is."

Ordway appeared on the screen. He was seated in a large leather chair; his face was sad, his voice low and soothing. Behind him on a huge wall screen, the face of Miles Cavanagh loomed. As Ordway spoke the image on the screen switched from one picture of Cavanagh to another and another and another . . .

"Miles is gone and he went in a way none of us could have predicted, none of us wanted," said Ordway. "Rather than remembering the manner of his death, we at MBC are looking back on his life. You out there who spent so many splendid hours while Miles Cavanagh brought you the glories of our games—you all know that Miles was a man who was larger than life. In some ways he saw sport as larger than life, too. His application of literature and theater to our games set a new intellectual standard for the industry. Miles Cavanagh was a fan, in his way, but he was also a critic and a philosopher about sport. Miles was a harsh judge at times, but he was a fair man, an honest man. We will remember him best for the rolling drums of theatrical thunder—his own personal brand of thunder—that he added to the drama that is a natural part of this nation's games. So long, Miles, and thanks."

The light on Ordway faded quickly when he finished speaking. The screen behind him remained lighted with the face of T. Miles Cavanagh looming still and ghostly. Ordway's figure remained silhouetted against it for a moment, then the screen went black and a commercial flashed on.

Maggie looked at Ordway in surprise. "Good God, Joe, who wrote that?"

"A news guy did the first draft, then Robin worked on it and I did, too. Why?"

"How could they force you to read it?"

"Force me? They didn't have to force me."

"You volunteered to do it?"

"No, I didn't volunteer. Robin decided I should do it. We really didn't talk about it much. It seemed the natural thing to do."

Maggie's voice was sharp. "Natural? But you made him sound like some kind of saint . . ."

Ordway stared at her, frowning. "So?"

"But, Joe, that's so hypocritical! You despised the man, yet you, you . . ." She gestured helplessly at the television set.

"It never occurred to me not to do it. I mean, you couldn't leave the whole country with its last image of Miles Cavanagh as a pederast and a sadist, could you? We had to lay the thing to rest as gracefully as possible. It was the only way to handle it."

She shook her head in bewilderment. "But it never struck you that you were trying to make people believe something that isn't even remotely close to the truth? Every word you said about that despicable man was really a lie."

"A lie? No it wasn't, not really . . ." He paused, then threw out the palms of his hands in exasperation. "Maggie, let's drop this! Now! I'm too damned depressed by it . . ."

Joe sat silent for several minutes, staring at the television set. A frown deepened on his face and at last he rose slowly like an old man and went to the door. "This isn't the night for us to be together. I shouldn't have come."

Maggie did not regret her criticism of his eulogy for Cavanagh, but he seemed so forlorn, so forsaken, that she felt a surge of sympathy. She said softly, "Joe, where are you going?"

He shrugged. "To my apartment. A bar. I'll get drunk somewhere."

"Stay here. I'll cook us something."

He shook his head. "I don't think so."

"Please, Joe. Stay at least for a drink and then we'll see."

He agreed but it seemed more out of weariness and resignation than desire. The conversation proceeded in a desultory way for a time. But he stayed past the one drink and she served a light dinner. They relaxed more and more, drinking without becoming drunk.

Now, as she lay in the sun-bright bedroom, she didn't

remember anything they had talked about. Her only memory
was of Joe putting his large hand over hers. She had been
surprised at how gentle it felt. He had folded her in his
arms. She had put her hand on his shoulders and been
surprised at how wide they felt. His embrace was unex-
pectedly tender and they had held the kiss for a long time.
There had been no sense of urgency, but she remembered
now that when the first kiss had occurred, she had never
considered any other possible outcome except this—waking
up in bed with Joe Ordway at her side.

He turned toward her, his eyes open. He grinned. "Hi.
How are you?"

She spoke with a husky chuckle. "How? Or *who?* You
gave me quite a start."

"Why? I thought we got along famously."

"We did, but I'm just not used to waking up with a
football player. A classics professor maybe. But a quarterback?"

"Is it so different?"

"Well, ah, yes, as a matter of fact it is."

"How?"

"Ah, bigger shoulders mainly, I guess. And a broad chest
and . . . well, you get the idea."

He put his hand on her bare shoulder, rubbed it tenderly,
then moved to her breast. Her nipples hardened and a tin-
gling sensation spread through her body. She turned toward
him and they embraced. He pressed closer and kissed her,
then gently slid his hand down her belly . . .

An hour later Maggie moved languidly across the bedroom. She was naked in the sunlight, and in other circumstances she might have been quick to cover herself. The
presence of Joe Ordway didn't affect her that way. Her body
seemed very good to her this morning.

Ordway stood in the door of the bathroom, toweling
himself after a shower. "You are a beautiful woman, Maggie," he said.

She laughed with pleasure. "I have never felt more beautiful, Joe."

She went to him and hugged him. She was so full of desire, so drunk with passion, so smitten with the splendid feel of this man. She held him tightly and murmured against his chest, "Joe."

PART IV

April 1984

PART IV

APRIL 10, 1984
Stockholm

Ordway and John Magnuson entered the lobby of the Grand Hotel in Stockholm and were immediately assaulted by a familiar voice bellowing: "Schmile! Schmile, Choe! Schmile, Chonny!" Ordway turned and saw the gargantuan figure of Vasily Kirchov moving rapidly toward him. The famed Russian super-heavyweight weightlifter, retired after winning gold medals in three Olympic Games, was light as a dancer on his feet despite his immense size. His huge, blue-jowled face was wreathed in a smile of welcome. However, his dark eyes, oddly beautiful with their long black lashes, seemed to glitter with something else—sadness, anxiety, perhaps even fear.

"Smile!" Ordway cried. "Smile, Vasily, smile!"

The weightlifter wrapped his massive right hand around

Ordway's. Joe's hand was large by any measure, but Kirchov's enveloped it as if it were a child's. "Schmile, Chon!" the Russian shouted as he shook hands with Magnuson.

The greeting had its origins four years ago before the Moscow Olympics of 1980 when Joe, Johnny Mag, and a small MBC Sports crew traveled to Kirchov's hometown in the south of Russia to shoot a *Sports Week* documentary about the champion. At first Kirchov had been in a brown mood, his face clouded by a brooding frown. Magnuson had been taking still photos along with the TV tapes and at one point had said rather timidly to the glowering Kirchov, "Smile?" The Soviet interpreter had translated the word for the weightlifter.

Kirchov had scowled, but then suddenly produced a wide, clownish grin. Delighted, Johnny Mag said again, "Smile!" And Kirchov responded with a beaming grin, this time bellowing back jovially, "Schmile! Schmile!" Beneath the blue stubble his plump cheeks soon glowed pink with the exertion of each massive smile.

"Schmile, Choe!" Kirchov bellowed again. He gripped Ordway by both shoulders and held him away as if he were a child who might have grown a few inches since their last meeting. The grin stayed fixed on his face, but now it seemed to turn a bit glassy. He looked drunk. Kirchov hugged Ordway to him with the embrace of a gorilla. He shouted "Schmile!" once more. Then with his lips close to Ordway's ear he whispered hoarsely, urgently, in Russian. The words were gibberish to Joe but he was surprised by the tone of alarm in Kirchov's voice.

The weightlifter held Joe away from him again, this time scrutinizing his face as if to see whether he had understood.

Ordway frowned, puzzled at this strange behavior. He knew that Kirchov was, by nature, a hyperkinetic, habitually theatrical fellow given to the same overblown flamboyance and bombast as a professional wrestler. He was a braggart and a swashbuckler, a man of high color and deep moods.

He was also a notorious drinker. Ordway had observed Kirchov in a variety of attitudes during that week at his home in 1980. They had drunk a lot together, toasting each other in tumblers full of icy Russian vodka or the magnificent caramel-colored Armenian cognac that Kirchov liked best. They had put away so much in those nightly bouts toasting international friendship that the Russian translator, a sallow, blond young man, inevitably became so drunk that he was unable to speak either English or Russian. Then Kirchov, Ordway, and Johnny Mag would be reduced to communicating only through repeated shouts of "Smile! *Schmile!* Smile!"

During those intoxicated hours Ordway had watched Kirchov ascend to incredible peaks of joy, whooping with laughter so overwhelming that he would fall to the floor and roll on his back. Then, without warning, he would begin to weep over some melancholy Russian tune that had generated black memories.

Now, as he gazed at Kirchov, Ordway saw tears rise in the giant's eyes. A look of desperation, something close to panic, swept across his face. Ordway wondered if the great Kirchov had suffered a breakdown of some sort. He said, "Vasily, what is it? What's the matter?"

At that moment Ordway became aware of the three men who had been standing in Kirchov's shadow. They were pallid and hard-eyed, all wearing lumpy dark suits with padded shoulders, worn hats, scuffed shoes. Obviously they were members of the unmistakable brigade of plainclothes KGB men who accompanied all Soviet teams traveling abroad. They were officially listed as coaches or trainers, but no one was fooled; they were secret police charged with preventing defection or any disloyalty among Russian athletes. In the past, Ordway knew, Kirchov had been allowed to move about on his own. As a loyal and heroic member of the Soviet Communist Party, this was his due. But now this trio of watchdogs was gathered tightly around him.

Ordway said again, "What's the matter, Vasily? What are you trying to say?"

One of the guards stepped toward Ordway. He managed to produce a thin, tight grin. He spoke English with a dense Russian accent. "Vasily is in black mood. Pet dog has died."

Still grinning tautly, the KGB man looked up at the mountainous champion. He spoke in Russian to Kirchov, his tone urgent, though his voice was soft, as if he were reasoning with an infant. Kirchov blinked and wiped the tears from his eyes. He gazed blankly at the KGB man for a moment, then nodded in resignation. After one sad glance at Ordway he turned and walked to the elevator. Ordway said to Johnny Mag, "What the hell was that all about?"

Magnuson shrugged his narrow shoulders. "He's a certifiable manic-depressive and a drunk, Joe. You remember him in '80. I imagine it's even worse now that he's a has-been. They're rough in Russia. They love you when you're on top, but they'll stomp you to a pulp the minute you fall."

Ordway nodded. "He's about as flaky as anyone I ever saw, but there's something wrong with him."

As they signed the registry at the hotel desk Ordway felt a light tap on his shoulder and heard a voice with a European accent at his back. "The famous Joey O has arrived. Now all the good times will begin."

Ordway knew who it was without turning. He said, "Herr Scheibl, I should have known I couldn't sneak into any country in Europe without your knowing about it." He turned to gaze bleakly down at the little man. "Just once I'd like to manage it."

Ludwig Scheibl beamed through his rimless glasses. "Herr Joey O and the incomparable John Magnuson. The MBC network has sent its best. Welcome to Stockholm, the land of suicide and winter night. And when will you allow me to buy you the finest meal in Sweden?"

Ordway looked at Scheibl with distaste. He had been

running into Scheibl constantly for several years at almost all of the dozens of international events he had covered for the network's *Sports Week Magazine*. Scheibl was as inevitable as jet lag. He had arranged a couple of minor television productions for MBC and had been useful in setting up interviews with foreign athletes—particularly Russian—but Ordway considered him a parasite and a nuisance.

Scheibl cocked his bald head and winked slyly. "I have a table at the Opera Cellar ready for lunch even now. I am prepared to bribe you with reindeer steaks and ice cold aquavit. Come, let me corrupt you."

Magnuson said impatiently, "What are you trying to sell? You know damn well you wouldn't be spending a thin dime on us if you didn't expect something in return."

Scheibl said lightly, "I do have business in my mind at most times. Possibly I have some in mind today, too."

Magnuson said coldly, "No lunch, Ludwig. We have to set up in the arena for the competition tomorrow."

Scheibl pretended an expression of pain. "Why is it you ostracize me?"

Ordway said lightly, "Ludwig, anyone seen hanging around with you becomes a suspicious character automatically. It's like associating with a famous criminal."

"Criminal? I? What have you heard about my so terrible crimes? That I torture nuns? That I commit sodomy with farm animals? What crimes, I ask you?"

Ordway laughed in spite of himself. "None of the above. But anyone who can move between the Kremlin and the real world as easy as you do has to have some kind of dark secret. How the hell do you do it?"

"Quick feet," said Scheibl, "very, very quick feet." He did a swift little soft-shoe shuffle that was surprisingly graceful.

"The Fred Astaire of con men," Magnuson said.

"I insist on it," said Scheibl. He arched one eyebrow. "And how is my fellow confidence man, the indomitable Robin Booth?"

Ordway said drily, "Robin will be ecstatic to hear that you were asking for him, Ludwig. You are his favorite business contact in all of the Eastern Hemisphere."

"Robin Booth still considers me vermin, then?"

"Worse," said Magnuson. "Since you took that deal for the U.S.–Russian basketball series to ABC back in 1978, he has considered you to be dead meat. You don't exist."

"I was under no promise or contract to deal only with MBC. I was a free agent with my own package to sell. I did nothing dishonest."

"All I know, Ludwig," Ordway replied, "is that when your name comes up he looks like he's been bitten by a rabid dog."

"He is the consummate actor. All the best businessmen are. Duplicity is what greases the wheels of capitalism, my friend."

"Is that what you are?" said Johnny Mag. "A capitalist?"

"If need be, yes, I am a capitalist. Or if needs be otherwise I can easily become a socialist or a communist. I am flexible."

Ordway was tired of this nattering. He said, "Let's go, Johnny."

Scheibl was unmoved by Ordway's rudeness. He bowed slightly and said with a smile, "I am not only flexible, I am patient. I will reserve the same luncheon table tomorrow— and the next day—and the next." He did another brief shuffle on his tiny feet and left the hotel.

An hour later Ordway and Magnuson were inspecting the arena where the championships would be held. It was a large, immaculate, brightly lit gymnasium with bleachers rising to the high ceiling on two sides. A raised stage had been constructed in the center of the floor for the weight-lifting events. It was circled by rows of folding chairs.

MBC's European unit had set up equipment for the *Sports Week* taping, which would begin the following day. Johnny Mag was pleased. "You guys are pros," he said to the unit chief. "This will be a piece of cake." He left Ordway to look at the control trailer outside.

There were only a few dozen people in the arena, officials of the International Weightlifting Federation, European TV technicians, a few coaches and trainers. The place would be filled with spectators the next day. Competitors from fifty countries would be performing. MBC's cameras would tape the entire event, but Ordway's assignment was not very taxing. He would do an introductory commentary in front of the stage to give an authentic on-the-scene flavor and a few spot remarks from time to time. Most of his narration for the competition would be dubbed in as the tapes were edited later in New York.

Ordway wandered idly around the gleaming gymnasium floor. Suddenly he spotted a familiar figure near the stage. Ordway cried, "Ivan! Ivan Bulov!"

The Russian spun around. His face remained fixed in a deep scowl. For a second or two he gazed at Ordway as if he had never seen him before.

Ordway moved closer and said, "You know me, Ivan. It's Joe Ordway."

Now the Russian's face broke into a glinting grin of recognition. He spoke in heavily accented English. "Joe Ordway! I am thinking too hard to know you. I have my brain in the clouds and here you stand on the ground where I should see you. How are you?"

Ordway said, "Fine, Ivan. Will we drink some vodka before this competition is over?"

"For sure," Bulov said. "For sure, just as in Copenhagen and just as in Salzburg and . . ."

". . . and Brussels and London and Oslo." Ordway had encountered Bulov almost as often as he had Ludwig Scheibl in his trips abroad. The ex-hockey star exuded a rough charm, a jock's *joie de vivre* that was full of physical vitality and crude jokes. They had shared a number of bottles of Russian vodka and fresh caviar, which Bulov carried with him wherever he went.

"Why are you here?" Joe asked. "I didn't realize you were tied up with the weightlifting federations too."

Bulov said, "I go where I am needed. It is my job."

Ordway nodded. "I saw Vasily Kirchov at the Grand Hotel. He is not the same man he used to be. What is his trouble?"

Bulov paused. A hint of a scowl crossed his face. "Trouble with Vasily?"

"He seemed very sad to me. Anxious, maybe."

Bulov gazed silently at Ordway for a moment, then shrugged his wide shoulders in an exaggerated gesture of nonchalance. "He is a man of black moods. He has been struggling with a sick stomach, too." Then Bulov took Joe's arm and spoke confidentially. "It is too much cognac. Too much time to do nothing. Too much time to think about growing old. Too much time to know that he will never lift weights again. Vasily is a man living with dark thoughts. He believes his life is behind him."

They parted, promising to meet before the end of the competition.

The next day Ordway stood in front of the weightlifters' stage, which was bathed in a glaring wash of floodlights. Behind him the bantamweight lifters were performing; they were tiny bulging men no taller than children but more powerful than donkeys. Joe looked into an MBC camera and casually ad-libbed a two-minute scene-setter narration. As he finished he saw Vasily Kirchov moving slowly, almost languidly, toward him. The trio of KGB "coaches" were at his side like three dinghies tied to a battleship. The super-heavyweight was staring blankly at Ordway. There were deep rings beneath his eyes, and when Ordway shouted out his name Kirchov ignored him.

Ordway began to move toward the giant, but the button in Joe's ear hummed with the Indiana inflections of Johnny Mag. "Joe, that was real good. One more retake, then we'll get some breakfast while the little guys are working, okay? The camera's on; do it when you're ready."

Ordway turned to address the camera once more. The thud of a weight crashing to the stage floor sounded behind him like the detonation of an explosive. The noise was followed instantly by rising cries of alarm. Ordway turned quickly to look at the lifters' stage. Several men were leaping onto it. Their faces were taut with anxiety. Then Ordway saw that a lifter was lying pinned beneath the fallen weight. He was moaning loudly and writhing and jerking in convulsions on the floor.

The stricken man was no more than twenty feet away and Ordway saw that his face was a ghastly white. As Ordway watched, the lifter's skin swiftly turned to a deepening blue. His eyes suddenly bulged open. The moaning stopped and was replaced by desperate gulping sounds. The man's convulsions grew more violent. He stiffened as if a bolt of electricity had shot through him. Then his body went limp. His bowels loosened and a brown, stinking stain formed beneath him as he died.

Ordway stood his ground as agitated spectators rushed past him to get closer to the stage. Suddenly Joe felt a powerful grip on his arm. He turned. It was Kirchov. The Russian was breathless, panicky, his dark eyes wild and burning. He was jabbering rapidly in Russian. Tears were streaming down his blue jowls. He grabbed Ordway in a great hug. Ordway tried to fight. At the same time Johnny Mag's voice was crackling through the button in his ear. "What happened, Joe? What the hell is going on?"

Still in Kirchov's grip, Ordway spluttered into his microphone, "He's dead! The little guy is dead!"

Kirchov let Joe loose again as suddenly and inexplicably as he had grabbed him. His escorts were pulling at his arms

like children trying to coax away a drunken father. Suddenly
docile, the Russian giant allowed himself to be guided away.
Then he turned once more to look at the cluster of people
kneeling around the dead man on the stage. His face twisted
uncontrollably and he began to sob like a heartbroken girl
as the KGB men led him away.

The dead weightlifter was a young Moroccan bantamweight. He was a brilliant new competitor who had recently
become dominant in his weight division, a certain star-to-
be.

Magnuson was speaking urgently to Ordway. "Joe, start
talking. Start telling what's going on. We've got the tapes
running. Give us some kind of explanation!"

Ordway climbed onto the stage. A man with a stetho-
scope had just risen from the weightlifter's prone body.
Ordway held out his microphone and the man said something
in Swedish, then Ordway spoke into the microphone. "I
assume this is a doctor. The situation is wild. No one seems
to know what has happened. The doctor examined the
man . . ."

Now Ordway saw Ivan Bulov standing on the stage beyond the doctor. The Russian's face was pale, his eyes
glittering, as he stared at the small corpse. Ordway shoved
his way to Bulov's side. The man seemed to have a passing
understanding of just about every language on earth.

"What did the doctor say, Ivan?" He held out the microphone to Bulov.

The Russian turned sharply toward Ordway. He seemed
startled when he saw the microphone. Then he relaxed and
spoke very slowly into the mike. "He say heart attack. The
heart failed, It was accidental death. Absolutely accidental."
Bulov moved away through the chaos.

Ordway continued to describe the pandemonium while
ambulance attendants arrived and carried the body away on
a stretcher. A short time later the official word was issued
from the hospital: Following an autopsy it was determined

that the cause of death was indeed a heart attack. Later it turned out that men in the Moroccan's family had a long history of heart failure at a relatively young age.

Back at the Grand Hotel, Ordway went into the small bar off the lobby and ordered a double Scotch. He was badly shaken. Ordway drank quickly and ordered a second double.

Johnny Mag joined him. "The tapes are terrific, Joe. Grisly as hell, but spectacular. I doubt like hell we'll ever get them on the air though."

"I hope not. I never want to see them again."

They drank deeply and spoke very little for a few minutes. Then Ludwig Scheibl joined them. He was very excited. "I have come from the Russian suites. Vasily Kirchov is very drunk and upset. He is weeping and stamping about. It is very frightening. When he saw me, he hurried over and grabbed me by the arms. It was very painful. Tears were falling down his face like waterfalls. There were KGB men everywhere. He whispered in my ear, 'Did Joe find my message? Go and ask him.' It is all he had time to say, I think." Scheibl paused. "Did you find a message from Vasily Kirchov?"

Ordway was a little blurry. "Message? No message."

Scheibl persisted. "Kirchov was most urgent, it seemed, about this message."

Ordway shrugged. "He kept trying to whisper stuff to me. It was gibberish. Russian."

Scheibl frowned. "I have a sense that it was important." He paused, then leaned forward. His eyes glistened behind his glasses. He spoke in a hushed voice. "I am leaving Stockholm in an hour. But first I have something to relate to you. It will cost nothing for the moment. But if it proves to be true, I would hope Robin Booth will remember me for giving him the earliest information so he can be prepared when it comes to pass."

He paused dramatically, then spoke in a confidential voice: "It is becoming more apparent that the Russians will send a team to the Los Angeles Olympics. I have seen the signs. I have heard the talk. I am certain it will happen."

Magnuson spoke with scorn. "You don't know what you're talking about."

The Liechtensteiner said, "If you do not pass this word on to Robin Booth you will be most wrong. He needs every moment to prepare for it. You must tell him whether you believe me or not."

Ordway was suddenly angry. The shocks of the day had been too much. "Goddamnit, I've had enough of you! Beat it or I'll throw you out myself."

Scheibl's eyes widened in fright. "You *must* tell Booth," he said. He hurried out of the room.

Johnny Mag said wearily, "Do you think he knows what he's talking about? Christ, if that's true . . ."

Ordway sipped at his Scotch. "It's not true. Booth says there's no chance."

"What's the stuff about a message from Kirchov?"

Ordway gazed gloomily at his drink. "None of it makes sense, John. Maybe in the morning." He rose and walked with a slight stagger to the elevator.

Bulov paced his hotel room. All around him was wreckage, broken furniture, shattered glass. His brow was furrowed. He was trying to sort out the possibilities, searching through the chaos of this error-filled day; to discover exactly where he now stood. Mistakes had been multiplying with frightening rapidity.

First the murder of the Moroccan had gone awry. Perhaps Bulov should have anticipated the immense physical powers of the little weightlifter. Perhaps he should have known to double the dosage so the man would die as planned in the privacy of his hotel bed. Bulov had measured the portion of the drug himself. He had been told it was enough to bring down a horse in an hour. Once ingested, it would seep through the bloodstream until it reached the heart. There it would cause the tissues to weaken until the powerful muscle turned flabby and eventually failed altogether.

Bulov had himself watched the night before in the weight-lifters' cafeteria as the Moroccan ate the bowl of soup that had been loaded with the drug. He had watched as the little man swaggered off to his hotel room, chatting animatedly with a teammate. He had assumed that in the morning the man would be found dead, the cause a heart attack.

Thus, when Bulov arrived at the arena for the morning events, he almost collapsed when he saw the Moroccan on the stage, dressed in his lifting leotards, calmly waiting his turn to compete. Bulov's heart began to thump crazily. It was as if he were seeing a man rise from his grave. True, the man did not look well. There were purple pouches beneath both eyes and his skin had a grayish cast and he did seem to be rather vague in his movements.

Yet he should not have been there at all. He should have been stretched out, growing cold, on his own deathbed.

Still, now, as Bulov reconstructed the grotesque public circumstances of the death, he did not see that anything truly crucial had been affected. Despite the sensation of it all, there were no more suspicions over the Moroccan's collapse in public than if he had expired in private. The death certificate bore the unmistakable verdict that the man had died of natural causes. There had been no sign of the drug, no reason to doubt the findings. Indeed, the fact that several thousand people had witnessed the death might actually make it even less suspicious than otherwise. So, Bulov breathed somewhat easier—but not entirely.

More troublesome, *far* more troublesome, was the situation concerning Vasily Kirchov. Here Bulov could feel the cold, slicing blade of K-1's vengeance poised at his throat. Bulov and Kirchov had long been warm friends. Both had been sports heroes in the Soviet Union for many

years. They were the same age and their stars had ascended
at about the same time. Both had been held up as models
for young Soviet sportsmen; both were popular as speakers
and banquet guests; both were welcome in the highest ech-
elons of the Kremlin.

Lately they had seen little of each other. This was largely
because of Bulov's constant travel, but also because Kirchov
had finally been forced to retire from active competition
due to age, injury, and incipient alcoholism. He had been
given an undemanding ceremonial job as a deputy minister
of the Sports Council of the Soviet Union. His function was
merely to perform as an honored elder statesman of sport,
giving inspirational speeches to youth groups, making appearances at soccer matches and bridge openings. He was
rarely sober enough to perform these functions, but he had
an office in the Sports Council building on Gorky Street
and it was there during a drinking spree that he had gotten
wind of the part of Operation *Igry* that called for the murder
of the Moroccan.

What had happened, Bulov now knew, was that a highly
placed KGB man assumed—wrongly—that Kirchov had
been a party to the *Igry* conspiracy because of his position
on the Sports Council. During an evening of heavy drinking
the KGB man had confidently mentioned to Kirchov that
the Moroccan weightlifter might well suffer an early death,
thus allowing the Russian competitor in his division to win
the world title in Stockholm as well as a gold medal in Los
Angeles. Angered and very drunk, Kirchov grabbed the
terrified KGB official and threatened to tear out his spine
unless the man told him everything he knew about the plot.
Fortunately the KGB man knew very little, but what he
knew he told to Vasily Kirchov.

The super-heavyweight had been devastated. He kept it
to himself until he got to Stockholm, then he cornered his
old friend Bulov and spilled it all. He had no idea, of course,

that he was speaking to the very man who would be the Moroccan's assassin.

Kirchov had pleaded, "Ivan, we must stop this horror. We cannot kill a man just because he may win a gold medal."

Bulov had been frightened by Kirchov's revelations but he carefully calmed himself and pretended disbelief. He said, "Have you invented these things? Is this a vodka dream you have had?"

The giant shook his great head. "It is true. It is no dream. There is a conspiracy to kill, a KGB conspiracy."

Bulov had opened a bottle of vodka, hoping to calm the man and perhaps to move his sotted mind onto less volatile subjects. Kirchov had drunk willingly enough but he did not become calm. He became more and more anguished. It was at this point that Bulov arranged for the trio of Russian agents to accompany the weightlifter wherever he went in Stockholm. He also considered contacting K-1 about the problem, but decided not to because of his long friendship with Kirchov.

The next day Bulov learned with a sinking heart of Kirchov's meeting with Joe Ordway in the lobby of the Grand Hotel. He was not concerned that the weightlifter had actually transmitted any information to the American. Kirchov could speak no English, and he knew that Ordway was as ignorant as most Americans when it came to any language but his own. He again considered contacting K-1 and again decided against it out of affection for Kirchov. And, of course, now that the murder was finally accomplished, Bulov felt much easier. But ominously enough Kirchov, consumed by grief and disgust at what had happened, began to drink heavily in Bulov's suite. After he finished a bottle of vodka, he began to show signs of anger. His uncontrollable temper when he was drunk was legendary. Bulov talked to him steadily, trying to reassure him that the death

of the Moroccan was indeed from natural causes. As he
talked Bulov managed to dissolve half a dozen sleeping pills
in the giant's glass of vodka and after quaffing this potion,
Kirchov fell into a stupefied doze.

Bulov was about to sink into an armchair to relax when
the phone rang. He picked it up, heard an operator's voice
in Swedish, another in Russian. Then the nasal voice of
K-1 droned through the receiver. Bulov's throat became so
dry that he could not croak a greeting, but it was not required. In brief words K-1 gave him his orders: "The giant
must be returned. A plane awaits at Sverige. His destination
is Gulinka."

K-1 cut the connection without waiting for a reply.
Slowly Bulov replaced his phone. Fear immersed him as
if he were underwater. It was a full minute before he realized
that he was actually holding his breath. He turned to look
at his old friend sprawled over the bed. Though he knew
Kirchov's fate would be terrible, Bulov actually envied him
for a brief moment. The giant lay in a beatific stupor, his
face so relaxed that it sagged like a deflated balloon. His
eyes were slightly open. They shone dully through the slits
of his eyelids, which blinked from time to time in the sleepy
movement of a child. He was a vision of innocence.

Bulov summoned the KGB trio. Briskly he told them to
remove Kirchov from the hotel to the Soviet plane waiting
at Sverige Military Airport, then he went to a Soviet trainer
to arrange for a car to the airport. Left alone, the three
agents discussed how best to accomplish their assignment.
They agreed that since they could not lift Kirchov's great
bulk while he was unconscious, they would gently rouse
him so he might walk by himself. At their urging Kirchov
stood drowsily, yawning like a sleepy child. Speaking in
soothing whispers, the KGB men guided him toward the
door. When he resisted slightly, they pulled harder. Kirchov
began to struggle harder and came more awake.

Alarmed, one agent hurried into the bathroom and returned with a hypodermic needle. Stealthily he approached the weightlifter from the rear, but some deep and primitive reflex warned Kirchov that he was in danger. He could scarcely raise his eyelids, yet he began to flail wildly with arms as thick as tree limbs.

He knocked one KGB man to his knees with a single blow. The man's nose was smashed, a cheekbone shattered. He began to squeal in pain. This enraged Kirchov. He charged madly around the room. He broke the bed; he smashed two chairs.

Bulov burst back into the room at these sounds of mayhem. Another KGB man tried to bring the giant down with a chair from behind, but the groggy Kirchov shook off the blow, spun around, grabbed both the man and the chair, and flung them across the room. The man's head shattered a mirror and he fell to the floor unconscious and bleeding copiously. Terrified by the catastrophe bursting around him, Bulov rushed back into the corridor and began to pound on doors. Other members of the Russian team responded and Bulov shouted that Kirchov was into one of his notorious drunken tantrums.

A dozen weightlifters followed Bulov to the room. It was a shambles. One KGB man lay bleeding beneath the broken mirror. The man with the broken face cowered in a corner squealing like a run-over dog. The third man was still upright, but he had been cornered by Kirchov. He crouched, trembling, the hypodermic needle in his hand, as the giant moved unsteadily toward him.

Bulov bellowed from the doorway and Kirchov turned his bleary eyes to him. Now the phalanx of weightlifters steathily advanced while Bulov spoke in low soothing tones. Kirchov's half-conscious attention was now riveted on the advancing lifters. Swiftly the KGB man crept up behind and plunged the needle into the flesh at the base of Kirchov's skull. The giant collapsed as if he had been shot.

Moments later, like pallbearers, the cadre of weightlifters

carried their fallen hero out a rear door of the hotel. They
loaded him into the back of a van, accompanied him to the
airport, and tenderly bore him aboard the small Russian air
force jet that would take him home. Bulov explained that
Kirchov would be hospitalized for alcoholism and mental
problems. The weightlifters expressed sympathy and sadness over this depressing demise of the greatest of them all.
They returned to the hotel. Bulov watched the plane take
off in the bleak dusk, then returned to his ruined room.

He wondered if K-1 would blame him for all of the day's
mistakes. Would they imprison him in the insane asylum
at Gulinka? There was nothing he feared more. But he had
been loyal and obedient, had he not? He had in no way
resisted the authority of K-1. Perhaps he had been slow in
informing K-1 of the trouble in Stockholm, but ultimately
he had been so unswervingly loyal, so abjectly obedient,
that he had delivered a good and true friend into the depths
of Gulinka without even questioning the order to do so.
Certainly K-1 could not doubt the strength of his allegiance.
Could he?

In truth Bulov did not know the answer, and from habit
he moved to the mirror to try and puzzle out where he stood.
But of course the mirror had been shattered by Kirchov,
and Bulov could barely recognize himself in the shards of
glass that remained. Still, he stood there automatically examining the cracked fragments of his reflected features as
he tried to analyze precisely his probable future.

A single word kept pounding in his mind. Gulinka, Gulinka, *Gulinka!* His eyes suddenly widened in horror.

Gulinka!

Gulinka was where Natasha was imprisoned even now!

As Bulov searched the broken shards that showed his
face, he began to recall for the first time in many years the
details of that betrayal. He did not *want* to remember. But,
alas, it was all coming back . . .

In the winter of 1976 it had become unmistakably clear

that his salad days of hockey were at an end. His knees had betrayed him. They ached constantly and he could only skate at all if they were bound in stiff, tight braces. Already he had undergone surgery eight different times—five on the left knee, three on the right. There was no more to be done. Night after night he lay awake with his throbbing knees, plagued by the nightmare that his days of stardom were over and he could no longer look forward to any future except eventual transport to a labor camp or an insane asylum. He was useless, he was finished.

It was while he was in this intensely paranoid condition that he was summoned to the incubator-office of K-1. Bulov was convinced that his end had come, that this audience with the most powerful secret policeman in Russia signaled certain exile or certain death. But K-1 had something else in mind. He asked the ashen Bulov, "Are you absolutely loyal to the Communist Party in the Soviet Union?"

Thinking this might be a last desperate chance to save his life through a display of doglike devotion, Bulov launched into a very long, very impassioned dissertation concerning his love of communism. K-1 cut him off sharply. "Would you do anything for the party?"

Bulov replied in a quavering voice, "Yes, sir."

"Would you help the KGB bring down a potential defector?"

"Certainly, sir."

"Any defector, no matter who the person is?"

"Of course. Defectors are enemies of the state and corruptors of party values . . ."

K-1 waved an impatient hand. "Stop the orations, Bulov, you are a hockey player. Just listen to me and answer only very briefly when I ask you a question. Otherwise say nothing."

Bulov nodded.

"You would assist us no matter who the defector might be?"

"Yes."

"In this case, for your information, the defector is someone you know very well. That does not matter?"

Bulov shook his head vigorously. "No!"

"In this case the defector I want you to deal with—deal
with quite violently—is a figure skater named Natasha Penska."

Involuntarily Bulov blurted, "No! Not Natasha!"

K-1 rose threateningly. "Yes! Natasha!"

Bulov stammered, "I mean, I, I, did not mean . . . It
cannot be Natasha. She has said nothing to me about defection, and we are, we are . . ."

K-1 nodded. "I know precisely what you are. That is
why you have been chosen."

Bulov had buried his head in his hands. She had said
nothing to him about this. They had talked recently of getting married, of finding an apartment in Moscow. For two
years they had been lovers. It was a passionate, powerfully
sexual affair, and Bulov was in love with Natasha as he had
never been with the dozens of other women he had wooed
and bedded over the years.

She was beautiful, dark, and joyous, with a quick bright
smile. As a skater she was as light and lovely as a firebird,
one of the best three of four figure skaters on earth. As a
lover she was passionate and imaginative, often taking
charge of their lovemaking with an authority and originality
that left Bulov thrilled and delighted. He raised his head
and spoke carefully to K-1. "She has said nothing to me
about defecting. I can't believe she would keep such a
secret."

"We have information that she has already completed the
preparations. She will do it immediately after the Olympics
in Innsbruck. Do you not believe us?"

"Yes, yes, I believe," Bulov spoke hurriedly. "I believe
whatever you tell me."

"Then you must do as I tell you."

Bulov did exactly as he was told. The Russian Olympic team arrived in Innsbruck in late January 1976. He and Natasha were assigned to different sections of the Olympic Village. They arranged to meet each night in his room so they could make love, and it was during their first assignation that Natasha told Bulov of her plan to defect. She told him of all the arrangements she had made—of transportation to the United States, of friends who would meet her there, of the promise of a job performing with an American ice show. She pleaded with him to join her.

Bulov promised he would. For the full two weeks of the Games, he asked eager questions, pretending to be excited about their coming adventure. He listened to her answers with feigned enthusiasm. Yet it was a time of such fear and anxiety for him that he ate little, rarely slept, and sometimes when alone he retched uncontrollably for many minutes at a time. Furthermore, his knees were the worst they had ever been. The pain was grinding and constant. He was now a slow, lumbering skater, useless to his team, useless to his country. So frightened was he at the prospect of life in the Soviet Union without the protective cover of hockey that at one point he actually considered defecting with Natasha.

That idea lasted for only a few minutes. He knew that K-1's warnings were not to be taken lightly: the KGB would track him and kill him no matter where he went. He would never sleep soundly again if he defected with Natasha.

The Russian team won the Olympic gold medal in hockey at Innsbruck, but Bulov stayed on the bench. It was clear he would never play again.

Natasha skated superbly and won the silver medal. Then the lovers met outside the gates of Olympic Village the night after the closing ceremonies. They carried no bags. They hired a taxi, which carried them to Munich, eighty miles away. They checked into a seedy hotel in the Schwabing district and waited for the delivery of the airplane tickets in the morning. They could not sleep and were too nervous to make love. They lay tensely, silently awake in each other's arms. Suddenly there was a sharp knock at the door. It was too early for the ticket delivery. Natasha pleaded with Bulov not to open the door but he reassured her that no one could possibly know where they were.

When he opened the door, five burly Russians burst into the room. One of them carried a thick black-rubber truncheon. He said to Bulov, "Good job, Ivan. If you are not still a hockey star, you are a star at bringing down traitors. Hold her so she doesn't scream."

Natasha turned her large brown eyes on Bulov. A look of horror twisted her lovely face. Her skin turned a ghastly gray. She opened her mouth but the sounds that came out were incomprehensible—gaggings and gulpings as if she were strangling.

Bulov said to her, "I'm sorry. I'm sorry. I had no choice, I . . ."

Then Natasha began to shriek. It was a fierce animal screech that made Bulov's hair rise. The KGB man rasped in a hoarse whisper, "Shut her up, Ivan! Hold her tight."

Bulov grabbed Natasha from behind and clamped his hand over her mouth. He thought the policemen would now simply bind her and gag her. To his horror, the man with the truncheon took Natasha's left foot in his left hand, placed the heel on a table top, and held it firmly. Her leg was stretched straight and stiff before him. He raised the truncheon and brought it down in a swift, cruel arc that shattered her kneecap as if it were an overturned china cup.

Bulov felt his lover convulse in a single spasm of pain. She bit his hand so hard he trumpeted with the pain. Then she went limp and Bulov began to retch.

Quickly and efficiently the KGB men carried the unconscious Natasha along the dim hotel corridor and down the stairway. It was the last time Bulov saw her. He lay weeping and retching in the Munich hotel room for three hours, then he took a taxi back to Innsbruck. He was with the Russian Olympic team the next evening when it returned in triumph to Moscow. He later heard that Natasha had been imprisoned at Gulinka, that her hair had turned gray, that her left leg was permanently as stiff as a wooden post.

He peered closer at the fractured sections of his face in the mirror. Of course, his features made no sense; the distortion was monstrous. One eye glared out of one shard of mirror, the other was two inches lower in another. The scars on his face made zigzag lunatic patterns. Bulov was frightened. He felt a chill pass through his body. What had he done? What had he become?

There was a knock at his door. Startled, he shouted too loudly, "Who's there?" A woman's voice replied in Swedish, "Shh. It is Mai, Ivan. I am keeping our date."

He moved like a robot to the door. The woman who entered was tall with silky blonde hair, high cheekbones, china blue eyes, a radiant, expectant face. When she saw the shambles of the room, her look changed to fear. She asked anxious questions. Bulov explained numbly that it had merely been a party for drunken weightlifters. She accepted this and hurriedly undressed. She stood before Bulov—a statuesque, eager nude. He gazed at her blankly. She had disrobed so quickly that he had no time to tell her he had no inclination to go to bed with her tonight. He undressed automatically and lay next to her. He sighed and she assumed it was in anticipation of ecstasy. In reality it was a sigh of despair, for Bulov knew perfectly well there was nothing in store for her but disappointment and for him, only humiliation.

APRIL 12, 1984
New York

Ordway shifted uncomfortably in his chair as he and
Booth and Johnny Magnuson scrutinized the wall-sized television screen in Booth's office. It glowed in sharp-focused
living color, filling the room with terrible moments of the
weightlifter's death in Stockholm. Ordway felt queasy all
over again as he watched the sturdy figure of the Moroccan
collapse, twitch in convulsions, stiffen, then flop limp in
death.

Booth shook his head. "It's dramatic, but *so* grotesque."

They watched the shouting, shoving crowd gather around
the inert form. They heard Ordway's voice declaring that
something tragic and inexplicable had occurred, then saw
Ordway interview the old Russian hockey star Ivan Bulov

and heard his flat declaration that the doctor had declared the cause of death to be a heart attack.

Johnny Magnuson looked over to Ordway. "How could the doctor tell it was a heart attack so quickly? The guy hadn't been dead five minutes. They can't tell that fast, can they?"

Ordway answered, "I don't know. The doctor spoke in Swedish. Ivan understands it, I guess."

Booth said softly, "It doesn't matter. It was a heart attack. They said so after the autopsy."

They watched the entire tape, which included ambulance attendants carrying the corpse out of the arena and the later press conference at the hospital where a doctor made his report. The screen went black at last and Ordway sighed. "It was like some kind of crazy man's nightmare. Weird stuff was happening all the time. Vasily Kirchov was sobbing like a baby when that little guy died. He grabbed me and shook me and almost tore my coat off."

Magnuson said, "And there was that little ferret, Ludwig Scheibl, and his swindles. What a trip!"

Booth spoke sharply. "Scheibl! What did that snake want?"

Ordway said, "He told us he had an idea that the Russians were getting ready to come to the Olympics after all. He said they've been getting ready for it and figure to make a big propaganda coup out of it."

Booth's voice was heavy with scorn. "That little bastard will say anything he thinks will get him some payola out of us. Anything."

"I agree," Ordway answered. "For what it's worth, Scheibl did say he wouldn't expect any dough from you until the Russians actually show up. He figured his early warning—giving you a chance to get ready if they come—might be worth a few schillings when the time comes."

Booth scowled but then said, "Just for your information, we *are* ready. I have a special section of the master control system set up for a direct feed to the Soviet Union from Los Angeles if by some wild chance they do come. I have dossiers from MBC correspondents in Moscow on the best Russian athletes. Also I have all I can get on the current situation from the State Department and the CIA." He paused, then said evenly, "And there still isn't one scintilla of evidence that they're going to come."

Magnuson said, "Isn't it awfully expensive then, Robin? I mean, all that preparation will be wasted if they don't show up. Can the network afford it?"

Booth shook his head in resignation. "We really can't, but we have no choice. We can't afford *not* to be prepared for everything."

"Well," Magnuson said, "it's your bucks. I'm just the guy in the chair. Now what about this tape on the dead weightlifter? Do we include it in the *Sports Week* package or not?"

Booth didn't hesitate. "Oh, no, John. It's incredible stuff but it's too macabre. We're dealing in entertainment, not death."

"I agree," Magnuson said. "Besides, I checked and the story got no more than a paragraph or so of coverage in the States anyway."

Magnuson rose and left the office. Ordway picked up his briefcase to follow, then recalled that he had a contract in it involving his endorsement of a breakfast cereal. He had been carrying it with him for a week, meaning to show it to Booth, as he was required to contractually. He set the briefcase on Booth's desk, snapped it open. Lying on top of the other papers in it was an envelope from the Grand Hotel in Stockholm. A single word was printed in shaky, childish block letters on the front: JOE.

Ordway found a folded piece of hotel stationery inside the envelope. The sheet was covered with painfully scrawled block letters obviously done by someone unfamiliar with English. It read:

ABBA KILL
HELP STOP
K.

Ordway looked up at Booth. "This must be from Vasily Kirchov. Scheibl mentioned something about a message."

Booth took the sheet of paper. "It doesn't make sense. 'Abba'? What the hell is Abba?"

"That was the name of the little Moroccan who died."

Booth examined the paper. "It's gibberish. But then you said Kirchov was practically crazed. He doesn't even speak English, does he?"

"Not that I know of. This looks like he labored like hell over it." Ordway frowned.

Booth put the piece of stationery on his desk with Ordway's breakfast food contract and rose casually. "Forget it, Joe. It was all part of a nightmare."

Ordway nodded. "To hell with it." He left the MBC Building and took a taxi to Maggie's apartment. He was determined to erase every vestige of Stockholm from his mind.

Paris

The money crackled in the pocket of his jeans—35,000 francs in 1,000-franc notes. It was a fine, satisfying sound and it gave him a sense of well-being that nothing else could do. Not even the world title. Not even the Olympic gold medal from Moscow.

Ian Robertson was twenty-eight, the premier decathloner in the world. He was the pride of New Zealand, even though he found it impossible to spend more than a few weeks a year in that faraway outland of sheep and scrub hills. Most of the time he was in Europe or America, a handsome, swaggering figure whose presence graced every track meet, indoor and outdoor, year-round on both continents. His price to appear was well known, no less than $15,000 for major meets such as this one, the Prix de Champions in Paris, and at least $8,000 for all others. Many people argued, but all paid eventually. He was worth it, as he well knew.

Ian Robertson was nothing if not an opportunist and a businessman. He had figured all the angles involved, in developing himself into a prized public property whose monetary value would reach its peak at the 1984 Olympics in Los Angeles. At that time, winning his second gold medal in the decathlon, he would be a world-renowned figure— and particularly popular in the United States. Already he had been recruited as a client by International Merchandising, Inc., which would endeavor to market his person in a variety of prosperous endorsements after the Olympics. Following IMI's expert advice, Robertson was carefully constructing his image as a dashing, amiable roué, one of those brash but terribly attractive athletes who come along once in a great while and captivate the world with an amazing combination of charm, good looks, and high-spirited swashbuckle.

Of course, his future lay in television. To that end he had had his teeth capped and his long hair bleached lighter than it really was. He had taken a course in speech elocution to knock off the harsher sounds of his near-Cockney New Zealand accent and yet hang on to the British-like inflections that would make him more appealing to the American public. He had even had a slight curve in his nose removed.

Robertson's role model was Jean-Claude Killy, the immensely likable and handsome French skier who had swept the 1968 Winter Olympics. He had also carefully studied other athlete-actor-salesmen millionaires who had emerged from the Olympic melting pot—specifically Mark Spitz, the 1972 swimmer who won seven gold medals, and Bruce Jenner, the 1976 decathlon winner. He had recognized their shortcomings, understood their strong points. Spitz had been an inept and wooden performer on TV who still managed to seem arrogant. Jenner had succeeded, it seemed, yet to Robertson's way of thinking, his endlessly grinning, toothy good looks made him seem a bit simple-minded.

The money crackled in his pocket as he walked down the Rue St. Germain de Pres toward his destination—a window displaying Jaguar automobiles.

He halted to admire the gleaming machines parked in the window. He swallowed once involuntarily at the sheer, stark beauty of these things, then he entered the building. He was so excited that he did not even notice the small, intense group of men who had been following him down the boulevard. There were five of them, all well-dressed but rather grim looking. One was Ivan Bulov, three others were Bulov's fellow members of the International Track and Field Federation committee on amateurism and anti-corruption. The fifth was a detective from French Sécurité.

Inside the auto showroom Ian Robertson walked up to the manager's desk and gave the man a letter and a check. The letter bore the stationery mark of a Paris bank. It introduced Robertson as a "client of International Merchandising, Inc., and public relations representative of the Apollo Athletic Shoe Corporation." The letter declared that the check Robertson carried—written in the amount of 105,000 francs on the Apollo shoe firm's account at the Paris bank—was to be honored in return for an XJ-3 model Jaguar that had already been ordered in Robertson's name. The auto agency manager skimmed the letter, examined the check, and looked up at Ian Robertson with a face wreathed in smiles.

The beaming manager reached out to shake Ian Robertson's hand. Just then the Paris detective and his entourage of avenging angels appeared behind the decathloner. The detective held up his police credentials and explained that the four august sports officials with him were interested in charging Monsieur Robertson with fraud. The check, said the detective, was a forgery.

Robertson spluttered in confusion. The check had been given to him by an IMI man in person. The deal with Apollo Shoes had been legally signed and sealed a week before. There was no doubt the check was legitimate, he protested.

But it turned out the check was indeed a forgery. So was the letter from the Paris bank. Robertson claimed they must have been planted on him. He insisted he was innocent. Nevertheless, he was charged with the crime, and this fact was duly splattered over newspapers' front pages around the world. Then, oddly enough, it turned out that the Paris bank had *indeed* sent such a letter to Robertson and that the Apollo shoe firm had *indeed* written an identical check for 105,000 francs to Ian Robertson in order that he might purchase an XJ-3 Jaguar.

So there was no actual forgery, no actual crime committed. Was there? Well, in a way there was. The committee on amateurism and anti-corruption had an open-and-shut case against Ian Robertson for a crass violation of the federation's code of ethics. It was true: Under-the-table appearance payments from track-meet sponsors were commonly given to almost every major star athlete. Also true: Gifts or cash or automobiles were at times—though not frequently—given to "amateur" athletes in return for their promise to use certain brands of equipment. And usually all of this was conveniently overlooked by the authorities. But this case was vastly different.

Exactly where the committee on amateurism and anti-corruption had learned that the original letter and check carried by Ian Robertson were forgeries, no one ever knew. But because his flagrant and cynical violation of amateur athletic ethics had come to be so heavily publicized—and so widely criticized—there was nothing to do but ban him for life from amateur competition. This, of course, included

the Olympic Games of 1984. The IMI group dropped him
immediately, as did Apollo Shoes. There was no commer-
icial currency to be found in an athlete who had been publicly branded as a cynic, an opportunist, and a hypocrite.
Ian Robertson would be returning to the bush country of
New Zealand.

New York

They embraced at her doorway. As she stepped back her laughter was as light as a child's. "It seems eons since you left. I thought about you all the time."

He put his arms around her again and they pressed together. The top of her head came to his lips and he could smell the faint fragrance of her hair. He blew on the curls lightly, then kissed her hair. She turned her face up to him, they kissed softly, and she said in a whisper, "Let's go to bed."

It was three in the afternoon and they did not get up again until almost eight that night. He had never been more aware of the pure sensuousness of sex. He and Maggie did things that afternoon that were as delicious as anything he had experienced with any woman. There was a selflessness in lovemaking with Maggie O'Rourke that moved Joe Ordway very much.

They went to dinner at Gino's on Lexington Avenue. She was uncharacteristically silent for a time, her brow knit in a thoughtful frown. At last she put her hand over his and said, "Joe, I'm not going to be able to write about you. It's impossible now. I never planned to cut you up, but I did plan to write you as rather an absurd figure, a hero in a time when the only heroism available is ersatz. Obviously I don't see you that way anymore. You're Joe Ordway, the man in my bed. There's nothing ersatz about you at all."

"Frankly, Maggie, I'm a little disappointed. Those interviews were getting to be a kind of purge, I guess. I've never talked about myself that much in my life. I was learning something although I'm not sure what . . ."

"Well, you don't have to stop talking, Joe. Obviously I'm even more curious to know about you now. The reasons are different, but they are also a whole lot more compelling." She paused, then said almost shyly, "Would you tell me about your marriages?"

Ordway found that his memories were surprisingly dim, perhaps repressed because of the failures that all his ventures into wedlock had come to be. For some reason he had never considered his marriages as an intertwined combination. They seemed to be utterly separate and isolated from each other. Indeed, his own personality in each of the three seemed totally different, from one marriage to the next, and certainly different from the man he was today.

With Janet, the first, he had been the classic dumb athlete who refused to join a world of grownups. With Mimi he had been a living phallic symbol, willing sidekick in any orgy of dissolution and dissipation that happened to come along. And with Jackie, as she had said herself, being married to him was like being the wife of Jesus.

Joe had to concentrate hard to recall Janet's face, even

though she had been very beautiful. Tall, with tawny hair, radiant skin, and a magnificently wide and toothy smile, she had been the classic rich girl of the 1950s, daughter of a Chicago doctor, president of the best sorority at the university, a very sophisticated lady—she drank brandy and soda and drove a red Buick convertible. When they were married in the winter of 1961, a month after he had won the Heisman Trophy, the papers in Chicago referred to it as "the American Dream Marriage."

"What went wrong?" Maggie asked.

"Somehow Janet got it in her mind that I intended to go to law school. She had mentioned it in a glancing way before our marriage, but I didn't take it seriously. It was an absurd idea. Sure enough, as the spring of our senior year came along and we'd been married five months or so, she said it was time to apply for law school. I said I wanted to play professional football. She claimed I had misled her—and her family. I denied it. I convinced her to try pro football with me. Well, of course she couldn't stomach the people she met. There were all those big, brutish men—a lot of them were really 'louts,' as she called them. She hated the players, but she hated the wives more. She called them Betty Boops. She wasn't totally wrong. There were one hell of a lot of beehive hairdos and y'all drawls and deadly serious discussions of meat loaf and tuna fish casseroles. I haven't even seen her since the divorce."

"And number two?"

Ordway frowned. He had never liked talking about Mimi Manning. Three years of marriage to her had almost ruined him—morally, emotionally, and professionally.

They were introduced in late 1963 at an *Ed Sullivan* show. She had appeared wearing a tight, glittering black gown and sang "Daddy's Little Girl" in the babyish voice she had adopted for her public role as a sex kitten. Her gleaming platinum hair was shoulder length, her skin was creamy. Ordway and three other National Football League quarterbacks had performed in a comic barbershop quartet, then threw footballs through a hoop. The climactic act of the show was a production number in which they were vamped by Mimi Manning. After the show the four quarterbacks went out on the town with a few people from the show—including Mimi Manning. They drank happily at several bars until they wound up, relaxed and bleary, at Downey's at about four A.M. The other three quarterbacks, all older than Joe, had made passes at Mimi during the evening and she rejected them all sweetly enough. Joe Ordway had refrained from any advances although he had become more and more intrigued by her.

As the evening—and the drinking—progressed, instead of becoming brash and noisy, she became gentler, softer, more feminine; a sleepy, sexy kitten. She and Ordway sat together in the booth at Downey's. Ordway felt her thigh press against his, at first languidly, then more firmly. The invitation was unmistakable. Mimi turned to him with a small, almost shy smile, her eyelids lowered, her eyes glistening. She said nothing, but he felt her hand rest lightly on his thigh. It seemed almost weightless, but then it moved, light as a bird, until it rested with an almost imperceptible pressure on his penis for a few seconds. Then it fluttered over his thighs again and reappeared on the table.

They left the restaurant together and spent the morning in bed in her hotel suite. It was a wild yet oddly sweet experience, filled with Mimi's shrieks and murmurings. She was tender yet passionate, and she led him into various acts of love that made them both whimper with joy. He had by then experienced sex with innumerable women, but many had been forgettable one-night stands, often so drunken or so brief that they left no impression at all. Even with the best he had never experienced anything like this. Here was Mimi Manning, *the* Mimi Manning, American's sex kitten of the sixties—and she was *his* this day.

They lunched in her room late that afternoon—two cold pitchers of Bloody Marys and eggs Benedict from room service, followed by an icy bottle of champagne. Early evening was spent in bed, then they went to "21" for a midnight supper. The sight of them together triggered a buzzing even among the world-weary regulars at "21."

As they dined Mimi spoke in a confidential, sultry voice: "I can't remember the last time I was fucked and sucked like that, darling."

Ordway was jarred by her casual use of these crude words, but he grinned and said, "It was like a dream."

She smiled and floated her hand gently up his thigh. She cooed, "It's real, babe, and it's just the beginning. We don't have to stop. Ever."

He flew to Los Angeles with her three days later and moved into her house in Beverly Hills. From the start columnists and paparazzi dogged their every step. He recalled for Maggie, "We were front-page news in every tabloid in the country. Every garbage-mouth writer and show-biz weekly sleaze touted our romance. We got as much coverage as Joe DiMaggio and Marilyn Monroe. The superjock and the sex siren! Another Joe and MM combo! I got so sick of it."

But for Mimi the publicity was important. She had been dubbed a likely replacement for the late Marilyn Monroe but had not yet made a significant movie hit. Neither had she proven that she possessed the magnetic presence of the inimitable Monroe. Indeed, so far her major appeal was her sheer transparent sexiness—sashaying walk, bouncing breasts, undulating buttocks.

Her romance with Joe Ordway was wonderful grist for studio publicity mills and they produced a storm of press releases about the couple. Mimi had just finished shooting a film when she and Joe began their romance. It was released in March 1964, a frothy bit about a chorus girl and a king.

Mimi's reviews were generally favorable and it seemed possible she might at last have been launched.

Whatever her prospects, Joe Ordway had fallen headlong in love with her and was enormously happy. He was twenty-five, and the excitement of life with Mimi Manning was like nothing he ever could have imagined. When they got married in the spring of 1964, their wedding produced a mob scene at a church on Wilshire Boulevard. Ed Sullivan gave her away. Bing Crosby sang. Elvis Presley was the best man.

By the end of 1964 Mimi had finished another picture, which her studio hoped would do for her what *Some Like It Hot* had done for Marilyn Monroe. Alas, the movie was bombed by the reviewers and Mimi's performance was greeted with disdain.

Ordway hesitated. Now how much of what came next did he want Maggie O'Rourke to know? He had to move carefully. This was a mine field.

He said, "Mimi always liked her dope. Pills and grass at first, mescaline and some razzle-dazzle stuff she got from Mexico now and then. Then she upped her intake. Cocaine, of course, and I think a little heroin once in a while. Well, I wasn't into that stuff but I was into her life . . . I mean, I had been really swept off my feet by her." He hesitated, then plunged ahead. "It's hard to imagine now, but I was *proud* of being Mimi Manning's man. Other guys envied me. They thought I was the luckiest guy in the world. It even added a dimension to my stature as a football player. I was a star on the field and now they all figured I was also a star in bed. I don't care how straight you might be, having a reputation as a competent cocksman on top of being a ranking pro quarterback is one hell of a combination . . ."

Ordway stopped and sipped his drink, brooding for a moment. Much of the last year with Mimi seemed to be blank. He supposed it was a psychological trick, erasing those memories, for it had been a year full of pain, anger, confusion, jealousy, shame. They were separated often. She played a series of dates in Las Vegas. Her act was built almost entirely on sex and innuendo. She gambled a great deal during these visits and, as Joe later learned, lost enormous amounts of money. She also slept with a large number of men there, too, but Ordway had known none of this at the time, and he had remained powerfully, neurotically, in love with her.

When the 1965 football season began, Ordway's concentration was impenetrable during actual games, but when he was not playing, his mind was consumed by Mimi. He had been informed that while he was in training camp that summer she had run up huge gambling debts in Vegas, more than $50,000. He had also been told that she would not be allowed to perform in Las Vegas again unless the debt was paid. Indeed, she was in danger of being blackballed by clubs all over the country.

"We managed to pay off her debts that fall and she went back to Las Vegas in late November. She was drunk or high on something the whole time. I'd try to phone her every day. Half the time some guy would answer her phone and say he was from room service. They fired her the first week in December. I still couldn't break from her.

"We lost four games that season, but we made it to the league playoffs. We were in Miami at some tacky motel— all the players and wives were there. Mimi was drunk and stoned for days—at night she'd curse the other wives."

"One afternoon I found Mimi in bed with a lifeguard. I beat the hell out of him. I even broke a knuckle on my throwing hand."

The press was duly informed that it had happened when he slammed his hand in a car door. No one doubted the story. Ordway didn't play at all and the Icemen were badly beaten. Later, the lifeguard sued for aggravated assault and the true story became public. Ordway figured his career was over.

"I was as low as I've ever been," he said to Maggie. "I was completely degraded. Finally Robin Booth called me."

"Your own Svengali coming to the rescue?"

"What? No, listen, Robin is a friend. When he heard how bad things were, he started moving. First he paid off the lifeguard and got him to drop his suit. Then he convinced me that the only way I was going to regain any kind of sanity, the only way I was ever going to be able to play football again, was to get rid of Mimi. I knew he was right. I just hadn't had the courage to cut it off for good. Robin hired a tough, mean divorce lawyer. It wasn't even necessary. By that time Mimi was so far gone in her dope and her booze she could hardly remember who I was." He paused.

"She was killed a year later in a car accident. I hadn't seen her once that whole year. I still felt as if I had lost the love of my life. I cried for a week. It was pure insanity. When I told Robin Booth how bad I felt, he told me that if I'd stayed with Mimi another year I'd have been drummed out of the NFL."

Maggie shook her head in sympathy. "God, how could you face the idea of another wife?"

Ordway was relieved that the sordid tale of Mimi Manning was finished. "Her name was Jackie," he continued. "She was a big, beautiful redhead—really beautiful. A sunny face and a great smile and about as gentle and passive as a rabbit. She was one of the Ice Maidens. She had a terrific figure and she was like a sack of flour in bed. It was exactly what I wanted. Blandness. Niceness. *Boredom!* Jackie was like being married to a sweet child. She loved cartoons on television. She was a Jesus freak. She said that marrying me was like marrying Jesus Christ because I seemed so good and so brave and so strong playing football.

The marriage lasted three years. Then we split, very gently, very passively, with a lot of mutual good wishes. I think we knelt and prayed together the night before I moved out."

"She was your defense against getting involved with another harridan?"

"I suppose in a way. I haven't been very involved—with harridans or anyone else since then. Affairs of convenience. But nothing serious."

"It all sounds very detached, Joe. Is that really the way you are?"

There was an odd note in Maggie's voice and Ordway glanced at her curiously. Her eyes were wide and shiny. She suddenly appeared very fragile, and Joe placed his hand over hers. He was silent for a long moment, then said softly, "No, Maggie, I'm not really that way." He leaned over, took her face gently between his hands and kissed her tenderly on the mouth.

She looked at him in surprise, then dabbed quickly at her eyes with a napkin. "I'm glad, Joe. Really glad," she said.

PART V

June 1984

JUNE 5, 1984
Brussels

Ordway sipped his Scotch and settled back as the airliner leveled off above the Atlantic. In six hours he would be in Brussels to cover the world wrestling championships.

In the seat next to him, Johnny Magnuson turned and said, "Do you know this is our eighth trip to Europe since January?"

Ordway said, "I feel like I haven't been without a case of jet lag for years. I look down out the window and I never know whether to expect to see Nebraska or the Alps."

"Once the Olympics is over we can settle a bit."

"Like hell! We move right into football season. I don't think there's even two weeks between the Games and the first NFL exhibition games." He groaned.

"Your problem is that Booth is making you into the world's resident expert on everything, Joe. It might be too much. You're doing all this international event coverage as a buildup to the Olympics. You're doing all the on-air promotional spin-in to the Games, all the public relations appearances, and this *Sports Week* stuff besides."

Joe sighed. "I'll be okay."

Magnuson said, "It's a question of how much you can cram into one life. You've been burning yourself at both ends." He paused. "The romance with Maggie O'Rourke isn't exactly light and easy on you either. It's one hell of a commitment, Joe, to get involved with someone like that."

Ordway looked at him sharply. "Have you been talking to Robin?"

"No. Why?"

"He's said a thing or two about Maggie." He looked at Magnuson and said softly, "She's something else, John."

Magnuson said nothing. He turned to look out the window. The tacit disapproval was clear. Ordway's affair with Maggie had not been received with warmth around the network. Most of his colleagues considered her an egghead and, therefore, a snob and an alien.

He sighed and picked up his newspaper. Three minutes later he was asleep and he did not waken until the familiar bump and screech of the tires told him the airliner had hit the runway in Brussels.

He and Johnny Mag took a taxi to the Adios Hotel, a discreet and luxurious establishment in the center of the city. A message was awaiting Ordway at the desk. It was a small folded note that said, "I must see you. Tell no one I am here. Scheibl."

Ludwig Scheibl again? Ordway sighed. The message seemed to have been scribbled in haste. There was no indication of how or where Scheibl could be reached, and there was the cryptic warning not to disclose his presence in Brussels—quite a break from the normal habits of the ubiquitous pest who was ordinarily so persistently under-foot.

"He's certainly being coy," Ordway said.

Magnuson replied, "Maybe he's learned some manners."

Ordway went to his room, showered, shaved, changed his shirt, and tried to shake his onrushing fatigue. The phone rang. Ordway said, "Hello." There was a silence. Ordway spoke again. A soft click sounded as the other party hung up. A moment later the phone rang again and this time a voice with a European accent said, "Is it Ordway? The MBC man?"

"Yes," he said. "Is this Ludwig Scheibl?"

There was a pause. "Scheibl? This is Ivan Bulov of the Soviet Union."

"Ivan! Good to hear from you."

"Yes." There was a tick of hesitation. "You were expecting Ludwig Scheibl?" Bulov's voice had an edge to it.

Ordway paused. He decided that, however foolish or selfish Scheibl's reason might be for not wanting anyone to know he was in Brussels, he would honor it. He said, "No. But he always calls me at the exact minute I try to get some rest. So I assumed it was Scheibl again."

Bulov's voice crackled jovially. "So you are wrong. It is I, Bulov, who is disturbing you. If you hear of Scheibl being in Brussels, please tell me where he is. Very important."

Ordway decided to change the subject. "How is Vasily Kirchov, Ivan? He looked bad last month in Stockholm."

Bulov sounded surprised. "Vasily? He is in very poor condition. His mind has snapped. There is no doubt. The drink and the pain of retirement did him in."

"I would like to send him a message."

"Message? To Kirchov?"

"Only a message of sympathy. I like Vasily. I'd like him to know Johnny Mag and I are thinking of him."

"It is not possible. He is in hospital for the insane. Sorry."

Bulov's voice was curt, dismissive. "But I wanted to discuss with you this wrestling competition and other things. When is good?"

"Tonight?"

"Yes." Bulov hung up with an abrupt click.

Ordway was pleased there would be a meeting with Bulov. Perhaps he would quiz him about Scheibl's theory that the Russians would be in Los Angeles. Certainly he would bring up Kirchov's strange message in Stockholm. Robin Booth and Johnny Mag had convinced Ordway that it was the scribbling of a madman or a drunk. Now that Bulov had reported that the super-heavyweight had been hospitalized as insane, this certainly seemed to be the truth of the matter. A question or two in person might clarify things. Yes, Ordway welcomed a talk with Ivan Bulov.

But what of Ludwig Scheibl? Ordway assumed that all he would have to do was wait in his room and Scheibl would materialize within minutes. After an increasingly impatient hour in his room, there was a tap on his door. A bellman gave Joe a small sealed envelope. In it Ordway found a scribbled message: "Come to the Square of Napoleon now. I will approach you there. Tell no one! Scheibl."

The writing seemed rushed, even panicky. Had there not been the feeling of desperation to the note, Ordway would have ignored it, but his curiosity was piqued. By the time he got to the square, it was growing dark. There were many people, most of them strolling slowly in the warm spring air. Flowers bloomed everywhere. Ordway stood beneath the statue of Napoleon and waited. Soon there was a tug on his sleeve. A small, hunched woman stood at his elbow. She wore a bandanna over her head and carried a large shabby purse over her arm. She said in a hoarse whisper, "Come with me, Joe."

It was Ludwig Scheibl. Ordway began to ask a question but Scheibl said in a frightened voice, "Say nothing. Follow me."

He led the way into an alley, then through a door that opened into the back of a shabby old coffeehouse and to a table in a dim rear corner. They sat down and Ordway peered at the cherubic face framed by the foolish bandanna. The rimless glasses glinted in the light as usual, but Scheibl's usually glowing skin was pale and there were bruiselike circles beneath his eyes. He looked exhausted and terrified. He spoke in quick, urgent tones. "Someone is trying to kill me. Twice. Here, tonight, as I came earlier to the Adios to find you. Two weeks ago, again, in Copenhagen."

"Who is it?"

"I don't know. The techniques are professional. The KGB perhaps. The CIA perhaps."

"Why would they want *you?*" Ordway could not keep the scorn out of his voice.

Scheibl gazed at him evenly. He seemed to be considering a more complete reply, then said curtly, "There are reasons for both sides to try."

"To kill a shoe representative, an impresario?"

Scheibl sounded resigned. "There are reasons. But I needed to see you, Joe, for two points of information. First, what did Kirchov tell you in Stockholm?"

Ordway was cautious. Ludwig Scheibl was not a man to be trusted. The ludicrous disguise, even the ashen, fearful face, did not convince Ordway otherwise. He said, "Kirchov didn't say anything I could understand. He babbled in Russian."

Scheibl was tenacious. "Joe! He gave to you something! A message. On paper, I think. What did it say?"

Ordway decided to avoid the question. "Kirchov was certifiably crazy in Stockholm. They put him away when he got back to Moscow."

Scheibl seemed startled. Tension pulled his face into a taut mask. "Who told you that? Who?"

"Ivan Bulov."

"Bulov! When? Where?"

Ordway told Scheibl of the call to his room. Scheibl seemed overcome with fear. He was trembling and there were tears in his eyes. "You did not tell him that I wanted to see you?"

"No, I didn't."

"Did my name come up?"

"Yes, in passing."

"Not about the Russians coming to the Olympics?"

"No. It was nothing. Believe me."

Scheibl seemed to relax slightly. He fell into a brief, bleak silence. Then he said, as if to himself, "Bulov. It might have been Bulov."

Ordway was puzzled. "What might have been Bulov?"

Scheibl gazed at him, blinking his moist, weary eyes. "The man who tried to kill me. Here, yes. And in Copenhagen, too. There was a bomb in my car in Denmark, my rental car. It exploded as I opened the door. Just before I climbed into the front seat in the hotel garage. Miraculously it did not hurt me. The explosion was timed wrong. I ran and have been hiding. Bulov was in Copenhagen, too. And now he is here, and I have narrowly escaped again."

"What happened?"

"It was two hours ago as I approached the Adios to see you. I was very careful. I had a false beard, sneakers, a rucksack, a wool cap. He could not have known it was I, unless—unless they were expecting me." He paused. "A car tried to run me down in the street."

Scheibl was breathing heavily. Perspiration glistened on his forehead.

"Bulov couldn't have known you were here from talking to me," Ordway said. "I said nothing."

"Perhaps not. But the message I left for you at the desk. Was it sealed in an envelope when you got it?"

"No, it was only a folded paper."

Scheibl sighed, nodding in resignation. "Someone knew."
"Bulov?"

"Possibly. It could be anyone. Many anyones."

Ordway leaned forward. "Tell me one thing. Do you still
think the Russians will come to Los Angeles?"

Scheibl nodded. "I am positive."

"Positive? What is your source?"

Scheibl became suspicious again. "Why do you ask?"

Ordway paused, then decided to lie. "Robin Booth is
willing to pay you a good deal of money if you can convince
him that you are telling the truth."

"There is no single source, Joe. It is based on my knowledge of what is happening inside Russia, from many people,
from many observations. They are preparing in ways that
can only be for the Olympics." He paused. "Also, Kirchov
told me in Stockholm that he thought this was happening.
Something he had seen at the Sports Council, something
in the computer readouts. He said the Soviets were using
computers to compare their teams, their stars, to other
teams, other stars around the world. They are like an army
preparing for war. It is for the Olympic Games, Joe, believe
me."

"Kirchov was your source? You believed him? You
didn't think he was insane?"

Scheibl shook his head sadly. "No, Joe. Vasily was
drinking a lot. He was very troubled in Stockholm. But he
was not a crazy man."

Ordway paused. He decided to tell Scheibl about Kirchov's weird message. He was about to speak when Scheibl
stiffened and gripped his arm. His voice was a frightened
whisper: "Wait! Those are KGB men! I'm sure."

Ordway turned and saw at the front of the coffeehouse
two burly men dressed in dark, lumpy suits, wearing wide-
brimmed hats. They stood at the door surveying the crowd.
Scheibl pulled his bandanna tighter around his face. He rose

from the table and said, "Joe, I will disappear. I will contact you. Tell no one you have seen me." He glided across the floor into the door marked *Damen*.

Ordway left the coffeehouse by the rear door. At the Adios he found Johnny Magnuson in the bar. He told him of his strange meeting with Scheibl, the confirmation from Kirchov that the Russians would be at the Olympics after all. As usual, Magnuson was skeptical. "It all boils down to whether or not you believe Kirchov was crazy. It's all so farfetched. Maybe Bulov will know."

Ordway nodded. "I think he's probably in on everything they're doing. We'll ask him tonight."

But the meeting with Bulov was canceled. The Russian called to say that he had urgent business and that he could spare no time until the following day. Ordway did not see him again during the three-day meet. When he tried to phone the hotel where Bulov had said he was registered, he was told he had never been there. Magnuson and Ordway flew home on Saturday.

It was while they were aloft over the Atlantic that the stunning story broke from Moscow. The Russian Sports Council announced that the Soviet Union would send an Olympic team to Los Angeles, as would all of the satellite nations in the European socialist community. The International Olympic Committee had been consulted and had agreed to waive all restrictions even though the entry deadline had passed. The confrontation between East and West would take place six weeks later in Southern California.

JUNE 13, 1984
Moscow

Igry had now become an unmitigated operational success, yet K-1 still had more to do. For one thing Vasily Kirchov had to be executed—now there was no choice. He had definitely spilled some information to Ludwig Scheibl about the computer operation at the Sports Council.

Even the icy mind of K-1 was slightly saddened by the fact that a man who had been such a rollicking and beloved hero to the Soviet populace would now die so ignominiously and in total anonymity. Rumors of suicide would be spread efficiently. It was ironic that he had to die at all, for Kirchov had really understood only the smallest bit of the vast *Igry* iceberg.

Indeed, K-1 still believed it was impossible for anyone

to crack the truth of Operation *Igry*. The plot was too well conceived for that. Only the tightest knot of Kremlin insiders—plus, of course, the Gamesman himself—would ever totally understand the grand plan.

Even K-1 had not been aware of the actual genesis of the conspiracy. When it was first revealed to him, he had been stunned by the audacity and grandeur of the scheme.

He recalled clearly that he had first learned of it on the afternoon of August 13, 1980, the final day of the Olympic Games in Moscow, when he was summoned into the august presence of the Presidium. The five men, the elite peak of the pyramid of Soviet communist party power, were gathered in a cavernous conference room in the Kremlin, a chamber with walls of burnished wood, a ceiling fourteen feet high ornamented with a lavish crystal chandelier that had once emblazoned these environs for Czar Nicholas himself. The five of them were tough old men, all gray faced, all gray haired. They wore heavily tailored dark suits and black shoes, the trademark wardrobe of the Kremlin patriarchy. They sat glumy around a long, polished table.

A television set, a massive forty-eight-inch screen in a rich walnut cabinet, was turned on. K-1 was mildly surprised to see that they were watching the closing ceremonies of the Olympics at Lenin Stadium. It was a moment of pain, not triumph, for the Russian leaders. Their great Games had been reduced to little more than a very expensive track meet among the communist nations of Eastern Europe and a smattering of athletes from the West. The boycott, led by the Americans, had depleted both the quality and the quantity of competitors in Moscow. What had been intended as further grand proof of the superiority of East over West had degenerated into insignificance, a sporting as well as a political dud.

As K-1 entered the room the chairman of the party was speaking in his harsh Ukrainian accent: "Shit! It is like playing with ourselves. The goat licking his own schvantz, the bear sniffing under his own tail."

Gritsky, the deputy chairman, spoke caustically: "They have made us spend millions of rubles, then forced us to play upon a pile of our own dung."

The chairman growled again, "It is pointless, joyless! The masturbations of an old man."

There was a moment of silence as they gazed at the television. The emptiness of the 1980 Olympics was perfectly reflected in the desultory nature of this ceremony. Even on Soviet television, which was striving mightily to glamorize and glorify these events, everything was permeated by the stink of defeat.

The chairman spoke again through clenched teeth. "What about this idea—the suggestion from the other side?"

K-1's ears pricked up at this odd phrase. Other side?

The chairman went on as if K-1 knew what he was referring to. "The *Igry* plot could be workable. But would it guarantee us the results we must have?"

Gritsky said, "The contact was very genuine. There can be no doubt of his commitment. He needs us more than we need him. His intelligence sources sound foolproof."

The chairman squinted, his large black brows meeting above his nose to form a single furry V. "We have already suggested that our presence at the Los Angeles Games is as likely as a donkey giving birth to a sparrow. We will make that official tonight—we will announce an uncrackable boycott. No Russians, no members of any European socialist state, will send any athletes to Los Angeles. The cold-blooded destruction of the 1980 Olympics by the opportunists of the United States has guaranteed that we will not compete. Never!"

Gritsky smiled thinly. "But if *Igry* works as we expect, then we perhaps shall change our minds."

"In an abrupt and dramatic reversal at the last moment,"

the chairman said, "but *only* if the results have been pre-guaranteed. *Only* if the Americans and the West are guaranteed to be left in broken pieces—utterly defeated—in 1984."

Gritsky went on as if reading from a script. "They will be all but annihilated by an onslaught of Soviet and satellite triumphs. The political impact will be stunning. The blow to morale in the United States will be crippling. Think of it! Our magnificent socialist athletes invading the very core of hedonism and capitalist decadence—Southern California—and reaping there more gold medals than all other nations combined. And there will be a billion witnesses seeing it on television. It will be the most impressive coup of the Cold War!"

K-1 leaned forward, attentively, patiently, waiting to be informed of the details behind this incredible prophecy. If it was what he thought it might be, it would be a monumental and very risky undertaking. And, certainly, most of the responsibility for tactics and logistics would fall to his own department. He fixed a small polite smile on his lips and waited.

The chairman turned to K-1. "We have told you nothing of this new possibility, because the idea is so new and so radical that we have not even decided whether it lies in the realm of reality." He frowned, that single dark V forming again above his small eyes. He cleared his throat. "It is an idea advanced from the outside—from the West. You will find this hard to believe—especially in light of the fact that the thrust of the scheme is to allow the Soviet Union to gain revenge for the damage and insult done to our own Games."

The five leaders turned to gaze with cold, grim stares at the lackluster ceremonies on the television screen. K-1 maintained his thin smile, but his mind was racing. An idea for Russian revenge that originated *outside?* There were, of course, dozens of possibilities: It could be something developed by the oil producers in the Middle East; it could have originated among the lukewarm allies of the United States, such as France, even West Germany or Japan, who might hope to undermine American prestige; any number of international business interests might have been the source.

All these ideas seemed monumentally farfetched at first examination, but as K-1 well knew, the truth of international political life these days was often far more bizarre than one's imagination could ever invent. He would simply wait to hear what the Presidium would allow him to know.

The leadership considered K-1 a mechanic and a technician, he knew that. They rarely consulted him about the initiation of a major policy. To them, K-1 was neither a philosopher nor a politician. He was, just as he had once defined Ivan Bulov, an executor of policy.

The chairman continued to scowl at the television for a moment before he turned to K-1. "Although the *Igry* plot is intricate and complex in its workings, the tactic is very simple. It calls for the elimination of roughly three dozen young men and women—all of them athletes who might in 1984 be in a position to win gold medals from our own athletes."

"Americans?" asked K-1.

"Not only Americans. A few perhaps. The victims will be from many nations—and many sports. We will pick our victims carefully so there is no visible pattern, no suspicion that there is any connection among them. It is possible, is it not?"

K-1 blinked once. His nasal voice was like the hum of a computer. "I think it should be possible, but it will all be a matter of detail, of tiny differences. There can be no visible similarity in their fates. By that I mean, they cannot all be murdered by a sniper. In fact, they cannot *all* be murdered—not ostensibly. They must be done away with in many various ways." His technician's mind had already begun its familiar clickings, fitting proper pegs in proper holes, outlining a broad sketch of the logistics and techniques that might be necessary to accomplish this odd goal.

. The chairman leaned forward. "You think, then, that the arithmetic is possible? You think that it could be done somehow without being obvious?"

K-1 asked, "How many athletes must be destroyed?"

"We have not yet done the figures exactly. But the Soviets and the Eastern satellites must come out of Los Angeles with no fewer than one hundred fifty of the roughly three hundred gold medals involved. We will ignore the totals of silver and bronze, for they will fall our way in plentiful enough clusters once we have arranged for the golds to be harvested. We imagine that perhaps thirty-five or forty athletes would guarantee the result we require."

K-1 nodded. "Thirty-five or forty would be, I think, possible. Such a plot is so outrageous, so bizarre in its way, that no one would ever make the connection between them. There is, as you know, no single agency or organization that makes any attempt to keep track of all world-class athletes in every sport. Each sport has its own federation, and officials of these federations are jealous enough of the empires they have fashioned so that they do not venture into other sports. They are totally ignorant of each other. So if a swimmer were crippled, the weightlifters would never know—and vice versa."

The chairman said, "We would, of course, have to leave many of the missions until a year before the Olympics because there will be new stars, new potential gold medalists rising in many disciplines."

K-1 frowned. "I realize this, but we must be certain to spread this work over as long a period of time as possible. Are there, for example, a half dozen or perhaps a dozen whom we can earmark now and begin to plan their demise?"

Gritsky spoke up. "Yes, of course. The details, the mathematics, we will leave to you. You should have no trouble extrapolating early victims from the comparative computer programs of the Sports Council. They list all world-record holders, all world-class competitors and their potential versus our Soviet sportsmen. It is as simple as to push a button, I think."

K-1 said, "If we are to be so subtle about these missions, we must know a great deal more about these sportsmen than their rankings in the world. Death is not necessarily the best form of annihilation, but if it is death, it must have an absolutely logical, unquestioned cause. It cannot be outright murder. Personal idiosyncrasies, odd habits, perversions, psychological problems, congenital health problems—these are all the elements we may be able to utilize. The research must be voluminous. There can be nothing left to chance. Every nuance may be invaluable."

The chairman nodded. "Yes, the intelligence is a problem." He paused. "But this, it so happens, is where we have an enormous advantage. Our friend from outside—our Gamesman, as he has called himself—has full access to precisely such personal nuances concerning any athlete you might select."

K-1 was puzzled. He knew of no intelligence organization capable of producing this kind of background material without long, tedious research on each individual. Such intelligence would require weeks of circuitous questioning of friends, family, teammates. It was a difficult assignment for even the most sensitive and subtle operatives. He had hundreds of intelligence experts at his fingertips. For this particular complex and intricately detailed assignment he could think of only two or three with the capacity to carry it off, and they were accustomed to working with political targets, not athletes. They would know exactly what to look for in dealing with a troublesome CIA man or a right-wing dictator or a Soviet traitor. But to probe for the key to the demise of a pole vaulter or a swimmer—that was something else again.

The chairman was talking again. "I do not entirely trust

this scheme. The Gamesman is highly intelligent and his idea intrigues all of us." He turned to K-1. "But it will be up to you, after you talk to him, to decide whether the project can actually be accomplished."

"Talk to him? When? Where?"

"He is in Moscow as an observer at the Olympics. He will visit you in your office within the hour to discuss the nature of the intelligence, as well as the basics of the plot. We will await your verdict," the chairman said.

As he looked back on it all now, K-1 marveled at how well everything had fit into the original overall pattern as it was designed by the Gamesman and himself that first afternoon. The intelligence produced by the Gamesman's global network of sources had served as the essential basis for selecting specific victims and for choosing specific— and extremely varied—methods for individual extermination. The material had consisted of voluminous and extraordinarily accurate information about each athlete's personal habits, psychological quirks, family traits, romantic entanglements, sexual proclivities, and so forth. Some of it was at a level no higher than gossip, yet all of it proved to be exceptionally valuable.

Thanks to the brilliant reporting from the Gamesman's correspondents, Operation *Igry* had already taken a toll of thirty-five Olympic athletes, each a likely gold medal winner in his or her event. And no one in the world was the wiser.

As K-1 had understood from the first, the victims would come from sports so diverse, from countries so far apart, from backgrounds so diffuse, that to discover a logical connection among them would be impossible. Even when K-1 himself examined the master list of victims and the causes of their elimination, it all seemed absolutely random.

Less than half had actually been killed, only fifteen, and none *seemed* to have been murdered. Three were apparent suicides. Twelve died in "accidents" or of "natural causes"— car mishaps, drownings, food poisoning, heart failure; one had fallen from a cliff while rock-climbing alone, another had disappeared during a solo cross-country ski trip . . .

These things had occurred over the past three years, each apparently isolated and disconnected from the others. K-1 was certain there was no way to tie any one of them to any other; that it would take a true psychic to uncover the whole truth. The computer at the Sports Council had been secretly programmed to produce ongoing estimates of Soviet Olympic potential vis-a-vis the newly changing structure of competition around the world. The computer now indicated that no further missions were necessary. The Soviet and Eastern European Olympic teams would absolutely sweep the Los Angeles Games—probably winning no less than 150 of the approximately 300 gold medals available.

Ivan Bulov would soon be able to rest. K-1 had ordered the execution of Ludwig Scheibl a month earlier, and the slippery little Liechtensteiner had twice evaded Bulov's attempts on his life. Scheibl's death was the last bit of bloodshed necessary to the *Igry* conspiracy, but it was a critical assignment. He simply knew too much—or thought he knew too much—to be allowed to live.

Even the Gamesman had been alarmed at the apparent extent of Scheibl's information and had taken the unprecedented step of contacting K-1 via the direct scrambler telephone connection through the Soviet United Nations Mission in New York City. It was an emergency system, with a complex code to be used only in the direst circumstances, but it had enabled the Gamesman to report directly to K-1 the startling information that Ludwig Scheibl had managed to impart to Joe Ordway in the cafe in Brussels.

The Gamesman! That brilliant and manipulative genius who had originated this entire magnificent, convoluted conspiracy. K-1 recalled again that day in August 1980 when he had first learned of the existence of *Igry* and the Gamesman. When he left the assembled Presidium, he hurried to his office to prepare for the meeting with the mysterious

creator of *Igry*. He had spent the full hour preparing lists
of questions, probing for weaknesses in the plan. Time had
passed quickly. He had been surprised when there was a
light knock at his door and his secretary silently opened it
to admit a tall, white-haired man dressed in a well-tailored
three-piece pinstriped suit. His bearing was dignified, his
stride confident. K-1 rose to greet him, then realized that
he had not been told what nationality the man was, and thus
he did not even know what language to use in addressing
him.

JUNE 19, 1984
Los Angeles

Booth surveyed the scene in the Beverly Hills Hotel ballroom. MBC had thrown a party and two thousand people had come. They were still babbling feverishly over the ten-day-old announcement that the Russians were coming to Los Angeles. What might have been a rather toothless competition among friendly nations had suddenly been escalated into a dramatic confrontation between East and West. The 1984 Olympics would be a bloodless Cold War battle as fraught with suspense and high stakes as anything since the Cuban Missile Crisis. Yes, there would be a truly epic quality to these Games.

Booth sipped his Scotch. Of course, he was very pleased. The timing of the announcement could not have been better although he had had nothing to do with it. The Russians had simply decided the right time had come to explode their bombshell. Booth did not know the reason for selecting the precise moment, but they could not have delayed much longer. Now that the news was gloriously public, excitement was building everywhere. MBC telecasts were expected to draw audiences that would break all ratings records. Nothing seemed impossible.

Booth spotted Joe Ordway across the room, his tall figure rising above the crowd. At his side was Maggie O'Rourke. Something would have to be done to break them up. Booth wanted to arrange it sooner rather than later, but he had no good idea how to proceed. God knows, Maggie was not going to be of any help.

Booth and Maggie had met to discuss the situation while Ordway was in Brussels. The meeting had taken place in a back booth at Costello's, and Booth had begun by asking her to keep it confidential.

"Why? Do we have something to hide?" She had been smiling, but her tone was arch, slightly irked.

"Not really. But I think it'd be more helpful if we can talk without Joe's knowing. I know I could be more open under that condition."

She frowned. "I really hate to compromise myself like that . . ."

He held up a hand, his blue eyes round and innocent. "Okay. Let's make some ground rules. If we get to something you feel you have to talk to Joe about, let me know and we'll change the subject. The whole damn thing is so terribly sensitive—for me—because it's meddling in his private life. But I'm a lifelong friend of his, Maggie. I'm a lot more than his boss. You know that."

She said nothing, and he went on. "I'm worried about what's happening to him. He seems distracted, unhappy with his work. He's got the biggest three weeks of his life coming up in July. What Joe does there could turn him into one of the most influential people in the world. Has he told you about the plans we have for the future?"

"Yes. They sound inspired, Robin. Joe makes you sound like an Old Testament prophet."

"I expect we are going to lead a revolution, Maggie. But that's not what we're talking about." He paused, then decided to plunge ahead directly. "Since he met you, Joe has gotten a new perspective that's causing him trouble. He no longer trusts his reflexes. He's beginning to think too much. You have caused that. Ordinarily it's a good thing: the more a man knows about himself, the better."

"But?"

"But . . . well, with Joe it's an insidious thing. The effect is negative. He is beginning to bridle at certain things he has to do on air . . ."

"He's not a professional actor."

"That's the point. He's a *natural*. And because Joe has started to doubt his role, that natural spark and genuine warmth is fading. Unless he is perfectly natural, perfectly at ease with things, Joe fails—exactly for the reason you're saying: he's *not* an actor."

"Joe never made a conscious decision to become such a supercharged TV star. It just happened. Now that he realizes he actually has some choices in life, he's beginning to wonder what exactly it is that he has been up to."

"Maybe that's good for an insurance adjuster or a taxi driver or a writer, but this man is operating in a very treacherous place. He's in the public eye. He is only as good as people perceive him to be. They used to trust him to win football games. Now they trust him to tell them what to buy, what to eat, what to think. Joe could easily ruin that image and destroy that magic if he begins to question his role. It's that simple."

"It's not simple at all," Maggie said. "Joe is a bright,

articulate man. We've had some very intense conversations these last months and, yes, he is beginning to see himself more critically. Is that so bad?"

Booth stared at her coldly. "Yes, it's bad. So bad that it could wreck one of the most brilliant careers this business has ever seen. It could also wreck his life. Joe Ordway is famous. He doesn't know how to be anything but that. He *needs* fame. If he begins to doubt the value of that, he doubts everything about himself—all his values. Everything he's been for twenty-five years goes to hell in a hand basket, Maggie. And what's left?"

"What's left? A man who has some independence. A man with a mind of his own, with a sense of *reality* rather than of image."

Booth shook his head vigorously. He was angry. "Maggie, you're operating with a closed mind. You have always abhorred commercial television. You have always judged it as brutish, cloddish, and tasteless. For a long time you've made it clear you think I'm a sell-out. Well, you're wrong. I'm not defending the garbage that's on prime time. I'm not defending the phoniness, the tastelessness, the garishness. I'm not defending any of it—*I'm trying to change it!* And I am closer now to doing it than I—than anyone—has ever been before!"

"But what about Joe Ordway? What is he? Just a tool in your grand design?"

"No, Maggie. He represents honesty in this business."

"You mean the *image* of honesty! The fact that he really is or isn't doesn't matter. You're saying that you have to keep him dumb to make him *seem* honest. You want him to be a ventriloquist's dummy for you to control!"

Booth said quickly, "I don't need to control him. But neither do you! Take a look at your own motivations. You're trying to change Joe so he will fit the cast of your prejudices. He was a football player and that is anathema to you as an intellectual. So you want to erase that fact, annihilate it. He is a commercial TV star and that is anathema, too—pure dirt in the eyes of eggheads. So you want to wipe that off the slate, too. You can't fall in love with this guy and then suddenly try to destroy everything he's been. All I'm saying is—watch out. Slow down. Take a look at *why* you're doing this to him."

She had gazed at Booth thoughtfully, frowning. Then she nodded slowly. "Okay, I've got some thinking to do, Robin. You're not entirely wrong. I don't like your motives very much. But then they may be no more suspect—or selfish—than my own." She stood up to leave. "I won't say anything to Joe about this."

Booth had not been satisfied by the talk. Certainly he had impressed Maggie on a couple of counts, and he was sure Ordway would not bolt from MBC. Not for a few months anyway . . .

The party swirled noisily around Booth, a glittering, jabbering maelstrom of movie stars, political figures, sports personalities, television celebrities. The deafening atmosphere of celebration suddenly became distasteful and he impulsively put down his drink and walked through the hotel lobby and the garden to his bungalow. There he phoned the maitre d' at the party and asked him to summon Ordway to the phone.

"Want to see the Olympic layout?" Booth asked. "A. J. and I are going to tour the grounds, the control center, the works. Come along. Bring Maggie."

Within the hour they were seated with drinks in the back of a Mercedes limousine—Booth, Ordway, A. J. Knox, and Maggie O'Rourke. The car wheeled silently down the palm-tree adorned driveway and rolled on through Beverly Hills. A. J. Knox seemed in the midst of a short sinking spell. His thinning gray hair was disheveled; his parchment face was lined and haggard. For once he looked his age, an old, old man, and in contrast to the rugged figure of Joe Ordway, the glowing face of Maggie O'Rourke, and the flushed good cheer of Robin Booth, the network chairman seemed almost mummified.

Booth said with ebullience, "You are about to view one of the electronic wonders of the modern world."

A. J. seemed to revive suddenly. He sat up straight. Pink rose in his cheeks. His thick glasses flashed, reflecting the passing palm trees. He spoke with hoarse vigor. "Wonder of the modern world? Bunk! It's a tangle of wires worth a hundred million dollars, give or take some. And if the Russians didn't come, it would be worth a whole lot less! You took a hell of a gamble, Robin. I should say *I* took a hell of a gamble! But tell me, what are those Red yeggs thinking? What do they have to gain?"

Booth replied calmly, "They figure they've got an edge, A. J. The propaganda returns from their Olympic success has always been enormous. They use it for domestic consumption. It also sells well in the Third World. Olympic gold medals give the Russians a prestige that all the missiles and space shots in the world can't match."

A. J. Knox shook his head vigorously. "Imagine that! Imagine that! Grown men and women running around in short pants can actually have an effect on the politics that operate this planet. Bunk!"

Ordway laughed. "I'd have clutched for sure if I'd thought another touchdown pass or two would change the complexion of the Cold War."

Booth said with a laugh, "You changed the complexion of American heroism—that's what Maggie says, right?"

Maggie said lightly, "Wrong, Robin. *You* changed it with all that television exposure."

A. J. Knox interrupted with a flourish. "Television changed everything, young lady! Everything! Goddamnit, I wish we knew what we were doing! Such crap we show!" He waggled his head sadly. "I'm too old to do anything different. All I ever knew was how to make money from it, and that doesn't take the brains of a blackbird. What a waste, what a waste."

The limousine turned off the freeway at last, rolled down the rainbow arc of an exit ramp, and arrived almost immediately before a gate of iron bars set in a fifteen-foot wire-mesh fence with triple strands of barbed wire along the top. The driver pushed a remote control button on the dashboard, and the gate swung open. It remained open until the limousine rolled through, then closed, with a final sinister automatic click. The car was now in a kind of corral, the iron gate behind, fences on either side, another iron-barred gate blocking their way. Three uniformed guards, all wearing mirrored sunglasses, appeared before the gate. Two more could be seen peering through windows from booths on either side.

"Bulletproof glass," Booth said. "This whole corral is capable of being electrified with enough volts to kill a herd of elephants."

Maggie said, "It's like a penitentiary."

"We've made sure that no kooks or terrorists will be able to get at our equipment. We've tried to make the place as airtight as possible. The Los Angeles Police Department is doing special patrols, and we have three hundred guards of our own."

Maggie asked, "Are things really that bad? You aren't being a little paranoid, are you, Robin?"

He shook his head. "After the killings at Munich, we can't assume that we'll foresee all the terrible things that could happen. We want to protect our own people and our equipment from every kind of trick and terrorism imaginable."

Maggie shook her head. "They call these games. I thought games meant *fun.*"

"Not for many years, Maggie, have the Games had *any-thing* to do with fun."

Booth showed the guards a plastic card. One of them inserted it in a slot in a small electronic box strapped to his waist. The box made a small chirruping sound and the guard said, "Okay, Mr. Booth."

Inside the gate the limousine rolled on through the MBC grounds, past a couple of office buildings, an equipment repair facility, a large garage for the network's fleet of cars and limousines. At last they came to the largest building on the premises. It was an old movie soundstage, a vast, arched-roof structure with no more esthetic appeal to its exterior than an airplane hangar. The interior, however, had been transformed by MBC's electronic architects into an environment that seemed to come from another world.

Booth led the party into the place. "Here is the electronic heart, mind and nervous system for the whole Olympic Games," he said expansively. "This is where all the ganglia come together. We call it Games Control."

Booth was immensely proud of the Games Control complex. It had cost $100 million and was equipped with the most spectacularly advanced television technology available. The cavernous spaces of the former soundstage had been transformed into an indoor village where 500 people could work. There were offices, editing cubbyholes, a large cafeteria. Video transmissions from the 300-plus cameras, scattered over 25 different Olympic venues, would be channeled through here. So would the sounds transmitted from more than 2,000 microphones planted to catch every pindrop of authentic noise—from the sound of a pole vaulter hitting the cushioned landing pit to the sizzle of the Olympic torch as it was ignited.

The lighting in Games Control was otherworldly, a kind of phosphorescent glow that produced no shadows. All the lighting was installed at a height perhaps a foot above a tall man's head. Beyond that, like an outer region of space, there was nothing but opaque blackness reaching into the highest caverns of the arched ceiling.

Their feet made no sound as they walked, and their voices took on a singular clarity devoid of any reverberation or echo. Booth explained, "We've soundproofed this place virtually into a vacuum. The walls and floors are lined with material that sucks up all extraneous sound, kills all echoes. You're dealing only with the purest resonances of the human voice."

Maggie asked, "Why go to that trouble?"

"First, it gives our on-air sound a purity that is exquisite. More important, it lets us use voice-activated computer equipment. Instead of punching typewriter buttons to set up a certain program, our technicians simply speak a set of codes into a chin mike and the computer obeys."

"How do you use it?"

"For setting up on-screen graphics, those printed bits of statistics or information that appear at the bottom of a picture. Also, we can vocally order up tapes we have catalogued in our tape memory bank. All the technician needs is the name of the subject and a number. These are listed in our master reference log. He simply says the tape title and the number in a low voice into his chin mike, and the tape is automatically racked up and ready to be edited, re-edited, cut, reviewed, or played on the air. It's more efficient than pushing buttons. There are fewer mistakes and quicker recall by the computer."

Maggie shuddered. "Do you *have* to give the place such an unearthly feeling to do that?"

Booth said, "If you think this feels like a *Stars War* set, come see the Games Control console."

The centerpiece to MBC's colossal Olympic assembly was the console. It consisted of a massive gleaming control panel eighty feet long, covered with a welter of dials, buttons, computer panels, toggle switches, blinking lights, tubes, lighted meters. During the telecasts it would be a workbench for fifty MBC technicians. Johnny Magnuson, as chief director for the whole production, would sit in the master control position—a horseshoe-shaped slot at the center of the console.

Beyond the console was a full wall, also eighty feet long, with row upon row of monitoring screens, some three hundred of them. Each provided a window that looked out from Games Control onto all the various segments of Olympic venues scattered around Los Angeles. Booth had ordered all three hundred cameras turned on for this visit. Thus each monitor glowed in color, showing the slice of Olympic territory that lay in its camera's line of vision. One beamed back a part of the Coliseum track; another was focused on a jump in the equestrian venue; another on a swimming pool, a diving tower, the soccer field at the Rose Bowl, the velodrome, rowing canals. Most of the scenes shown on the monitors were deserted, but here and there workmen were busy. From these three hundred glowing windows, specific images of the Olympics would be selected by John Magnuson and his assistants and transmitted to perhaps a billion spectators around the world.

Maggie gestured at the monitors. "It's Big Brother come to life. All those unblinking eyes, watching, watching." She turned to Booth. "It's 1984, all right, isn't it, Robin?"

"We're going to use those monitors as a Big Brother against the bad guys," he said. "Once the Games start, we'll leave the cameras on day and night as a security measure. They'll be like twenty-four-hour watchmen so no one unauthorized can enter the venues."

A. J. Knox had dropped wearily into the large leather chair that Johnny Magnuson would occupy during the Olympics. Now he revived. "What the hell is going on in the world when we have to hold the Olympic Games inside an armored truck?" he snapped.

Booth calmly answered, "Well, for those three weeks, A. J., this is going to be the center of the universe for almost all of the United States and for one hell of a lot of the planet besides. We will be feeding the whole world its nourishment, right from here. We have to protect—"

A. J. Knox interrupted fiercely. "Nourishment! A bunch of fools cavorting around on a glass tube? Fools no taller than a man's finger? Goddamn electric Lilliputians! Nourishment? From that?"

Booth said smoothly, "You are nourished by it, A. J.— with a lot of money—"

"Damned right! Profit, money, power! That's *real* nourishment. But do you think I'd spend half an hour—half a *minute*—watching this sort of bunk on a TV set? Hell, no! It's foolish. Stupid. Waste of energy, waste of time." Suddenly the anger drained out of his voice. "But if they want to watch it—hell, I can't stop them. I'm not my brother's keeper. Never was. Never will be."

"A. J., this is a high point of your career," said Booth. "In a way these Olympics are the pinnacle of what you have been doing—been *trying* to do—with the network ever since you started it. You have to realize that."

A. J. said sadly, "I know it, goddamnit, Robin, and I'm beginning to wonder if I spent a whole hell of a lot of wasted time. If *this* is what it all comes down to—"

Booth broke in irritably. "A. J.! This is going to make us number one! For Christ's sake! We are set to produce the finest sports journalism anyone has ever seen on television!"

The old man's voice was thin, struggling, but he went on speaking. "Yes, number one . . . maybe that's foolishness, too. Think of all this foolishness. You have these Games, all these people running around *working* at something that should be play . . . and you put that kind of bunk on a little picture tube no bigger than a dinner platter. And a billion people sit and watch it . . . and they . . . oh, my God, it's so absurd, so—"

His voice suddenly stopped. His face turned gray. He

swallowed once, a loud gurgling sound, then fell forward onto the Games Control console.

An MBC ambulance arrived with a doctor within moments, but A. J. Knox was dead. The old man's great muscular heart had simply worn out. They flew his body to New York that night. One thousand people attended his funeral two days later, and the following week his attorneys announced that he had left his fortune to the Sierra Club and the Audubon Society. They also said he had made it clear in his last will and testament that he wanted no one but Robin Booth to be chairman of the MBC board after his death.

PART VI

July 1984

JULY 26, 1984
Los Angeles

For the past six weeks Ordway had immersed himself in the politics, lore, and statistics of the Olympic Games with the devotion of a Talmudic scholar. He memorized the names and backgrounds of dozens of competitors; he analyzed individual approaches to individual events; he compared athletes to Olympians who had gone before. He studied four years' worth of files from MBC News correspondents on more than 200 Olympians. The material was voluminous, exhaustive, overwhelming in its detail. In some cases it included hours of taped interviews as well as written reports that ran to as many as a hundred pages. Every athlete's profile proved to be a mini-masterpiece of psychological insight and personality dissection. Each probed relentlessly

for the motives that drove the individual to a life-consuming
commitment to sports.

Condensing this immense volume of material to fit
MBC's daily Olympic programming was far more difficult
than gathering it had been. Robin Booth himself supervised
the editing as well as the scripting of the tapes. The majority
of profiles dealt with athletes likely to win gold medals. But
Robin Booth had provided an additional deft twist to MBC's
coverage by creating personality sketches of two dozen athletes who had no chance of winning *anything* in Los Angeles. Though their quests were hopeless, the profiles of
these certain losers were more poignant and, in many ways,
even more inspiring than those of the gold medal favorites.

The more Ordway worked with this material, the more
impressed he became with the genius of Booth's grand concept. As he neared the end of his period of preparation he
said to Booth, "It's awesome, Robin."

Booth replied with an oddly supercilious grin, "You
didn't expect anything less, did you?" He laughed as if he
had been joking, then went on, "Are you becoming a believer again, Joe?"

Ordway frowned. "Believer? What are you talking
about?"

Booth put a hand gently on Ordway's shoulder. "Look,
Joe, I know what you've been fighting your way through—
because of Maggie. I know you've been doubting a lot of
things about this operation; about yourself."

"Maybe that's true. I didn't think it was all that obvious—or all that big a deal, frankly."

"Maybe not. But I've been telling you from the start that
we were going to make history in Los Angeles. Now you
can see what I meant."

Ordway nodded. "I just hope I'm strong enough to go
with it. Sometimes I think it's so good it'll blow me right
off the screen."

Booth said, "You've got to scramble to keep up with it, I agree. But you can do it. Just keep your mind on your job, and don't let Maggie distract you."

Joe had spent more than half his time in Los Angeles during the final weeks of preparation. The otherworldly atmosphere of Games Control became as familiar as his own—or Maggie's—apartment. Maggie stayed in New York during his trips west. She was deep in the outline for a new novel. When he was in New York, he lived at her apartment. Each of their separations became slightly more painful than the last.

Finally she said, "What are we going to do when you're out there for a whole *month?*"

"I just assumed you'd be out there with me, Maggie. I've got a suite at the Beverly Hills, plenty of room. I'll be working like a fool. Probably twenty hours a day. But I never thought for a minute you wouldn't be there."

She smiled. "I'm glad that's what you assumed. I absolutely *love* it. But I think, my dear, that I'm going to stay here in New York. Frankly, I have a feeling there will be just too many tensions."

He had felt a sharp and immediate sense of loss when he thought of living for a month a continent away from her. "Maggie, I need you, your ideas, your jokes—my God, your body!"

She had hugged him and said, "Oh, Joe, so do I. Please try and talk me out of staying here. If you can convince me, I'll be there."

In the end he couldn't. Or didn't. Maggie convinced him instead. Thus, Joe Ordway was alone when he arrived at the Beverly Hills Hotel on Thursday night, July 26, two days before the Olympic Games were to begin. He checked in and was told by the desk clerk that Johnny Magnuson wanted to see him immediately in the Polo Lounge. Ordway went directly to the darkened cocktail bar off the lobby.

Magnuson was at the bar, perched like a small boy on a tall stool.

Ordway said, "You summoned me, sir?"

Magnuson turned a dark and frowning face toward him. "Joe. Damn! I'm glad you're here." He turned to look quickly over his shoulder. There were many drinkers in the room. Most of them were the usual preening crowd of Hollywood high-rollers, agents, executives, movie stars, and their sycophants. But also scattered around the place were many International Olympic Committee members, a haughty, aging, cosmopolitan crowd easy to pick out from the rest.

Ordway said, "What's the matter, John? You look hunted. One of your wives?"

Magnuson said in a hushed voice, "Sit next to me, Joe. Order a drink, then look around casually. Is that guy way at the other end of the room Ivan Bulov? It's so dark I can't tell."

Ordway ordered a Scotch, then said, "John, Ivan Bulov is one of the only people in the world you couldn't mistake for someone else. Especially when he smiles."

"This guy hasn't smiled for forty-five minutes. He's got a face like Frankenstein. I think it's Bulov."

Ordway turned and pretended to gaze absently over the room. At the far end he saw Ivan Bulov seated alone in a shadowy nook. Their eyes met. Ordway waved jauntily. "Yes. It's Ivan." He turned back. "Shall we invite him over?"

Magnuson kept his back to the room and spoke quickly through clenched teeth. *"No!* He's the one guy I'm trying to avoid. I figured the one place in the world where you'd never find a damned Russian would be the Polo Lounge."

"Ivan moves easily in strange circles," Ordway said.

"He's always given me the creeps, those Halloween teeth." Magnuson paused in suspense. "Is he coming?"

Ordway looked over his shoulder. "Yes."

"What I have to tell you will have to wait then."

Ordway watched as Bulov worked his way through the thickets of drinkers. He did not smile as he approached. He was wearing a well-cut blue blazer, soft gray flannel slacks, loafers that may have been Gucci, a muted yellow turtle-neck. His clothing suited the Polo Lounge precisely. Only the scarred, heavy-boned landscape of his face made him seem alien. He grinned slightly, showing the barest few of his metal dentures, and said to Ordway, "I have been sitting here wondering how a scarred old hockey player can make himself appealing to the actress Shirley MacLaine. She has been at the table at my elbow for an hour. I detect her fragrance with each move of her figure. I cannot bring myself to say even hello. What do you suggest?"

Bulov's words were easygoing, but his delivery was oddly heavy. He sounded as if he had memorized the speech. He produced a quick, stiff grin, then frowned and said nothing.

Ordway said lightly, "I can't believe this has happened, Ivan—we're here *together* at the Olympic Games. I still don't understand why you people suddenly decided to come. What changed?"

"I cannot say. I am far below the rings of Kremlin power."

"Didn't you know it was going to happen?"

"I? Certainly not." He grimaced. The metal pegs glinted slightly.

Ordway frowned. "We've been hearing for more than two months that you might come to Los Angeles."

"Yes? From whom, might I ask?"

"Ludwig Scheibl, for one."

Bulov's face darkened and one fist clenched. "That weasel. What can a thief like that say that honest men would believe?"

Ordway felt Magnuson's knee nudging him. He turned.

The director was gazing at his drink but, sensing Ordway's eyes on him, he shook his head in an almost imperceptible negative gesture.

Ordway did not understand, but he decided to drop the subject of Ludwig Scheibl. "Okay, Ivan, you're here now. Where is the Russian team quartered? Have you good rooms?"

Bulov was not to be diverted. "I tell you, no word from the mouth of Ludwig Scheibl is to be taken for truth. Do you know where he is?" His voice was harsh.

Johnny Mag interjected. "No one believed Scheibl, Ivan. Not one word."

Bulov stared at Magnuson with burning penetration, then spoke angrily. "Scheibl is a rodent. All that I can say good about him is that he has been out of my sight for many weeks. I have not seen the weasel even once since the wrestling in Brussels. For that I thank my stars."

Ordway said nothing, but his ears pricked up at this remark. As far as he knew, Bulov could not have seen Scheibl in Brussels—except for one occasion: when the Liechtensteiner was nearly run down by a car. Otherwise, the frightened Scheibl had been in hiding. Ordway remained silent. The Russian quickly finished his drink, rose from the bar stool, and said with a taut grin, "If you cannot advise me how to woo and win the heart—or the body—of Miss Shirley MacLaine, then I shall return to the dreary company of Soviet Olympic women. Good night."

Magnuson watched Bulov leave the room, then he turned anxiously to Ordway. "Joe, Ludwig Scheibl has been trying to reach you all day. He finally got me an hour ago. He's here in Los Angeles and scared to death. Says we have to come to him. He's still yapping about that message from Kirchov." Magnuson paused, then said quietly, "I think we better see him, Joe."

"Where is he?"

Magnuson lowered his voice as if the bartender at the Polo Lounge might be eavesdropping. "At the Palmtree Ritz, a cheap hotel in Santa Monica. He's been in hiding in Europe for the last month."

"Who does he think is after him?"

"The Russians."

An hour later they sat in the back of a bar across the table from Ludwig Scheibl. He looked like an old man; the lines in his face seemed indelible; and the bruised look around his eyes appeared to have sunk in permanently. Scheibl spoke with a slight tremor. "Thank God you have come. I am seeing shadows with death in them at every turn. I cannot sleep, I cannot rest. My life is a nightmare."

Ordway said gently, "You're not just imagining all this, Ludwig? A bad dream is only that—a bad dream."

Scheibl gazed steadily at Ordway for a moment. He seemed to gain a little strength now that he had allies with him. "Perhaps I have imagined some of it. But twice they tried to kill me. This I did not dream. I have been hiding now, like a wounded fox in a burrow, since our meeting in Brussels. Panic feeds from panic . . ."

Ordway began to speak but Scheibl held up a hand and said, "Please let us get on with our business. I must ask you again. Was there a message from Kirchov in Stockholm?"

Ordway quickly told Scheibl the contents of the message. "Is this what he said? 'Help. Stop.' Is this what he said?" Scheibl bowed his head as if the burden of this information was too much. After a moment he looked over the rims of his glasses. His eyes were haggard but his voice was sharp and accusing. "And you did not act on this information?"

"Act? How?" asked Johnny Magnuson.

"Tell the authorities. Open an investigation. See what the body of the Moroccan contained."

"Ludwig, there had been an autopsy. The doctor said it

was a heart attack," Ordway said. "What more could we need? Besides, you know Kirchov is in a mental hospital. The man was probably insane."

Scheibl wagged his head sadly. "Kirchov is dead. I have heard this too. A suicide, they say, of course . . ."

Ordway was stunned. "No one has told us about it. Good God! Vasily Kirchov was a world figure. He can't just die and never be heard from again."

Scheibl shrugged. "They have done exactly that. In Russia no one knows anything the authorities do not choose to make known. But the Moroccan . . . Kirchov must have been informed from the inside about the murder. Why would he invent such a thing? Even if he were becoming deranged—why invent such a maniac tale?"

Magnuson said, "We examined that tape backward and forward, over and over again. There wasn't a suspicious move on the whole tape."

Scheibl was very still. "You have taped the Moroccan's death?"

Magnuson nodded. Scheibl was breathless. "May I see it? If only to quiet my fears. If only to put to rest the ghost of Vasily Kirchov. Please?"

Magnuson frowned. "It's out at Games Control. The tape is in the computer bank with all the others." He turned to Ordway. "What do you think, Joe? Is it worth the time?"

Ordway hesitated. He was sure that there was nothing more to be learned from viewing those grisly scenes again, but the only humane thing to do was to let Scheibl see the tape. He said, "Let's go, Ludwig. Maybe it will clear up your nightmare."

Together they drove to the Games Control building. Once inside Magnuson moved knowingly among the myriad switches and dials on the console. From his chair in the U-shaped slot, he spoke with careful enunciation into a microphone at his side. "The computer will rack up the tape instantly," he said. "We can pull any one of maybe twenty thousand different tapes by simply talking to the computer in the proper code. We tell it the date the tape was made, the place where it occurred, and the name of the sport. I happen to remember the date on this one—April 11, 1984. So I said, '4-11-84–Stockholm–weightlifting.' That gets it. As for making new tapes, say, at any Olympic venue, I just speak the word 'record' and the number of the camera or cameras showing the pictures I want to tape into the computer. If I want every single scene showing on every single MBC Olympic camera to go on tape at the same time, I say 'record' and the word 'omni.' Then we've got everything being taped from everywhere going into the computer."

He looked up, his eyes glistening like a small boy opening Christmas packages. "This is the greatest damned television invention since the cathode tube. I can tape anything—*everything*—and we've got it in storage forever. Whether we use it now or use it later for a historical rerun of the whole Olympics, it'll be here. A whole hour of tape can be stored in a space smaller than the dot on an 'i.'"

Magnuson pushed a button on the console, and the tape of the Stockholm meet began to roll on a master monitor. Ordway placed his head in his hands. "I don't think I can watch that poor little guy go down again."

Magnuson sighed. "I've memorized every twitch of his body."

Scheibl hissed impatiently. "Shhh. Quiet, please!"

For the next five minutes they gazed intently at the image on the tube. They listened to the cries of alarm, to Ordway's recital of what might or might not be happening, to the anxious talk of the men gathered around the fallen lifter. Now the figure of the doctor rose from the body and spoke loudly in Swedish. Now Ordway shouted to Bulov and the Russian appeared at his side. Now Bulov gave his translation of the doctor's words: "He say heart attack. The heart failed. It was accidental death. Absolutely accidental."

Scheibl leaped to his feet. His voice was so shrill it was almost a shriek: "Stop! Wait! Stop! This is not correct!"

He turned to Ordway, his eyes wide with shock. "John! Joe! Play it back. Quickly! Quickly!" His body had stiffened as if it were charged with electricity.

Quickly Magnuson racked up the tape again. "Which part do you want, Ludwig?"

"The doctor! The doctor's words." Scheibl was trembling now, his eyes bulging behind his glasses as he waited for the images to appear again on the screen. Once again the doctor rose from examining the fallen athlete. Once again he spoke in loud, authoritative Swedish, then Ordway spoke, then Bulov. . . . After the Russian's translation, Scheibl turned to stare at Ordway and Magnuson. His face was grim. His voice was thin but unwavering:

"The doctor's words were these: 'He is dead. Call for an ambulance. We must take him to the hospital to find the cause. Hurry. Hurry.' That is approximately what he said. My Swedish is not perfect, it is only workable. But I know that Bulov told you wrong. The doctor did *not* say it was a heart attack. He did *not* say it was an accident."

Ordway was confused. "You mean that Ivan couldn't understand him? He just made up something to tell me?"

Scheibl shook his head. "No, Ivan could understand him. He speaks passable Swedish also. He knew what the doctor said, but he was saying it was a heart attack, an accident, to get rid of you."

"But that doesn't mean it *wasn't* a heart attack," Magnuson said quickly. "The autopsy was very clear about what happened. The cause of death *was* a heart attack."

Scheibl said calmly, "Perhaps this is so. But Ivan Bulov did not know from the doctor that it was a heart attack when he spoke."

"Then why did he say it?" Ordway asked.

"Because he knew the lifter was going to die. He knew

it would seem to be a heart attack. He wanted you to believe it. He wanted you to believe very badly."

Magnuson frowned. "You think Bulov was somehow responsible?"

Scheibl said, "Yes. Think of Kirchov's message now. Think of it! A killing. A murder—by Ivan Bulov."

Ordway said, "But what was the *point* of killing the guy? It doesn't make sense."

"No, it doesn't, does it?" asked Scheibl. He frowned. "But there is something here that we can't see. Something Kirchov perhaps suspected. Something, certainly, that Ivan Bulov knows."

Magnuson shook his head. "It's still just possible that Bulov did honestly misunderstand the doctor in all that confusion. It's possible he heard someone else say something about a heart attack."

Scheibl shook his head. "The coincidence is too suspicious. We must pursue this."

Magnuson disagreed. "I don't think there's anything to pursue. What is it we're supposed to be looking for?"

Ordway said, "I think you're right, John. We have nothing to go on."

Scheibl spoke anxiously. "But we have the answer to *something* here in our hands. We *must* try to find out what it is!"

Magnuson shook his head. "I've got too much to do now to think about this any further. We're on the air"—he looked at his wristwatch—"in less than forty-eight hours. I just can't get involved in this anymore. I just don't have the time—and neither do you, Joe."

Ordway said to Scheibl, "I'll take you back to the hotel, Ludwig."

Fear returned to Scheibl's face. "Please, you mustn't say I am here! I am leaving as soon as I can. I need money, Joe. Please, I have been of value, have I not?"

On the ride to Santa Monica, Scheibl agreed to remain hidden until the following day. In the meantime Ordway would arrange to get him some cash along with an airline ticket to Mexico City. When they parted, Scheibl was sad and resigned. His face was that of a very old man who had given up all hope.

Back at the Beverly Hills Hotel, Ordway was handed a message: Robin Booth had arrived from New York and was waiting in his bungalow. Ordway was relieved. He wanted nothing more than to discuss with Booth the latest revelation in the odd circumstances surrounding the Stockholm death. He hurried to Booth's bungalow.

JULY 27, 1984
Los Angeles

Bulov stiffened as his telephone jangled again and again. His room was dark. The lighted dial on the clock indicated that it was four A.M. He was afraid to pick up the phone. He was certain the caller was K-1 or one of his agents. His failure to bring down Ludwig Scheibl had caught up with him. This single stain on an otherwise perfect career almost certainly meant that Bulov was finished, even though it was not really his fault. The slimy Scheibl possessed an instinct for survival, a sixth sense that made his sleazy life charmed.

The phone continued to sound its alarm . . . At last Bulov picked it up. He said nothing. There was a silence at the other end, then a voice spoke in American-accented English: "Bulov! Ivan Bulov?"

Relieved that it was not a Russian voice, he replied breathlessly, "Yes, yes, it is Bulov here."

The voice was crisp: "This is the Gamesman speaking. You don't know who I am, but you certainly know of me."

Bulov was dumbfounded. He held the phone away from his ear and stared at it as if that might help him recognize the person at the other end. After a moment he whispered, "Gamesman? What does that mean?"

"The Gamesman of *Igry!*"

The unutterable word brought Bulov to his feet. His hand trembled. "I know nothing of what you speak." His English was suddenly failing him.

"You must believe me, Bulov. I have important information for you. It's about Ludwig Scheibl."

He knew this could be nothing except a trap, a snare designed by K-1 to reveal his weakness, his stupidity. Breathlessly he said, "I do not care nothing for Ludwig Scheibl. Or you."

Bulov wanted to slam the receiver into its cradle—to break the connection with this frightening stranger. But he held the phone tightly against his ear—waiting.

There was a moment of silence, then the voice said calmly, "I am going to begin listing names, Bulov. You will recognize them. You will then know that I am the Gamesman. Do not let the list go on for long."

The American began to toll the names of the doomed— Friedl Marx, kayaker . . . Kiki Ankeny, gymnast . . . Ali Abba, weightlifter . . . Ernesto Diaz, diver . . . Enzo Pavone, runner . . .

Bulov's face was suddenly drenched with sweat. It dripped off his brows, rolled in streams down his cheeks, off his chin. He cried, "Stop! Stop!" He swallowed hard, then stuttered, "W-w-wait." He went into the bathroom and dashed cold water over his face.

He returned to the phone. "You are the Gamesman of *Igry*. I believe it. What do you want with me?"

"I want you to complete your mission with Ludwig Scheibl."

"That is not so easy. He has been hiding like a mole in Europe."

"He is in Los Angeles, at the Palmtree Ritz Hotel."

Bulov shifted uneasily. "How is it you know this?"

The voice sharpened. "There is no need for you to know any details. Your business is assassination, not questions."

Bulov persisted. "He is there now? You are certain?"

"Yes. Tomorrow evening he is expecting a delivery of money and tickets that will allow him to run again. The delivery is to be made to a rental car in the hotel parking lot. License number is CSL 074. You have used a bomb before."

Bulov could not bring himself to submit completely to this disembodied voice. "Is this assignment from K-1?"

The voice was hard, chilling. "They were orders from K-1 two months ago, Bulov! Orders to kill Scheibl! You failed twice! No one has rescinded that order. It still stands. And it is K-1's order now as it was then."

"Yes, sir." The frightening bite of authority was in that voice. Suddenly Bulov felt as threatened by the Gamesman here in Los Angeles as he had ever been by K-1 in Moscow. He said again, "Yes, sir."

Bulov hung up the phone. At least he now knew a little more about the infamous Gamesman. An American! Bulov wondered how an American had gotten involved in the KGB's dark network. And why? But he had no time to ponder riddles. He went to a black valise and began to sort through the equipment there. Another bomb was the answer, but he did not feel confident. He was frightened, anxious, powerfully worried about his future, about his life. The way he performed the murder of Ludwig Scheibl could well dictate how he would spend the rest of his days—or if he would have any days left to spend.

Ordway paced his room. Nausea was a constant companion. It was almost midnight. In twelve hours the Olympic

Games would begin. The prospect of the day ahead loomed like a sentence of death. Again and again the grand music of the MBC Olympic theme thundered through his mind. It was Beethoven's Ninth Symphony, but to Ordway it sounded like a dirge for the doomed. He visualized the set in the control center, the large leather chair where he would rule as anchorman and oracle for three weeks of Olympic television. He would be the most visible—and the most vulnerable—man in the world there.

To make it worse, he could not forget Ludwig Scheibl and his ominous revelation about the Stockholm tape. When he had told Robin Booth about it, the network chairman had been predictably angered that Joe and Magnuson had allowed the hated Liechtensteiner to see the tape. Yet when Ordway went on to explain that Scheibl feared for his life, that he had been twice attacked, Booth agreed instantly to provide money and a plane ticket to Mexico.

"Let the creep have a break," Booth had growled. "But tell him we don't want to hear from him or *of* him ever again!"

That morning Ordway had phoned Scheibl to tell him the conditions under which the money and the ticket would be delivered. There would be a rented car in a parking lot at the Palmtree Ritz. Someone from MBC would place the money and the ticket in the glove compartment. Once the delivery was made, Scheibl would drive the rental car to the airport and take the midnight plane for Mexico City.

Ordway looked at his watch—11:54 P.M. Scheibl would be on the plane safe from whomever had pursued him. He thought of calling Maggie. No, it was close to three A.M. in New York. He had already talked with her earlier that night. He paced anxiously. His mind would not rest. He lay on the bed. His stomach churned. The Ninth Symphony thrummed through his mind. Again. And again . . .

The phone rang and Ordway sat up, startled and confused. He had fallen asleep for a few minutes. He looked at his watch—12:15 A.M. He picked up the phone. "Hello?"

"Ah, is this Joe Ordway?"

"Yes."

"Ah, *the* Joe Ordway. Of MBC Sports? *The* Joe Ordway?"

Ordway was irked. "Who is this?"

The voice was apologetic. "Mr. Ordway, this is Sam Morgan—ah, *Sergeant* Sam Morgan of the Los Angeles Police Department."

"Okay. What do you want?"

"We have had a killing here, sir. A couple of hours ago. An unidentified man who was, ah, blown up with a bomb. We don't know who he is. We need your help, I think."

"I don't understand."

"I'm sorry. Here's what happened, Mr. Ordway. This man—unidentified as of now—was the victim of a bomb in his car. It blew up shortly after ten o'clock. He didn't die right away, and the officers who came to the scene first heard him raving in German, then in what was probably Russian. Finally in English he mentioned your name. He said, 'Call Joe Ordway. Tell him what happened. Tell him . . .' Then he said a name our officers interpreted as something like Lionel Shabel or Lubbock Shiner . . . an odd name, sir."

Ordway stiffened; the hair on the back of his neck rose. "Scheibl? Ludwig Scheibl? Could that be it?"

"Could be, sir, could be. We wouldn't have called you at all. At first we assumed he was just some small-time guy, maybe a little nuts, who knew you from TV. But we found a piece of paper in his pocket with your phone number and room number there at the Beverly Hills Hotel. We were surprised he had that kind of confidential information. He had a passport made out for a West German named Willi Bremer from Dusseldorf. No other identification. It checked out as a forgery—"

Ordway interrupted. "Where is Ludwig Scheibl now?"

"He's in the morgue. What's that name again?"

"S-C-H-E-I-B-L. Ludwig Scheibl."

"You'd know him if you saw him?"

"Yes."

"I hate to ask this of you, Mr. Ordway. I mean it's a hell of an imposition, but is there any way you could, ah, come down and identify this man's body? We don't know anyone else who knows him and, ah . . ."

"I'll come as soon as I can. Did he say anything else before he died? Any idea who set the bomb?"

"Well, ah, it was in a rented car. We have a suspicion it might have something to do with some kind of terrorist operation at the Olympics. We sort of assumed he might be involved with one of those German terrorist gangs. Maybe a bomb went off by mistake. Pure theory, of course."

"You're dead wrong."

"We are? How would you, ah, know that, Mr. Ordway?"

"I'll tell you when I get there. Is there any hint as to who might have done it?"

"Yes, sir. The car was parked in the lot at the Palmtree Ritz for quite a while. A bellman says he saw someone tinkering with it during the afternoon. The car hood was up. A man was leaning into the motor."

"What kind of man?"

"The bellman is very vague. He recalls a tall man, big shoulders, blue blazer. His face was tough-looking, he remembers that. The guy was wearing dark glasses."

"Scarred face?"

"He didn't say that, but maybe that's what he meant. He has a memory of kind of bad teeth. He was never close to the guy and he never paid much attention to him—you know how those things are."

Ordway blinked in disbelief as he heard the description. It had to be Ivan Bulov. Good God! And what a mess this was going to be. If the Los Angeles cops tried to arrest him, the Russians would refuse to let him be taken. Ivan Bulov was a Soviet hero, a respected functionary in world sports organizations—including the International Olympic Committee itself. Ordway groaned. But there was no other possibility: Bulov had murdered Ludwig Scheibl.

Ordway said to the officer, "I'll be wherever you want me in half an hour." He listened to directions to the county morgue, then hung up and dialed Robin Booth.

Booth sounded stunned by the news, but was particularly alarmed over the possibility that a horrendous international flap could arise if the L.A. police went after Bulov. After a moment of thought he said that he would personally go to the hotel where the Russian ambassador was staying and try to arrange for some peaceable way to handle things. "I know the ambassador," said Booth, "and I think if I visit him in person, we might be able to arrange the whole thing quietly. God knows, we don't need a big Russian–American fuss over some cheap little creep to foul up the opening of the Games. I'll meet you in a couple of hours at Games Control to talk about what we should do next."

Bulov was dead asleep when the Gamesman phoned. He had to ask the man to talk slowly because he was confused by his rapid-fire English. The voice spoke carefully. "Ordway is convinced you killed Scheibl. I don't think the police will be coming for you for a while. There is a lot of confusion. But I think eventually they will try to question you today."

Bulov felt his heart drop. "They know it is me? How did they even guess?"

"A witness who saw you working on the car could only describe you as being tough-looking and something about your teeth. But Ordway knew immediately. Of course, Scheibl had mentioned your name, you know that."

Bulov felt a wave of panic sweep over him. They had him. The entire *Igry* conspiracy could be blown by this situation. K-1 would never cease hunting him. Something

close to a sob rose in his voice. "What can I do? How can
I be saved?"

The Gamesman's voice was soothing. "Settle yourself
down, Ivan. You have done a good job. Ludwig Scheibl
is no longer alive to point his finger. No one is certain that
you are the killer. No one knows anything for certain."

Bulov relaxed slightly. "Yes. There is nothing definite
to tie me to Scheibl, is there?" He paused and the fear
returned. "But the police will want to question me?"

The Gamesman was matter-of-fact. "I think our best
move is to get you out of Los Angeles—now."

"Isn't that more suspicious than if I stay and deny all
accusations?"

"Not necessarily. You can be recalled to the United Nations Mission in New York, urgent business of some kind."

Bulov thought for a moment. Yes, he could do this—fly
to New York, take refuge in the mission, contact K-1 from
there, and have him arrange an explanation for the Soviet
Olympic delegation in Los Angeles to cover the sudden
departure. It would make sense. There would be a stain,
yes, something less than perfection in the way he had executed his mission. But in the light of so many successes
over the past years, this could easily be forgiven.

The Gamesman went on, "I will deal with Joe Ordway.
Nothing will go wrong."

Bulov was skeptical that it would all be accomplished
so easily. Yet, like a small boy listening to a reassuring
adult, he wanted to believe every word the Gamesman uttered. So he said with a small sigh of relief, "Tell me what
to do. I will do it."

The Gamesman briskly outlined plans for a meeting between himself and Bulov, the purpose being to give the
Russian a plane ticket to New York.

"Drive your car to the peristyle entrance to the Coliseum," the Gamesman said. "I will meet you there at four

fifteen. The area will be deserted." He paused. "I would like to shake your hand, Ivan. You have been heroic."

Authority rang in the voice of the Gamesman, exactly what Bulov wanted to hear. He glowed with the praise. He said, "I shall look forward to meeting the Gamesman. You have been at the core of my life for a long time."

Booth hung up the phone and looked at his watch. It was three-thirty A.M. In eight and a half hours the opening ceremonies would begin. He was tired, but extremely exhilarated. He had never experienced quite such an intense sensation of well-being. He seemed to be breathing the sharp, pure air of something close to omnipotence. He poured himself a Scotch over ice. There had been flaws in the plan, but they were proving to be barely discernible hairline cracks. The killing of Scheibl had been an unnecessary complication; Bulov should have stamped out his life many weeks before. Booth was still slightly concerned by Ordway's suspicions, but he had no doubt that he could handle the ex-quarterback.

Ordway was no longer so malleable as he had once been, but even so there remained the old ugly secret that Booth alone knew. As always, this hung like a bright guillotine blade over Ordway. If Booth ever decided to let the blade fall, Ordway's career would be destroyed, his life permanently disfigured.

Booth was confident. Everything was working so well. The direct phone connection with K-1, patched up an hour ago through the Soviet Mission switchboard in New York, had been perfect. And K-1's reaction to the crisis in Los Angeles was, to Booth's way of thinking, also perfect. Without hesitation K-1 had decided to sacrifice Bulov. He would arrange for three KGB men who were in Los Angeles with the Soviet Olympians to grab Bulov when he arrived to meet Booth. They would drug the old hockey star, bring

him to New York on a private jet, then take him on Aeroflot
to Moscow—and Gulinka. Meanwhile, the Los Angeles
police would be encouraged to pursue Ordway's belief that
Bulov had killed Scheibl. K-1 had arranged it so that when
they came to the Soviet delegation looking for Bulov, the
Russian ambassador would diplomatically—and privately—agree that they had the right man. He would tell
the police that Bulov had been drinking heavily, that he and
Ludwig Scheibl had for many years shared a violent dislike
for each other. The Soviet representative would say that he
had questioned Bulov himself and that Bulov had actually
confessed to the murder. The ambassador would say that
it was a shame, an embarrassment, that a former Soviet hero
would kill a man in cold blood. Naturally the Russians
wanted to keep it quiet. They would like to deal with him
themselves with typically efficient Soviet justice. In fact,
Ivan Bulov was already on his way back to Moscow, the
ambassador would say, and now he would appreciate it very
much if the matter could be forgotten. Let the Olympics go
on . . .

Robin Booth left the Beverly Hills Hotel at fifteen minutes before four A.M. and drove to the peristyle entrance of
the Los Angeles Coliseum to see that Ivan Bulov was delivered into the hands of the men he feared most on earth—
agents of his own KGB.

Joe Ordway stared at the mangled remains of Ludwig
Scheibl. The bomb had exploded at the base of the steering
wheel and sent black powder and shrapnel blasting into his
legs, groin, and abdomen. His lower body had been almost
completely destroyed. That he had lived for even a few
minutes was amazing. That he had been able to speak was
miraculous. The police were anxious to know everything
Ordway knew about Scheibl.

"Could he have been tied up with some terrorist outfit?"
a detective asked.

"No, Ludwig was a private opportunist. He had no politics at all. He was out only for his own gain."

"Who could have wanted to kill him?"

Ordway paused. Booth had advised him against implicating Bulov until he had met with the Soviet ambassador.

Ordway said, "He was a pretty sleazy operator. He was probably harmless but a lot of people will think it's just as well he's dead."

"Well, Mr. Ordway, is there any individual you know of?"

"I couldn't pin it on anybody specific. I do know that he absolutely was not a terrorist. He had easy access into and out of the Soviet Union. That was the main thing that set him apart from a lot of other wheeler-dealers."

"You think the Russians might know something about him?"

Ordway shrugged. "Maybe. I don't know." The police thanked him for his cooperation. A morgue attendant asked him for his autograph and he signed a tag that would otherwise have been attached to a toe of the next corpse. When Ordway finally left the building, he breathed deeply of the Los Angeles night air. It was disappointingly warm and not much fresher than the air inside the morgue. He checked his watch—3:50 A.M.

He drove swiftly back along the freeway toward Games Control. The guard at the gate let him through and said Booth had not yet arrived. The vast premises were deserted except for an occasional parked MBC security police car with uniformed figures barely visible in the darkened interiors.

Ordway entered the cavernous spaces of Games Control. The lights were dimmed. The lower area was gloomy and the blackness rising to the arched roof was more opaque than ever. This place was deserted, too. He moved toward the eighty-foot console, which Johnny Mag and his platoon of technicians would occupy in the morning. The director's chair was situated in the horseshoe-shaped indentation with all the critical computerized controls within reach on the counter. Beyond the console panel was the long wall covered with monitor eyes. As usual, all three hundred cameras had been turned on for the night to act as silent, staring watchmen over the deserted Olympic venues. The monitors gazed steadily at a variety of environments—row upon row of empty seats in the Coliseum, the still, turquoise waters of a swimming pool, an empty track and jumping pits, the soccer field at the Rose Bowl, the velodrome, diving pools, equestrian jumps. . . . There was no human sign, no motion at all showing on any of the monitors.

Ordway sank down in the director's chair and gazed blankly ahead. The vision of Ludwig Scheibl's mangled body haunted him. His body felt as if it weighed tons. He realized that except for the brief nap before the police summoned him to the morgue, he had not slept in more than a day.

He concentrated on the monitors, hoping their lucid, motionless views might act as a soporific, but their cold light and vacant venues chilled him. Ordway wondered how Bulov had found Scheibl. How had he known his hiding place, the plans for him to take the car with the money to the airport for the trip to Mexico City, the location of the car? Only Ordway, Booth, and Magnuson had known all this. Wasn't that right? Who else could have known?

He closed his eyes to shut out the chill monitor eyes, but when the bloody corpse of Ludwig Scheibl rose behind his eyelids, he quickly snapped his eyes open again.

Suddenly, at the corner of one eye, somewhere down the line of monitors, Ordway sensed a flicker of movement. He turned quickly, startled. Which monitor was it? He forced himself to move his eyes methodically from one to another, over dozens of them, examining each. He had been wrong. Nothing moved, there was no life, nothing . . .

Then it was there again! Something moved on a monitor he had examined a moment before. He fixed his eyes on this single window and saw the figure of a man. A guard? A policeman? A stray Olympian out for a pre-dawn run?

Ordway rose from the director's chair and moved around the console counter to examine the monitor closely. There was a man. He was tiny, no more than two inches tall on the miniaturized TV image. The monitor was numbered 145. A small legend beneath the number indicated that this camera was located on a mobile derrick outside the Los Angeles Coliseum. The camera commanded a low aerial view of the eastern end of the stadium exterior—the famous peristyle—and a street with a palm tree—plus the lone figure who was now pacing, constantly pacing.

Ordway watched, almost holding his breath. The figure was so small, the area so gloomy, that he could not tell what the man looked like. The pacing continued. Ordway stepped back and checked to see if there was anything moving on other monitors. Nothing. But suddenly the pictures on all the monitors looked odd—different somehow.

Then he realized what was happening: The earliest beginning of dawn was breaking over Los Angeles. Through the lifeless eyes of those three hundred TV cameras, he was seeing daylight rise slowly like some kind of grand cosmic stagelighting.

As the gloom lightened steadily Ordway could see the pacing man more clearly. He stood at the entrance of the Coliseum and often glanced at his watch. Suddenly the man seemed to snap to attention, as if he had heard a sound. He raised his head abruptly. Now his face was illuminated by the soft morning light and Ordway gasped.

Bulov!

Ordway's first thought was to call the police, but then he decided there was no point in doing that yet. He found a pad of paper at Magnuson's working space and quickly jotted down the monitor number—145—and the camera location. He returned to the monitor and watched the Russian with a sense of helplessness.

Bulov still seemed to be staring intently off into the distance, but now the set of his shoulders changed. He lifted his head expectantly. Someone was arriving beyond the camera's range. Bulov stiffened. He spun around quickly and began to run. Three men dashed into the monitor's view. One threw himself at Bulov's legs. The other two men jumped on him.

Suddenly Ordway remembered that Magnuson had told him how it was possible to tape every scene in front of the MBC cameras just by speaking the proper code into the computer microphone. The words had stuck in his mind: "Record-Omni." Ordway sprinted to the console, grabbed the computer mike, and spoke the words. He heard a whirring in the innards of the console.

On Monitor 145, Bulov was still down beneath the three men. Then, as quickly as it had started, the fight was over. The three men rose slowly and stood for a moment looking down on the still form of Ivan Bulov. They grouped themselves around the Russian, lifted him, and carried him—arms dangling and head-lolling loosely—out of camera range.

Ordway gazed at the monitor. The street was deserted. There was nothing more to see. But he had taped the last minute or two of the episode. He could prove to the police that, whatever this bizarre incident was, it *had* occurred.

His heart was pounding furiously. He reached for the telephone again to—what? Tell the police? He held the phone absently for a moment. Suddenly he saw another movement flicker on monitor 145. A very tall man with hair so white it seemed fluorescent in the morning light emerged from the darkness of an archway, a few yards from the spot where Ivan Bulov had been attacked. This man walked quickly across the screen, hesitated slightly at the

place where Bulov had been brought down, then resumed
a rapid pace out of sight.

Ordway gasped in disbelief. He raised his eyes as if in
prayer to the opaque black spaces above him. He must be
losing his mind.

Booth was pleased. He reached into the glove compartment for the bottle of Scotch and gulped twice as he drove.
The clean morning light proclaimed a glorious day for the
Olympic Games, and the messy loose ends of Ivan Bulov
and Ludwig Scheibl seemed, at last, to have been tied up.
The KGB men had been more brutal, less cautious than
Booth would have liked. They were lucky, purely that, that
some police car or security guard had not come upon them
as they attacked Bulov. Ah, well, God knows he was used
to dealing with human imperfections.

Booth sighed as he spun the steering wheel and turned
off the freeway to Games Control. He had only to face Joe
Ordway now, listen to his accusations about Bulov, en-
courage him to tell the police. . . . It would be simple, it
would be neat. The final small flaw had been corrected in
the massive workings of the *Igry* conspiracy.

Booth showed his pass to the guard at the gate and drove
to the Games Control center.

Ordway was slumped in the large leather chair on the set
he would occupy during the telecasts. His eyes were closed
and he was breathing heavily. He looked oddly small and
insignificant, a pale, weary man slouched in resignation.
He was unshaven and his clothes were rumpled. The set
and the chair seemed to overwhelm him.

Booth took a deep breath, then said softly, "I'm here,
Joe. Sorry about the delay."

At the sound of Booth's voice Ordway bolted to an upright posture that fairly trembled with tension. His voice
was hoarse. "Robin? I didn't know when to expect you."
He seemed stricken, his eyes wide and haunted. He shrugged

his shoulders, rolled his head, rubbed his face. "I've been dozing, I guess," he said. "You woke me up." He looked at Booth with an odd, wary expression.

Booth forced his mind to slow down, to take this all with one cautious step at a time. Why was Ordway so tense? Booth's voice was low and very cool. "Relax, Joe. You need sleep. You've got the biggest day of your life coming up. What's the matter?"

Ordway sank back in the chair. His hands were trembling. "I just can't get the sight of Scheibl out of my mind. He was . . . he was just charred raw meat from the waist down."

Booth decided to play the role of the hard-nosed coach; Ordway would understand that. His voice was firm: "Get that out of your mind, Joe. You can't jeopardize everything we've got going tomorrow just because that little sleaze was killed . . ."

Ordway shook his head as if to clear the cobwebs. "Okay. Okay . . ."

But Booth sensed an uncharacteristic wariness in Ordway. It was more than shock or nervousness. It seemed to be directed at him. Booth looked at his watch—5:15 A.M. The MBC crew would begin assembling at seven. The technicians would meet first with John Magnuson. At eight the on-air performers, along with the writers and editors, would gather.

Booth spoke with urgency. "What did the police say, Joe? You didn't mention Bulov, did you?"

Ordway hesitated just a tick. His eyes darted toward the wall monitors. "No. They were trying to figure some kind of a terrorist angle. I told them, ah, I told them that was ridiculous, ah . . . I tried to convince them, I tried, ah . . ."

"Joe. What the *hell* is the matter? You're acting like some kind of a cornered animal."

Ordway shifted in his chair. Again his eyes flicked involuntarily toward the wall of monitors. "Nothing is wrong," he said. His voice was wooden.

Booth was alarmed. As he had always said, if there was one thing Joe Ordway was not, it was an actor. There was something very wrong. Booth turned to examine the wall of monitors. He moved slowly to the console by Magnuson's chair. He picked up the pad of paper on which Ordway had scrawled the words: "Monitor 145, east end of Coliseum." Casually, Booth moved along the wall of monitors until he came to number 145. He saw the street, the Coliseum wall, the archway where he had hidden during the attack on Bulov. He willed his mind to stay calm and efficient. He realized instantly what had been wrong: the mobile derrick had been rolled to this location the day before, a location he had not known about. It was an amazing coincidence. The derrick could have been at any of a hundred other locations around the vast exterior of the Coliseum. But it had been *there*, exactly where Bulov had been attacked, exactly where Booth had passed when he left the darkened archway. It was obvious that Ordway had witnessed what went on there.

Booth decided to stay on the offensive. He walked quickly back to Ordway, stood over him, and fixed him with a burning gaze. "You saw them take down Bulov and you saw me, too, didn't you?" Booth's delivery was sharp, accusing—as if Ordway were in the wrong somehow.

"What were you doing there?" Ordway's voice was soft, uncertain.

Booth felt confidence rising. He had no reason to fear Joe Ordway. He said crisply, "I arranged for them to take down Bulov. They were from the KGB. Bulov killed Scheibl. He had to be removed."

Ordway looked at him in alarm. "You *know* that Bulov killed Scheibl?"

"Bulov was with the KGB. It was part of a mutual arrangement, a setup that was done to keep that little creep from ruining the Olympics."

Ordway's eyes widened. "What are you talking about? 'Mutual arrangement' with the KGB?"

Exhaustion and confusion lent Ordway's face an abject, almost pleading look. He seemed to be struggling to hold himself together. By contrast, Booth felt energized, exalted, omnipotent.

He spoke calmly. "Joe, I not only knew about Ivan Bulov killing Scheibl, I knew long ago that the Russians were going to come to Los Angeles. I knew that this Olympics would be unmatched in the history of sports. I knew all of it, Joe, because I was the single major force behind it. I was the cause."

Ordway shook his head in bewilderment.

Feeling extremely relaxed and very much in charge, Booth sat back on the edge of the desk in front of Ordway. The set was dimly lighted; the vast building was silent. Booth spoke clearly, with careful, didactic enunciation, as if he were giving a slow learner a complex lesson. He began, "*Igry* is the Russian word for 'games,' Joe . . ."

Succinctly, efficiently, he sketched the genesis of the conspiracy and all that went afterward—his visit with the KGB chief K-1, the use of MBC News correspondents' reports as Soviet intelligence, the role of Ivan Bulov, the methods and manners of annihilation . . .

His step-by-step unraveling of the horrors of Operation *Igry* produced an increasing stillness in Ordway that was almost hypnotic. Methodically Booth listed each and every victim and explained with thumbnail brevity how each of the thirty-five athletes had met his or her demise. He concluded crisply, "The Russians and their satellites will run away with the Olympics. They will win more gold medals than ever in history. We will get fantastic ratings for doing a historic series of shows. Then in the autumn we ascend through the heavens, Joe, to our own new kingdom of good works on television. It is a thoroughly happy ending."

Now that he had finished, Booth experienced a surge of pleasure so extreme that he felt momentarily lightheaded. He also knew exactly what Ordway's reaction would be—and he knew exactly how to deal with it.

Just as Booth expected, after a thunderstruck silence Ordway suddenly leaped out of his chair and bellowed, "You son of a bitch!" His fists were clenched. "What makes you think I'll go along with this, this *massacre?* Do you think I'm a . . . a . . . do you think I'm like *you?*" He choked on his anger.

Booth did not move. Ordway fumbled at the telephone on the desk. Booth said quietly, "Don't pick up the phone, Joe. No one is going to believe you. It's your word against mine. There's no way I can be connected with any of it. Even if someone checks the list of athletes against what actually happened, there's no way of proving they were connected either. It won't stick, Joe."

"The hell it won't! I'll get someone to check out where Bulov was during every one of those killings. I'll check where *you* were. The correspondents' reports. I'll find some way to tie it all together, goddamnit . . . I'm not going to let you get away with it." He began punching phone buttons.

Booth's voice was sharp. "Joe! They won't believe you. I'll tell them you were trying to blackmail me! You were desperate, panicky, out of your mind. You were crazy to get revenge against me!"

Ordway paused. "Revenge? Blackmail? What the hell are you talking about?"

"Put down the phone and listen." Booth reverted to his schoolmaster's enunciation. "I have a safety deposit box in New York filled with a folder of documents and a roll of telephone tapes. It all refers to you. It refers to a certain time in your life, to the year 1965, to two football games in which you played for the Chicago Icemen. They were not crucial games, either of them. One was against the St. Louis Cardinals, the other against the New York Giants. The Icemen were favored to win both of those games, Joe, but they lost them. Do you know what I'm talking about?"

Ordway's face drained of color. His lips were gray, his features stiff with shock. Booth saw that his blow had been perfectly timed, perfectly thrown.

Booth went on, "You remember it well, Joe, I'm sure. You were married to that whore Mimi Manning. Her gambling debts had got out of hand in Vegas. You got a call from Jack Donatti, the man at the Palms Club there, and he told you that not only did she owe fifty thousand dollars but that her behavior had been so bad the Palms management was going to send out a nationwide blackball on her. No clubs would book her, no theaters, no movie studios. You knew, of course, Joe, that Jackie Donatti and his friends could make anything happen if they wanted. So he suggested—you know all of this, I know, but I just want you to have no doubt that *I* know it, too—he suggested that you could settle her debt and possibly keep her career alive if you just managed to do a favor or two for Donatti and some of his friends in Las Vegas. Remember?"

Ordway had not taken his eyes off Booth's face, but Booth could see that the man was being transformed as he talked. His eyes were gradually becoming more sunken. His features had begun to sag into an expression of immense melancholy. Ordway's expression was that of an old, old man facing the knowledge that he had been caught, at long last, by his own death.

Booth went on. "So you went ahead and did what they suggested, Joe. In the St. Louis game you faked an injury to your shoulder. It had happened before; no one was suspicious. The Icemen lost twenty-one to nineteen, even though they had been favored by ten points. A lot of money changed hands. Then there was the Giants game. Very close, a tough game to call. You guys were favored by one point,

right? It got to the last two minutes. You had had a fairly
good game, but again you missed a pass that could have
been a touchdown. You were behind by one point, but you
were driving toward a score, certainly a field goal. Then
you fumbled. You remember it, Joey, a fumble on their
twenty-three-yard line as you took the ball from the center.
You hadn't fumbled even once before that in the pros. Not
in—what was it?—three seasons, thirty games or so. But
you did now. A fumble that cost the Icemen the game. Do
you remember all this?"

Ordway stared out of receding eyes. Booth went on
briskly, "You may ask how I can prove all this, why I have
any better chance of making people believe all this than you
have of making them believe what I told you about *Igry*.
I do have proof. Jackie Donatti, you may recall, got in a
scrape of some kind with the mob and was killed. But before
that happened, he was trying to save his skin and he told
the FBI about what you had done. He told them about
Mimi's gambling and he told them about those two fixed
games. Also, he had taped his conversations with you, Joe.
Do you know what the FBI did with Jackie Donatti's tapes
and with the affidavit they got from his spelling out all the
details concerning you and your fixed games? The FBI gave
it to the league office. They asked the league if they didn't
want to do something about this quarterback who was willing to fix games for this whore-bitch of a wife he had. And
do you know what happened then?"

Ordway had not moved.

"The league took all that prima facie evidence, took the
proof that you—Joe Ordway, the dream boy of pro football—had fixed two games. They took it and examined it
and talked it over and then told the FBI to forget about it.
You see, the one thing pro football didn't need at that point
was a scandal. The game was on the brink of incredible
things. The biggest television contract in history was being
negotiated right then. The whole damned future of the game

was on the line right then, Joe. The league simply couldn't afford to blow the whistle on you at a time that was so crucial to the success of the whole sport."

Booth paused to let that sink in, then he went on softly, "You were in a position to bring down the whole sport, Joe. You could have ruined everything. So the league saved you, kept you going. They weren't wrong, Joe. You weren't a dishonest player, you weren't a gambler. You were just a dumb Nebraska kid smitten with fucking a famous sex bomb. Once you got rid of Mimi Manning you were yourself again and everyone lived happily ever after. Pro football went on to become a national institution. And so, for Christ's sake, did you. And the FBI didn't give a damn about it, because once Jackie Donatti was killed they didn't have to knock over a starry-eyed kid quarterback.

"However, one of the agents did come to me with an idea for a great TV exposé a year or so later. He had left the FBI, but he thought I might be interested in this little bit of rot on the pristine skin of pro football. I bought all the evidence he had. The phone tapes, the affidavits, the dollars-and-cents stuff from the Las Vegas books about how much and who bet what money on those two games. I bought all of it from him for fifty thousand dollars and then I buried it. I buried it, Joe, for all time, never to be seen again.

"I haven't mentioned it to anyone else since then. Almost twenty years. Of course, I never forgot about it either."

Booth was finished. Ordway's eyes were as unfocused as a dead man's. He was shaking his head from side to side in continuing negative movements that were almost imperceptible.

"I need a drink." His voice was hollow. Booth poured him a glass of Scotch. Ordway took two deep swallows. Booth waited.

Ordway squeezed his eyes tightly closed, as if to shut

out all that had happened. He took a deep breath and opened his eyes. "I'm okay." He stood up. "Okay, I'm okay. I need sleep. Two, three hours. That'll be enough. Tell John I'll be back by ten. I know all the setups. I'm okay, I'm okay."

Booth watched Ordway's broad shoulders disappear through the gloom. He heard the door close with a bang. Booth sipped his Scotch. Ordway had reacted precisely as he had expected. Booth looked at his watch. Ten minutes to six. What the hell was he doing drinking in the morning? On this morning of all mornings. He had all the pre-broadcast meetings, the opening ceremonies . . . Christ, he had almost forgotten that he was going to watch the ceremonies with the president of the International Olympic Committee and the President of the United States.

The gate slowly swung open, activated by the guard in his bulletproof booth, and Ordway slammed the accelerator to the floor. He burst out of the security corral, and swung in a screeching turn up the curving ramp to the freeway. Which freeway it was, he did not now remember nor did he care. His head was throbbing and suddenly he experienced a sensation of suffocation that made him physically gag. Desperate, he rolled down the window to let in some fresh early morning air. But this was Los Angeles, and even at this early hour, he found the air warm and acrid. He rolled up the window and turned on the air conditioning. Then, shut away as if in his own personal incubator, he slammed the accelerator to the floor again.

His mind was functioning only insofar as it was required to keep him hurtling along the freeway. Time passed. Traffic grew thicker. He pounded the horn again and again, dodging in and out of traffic lanes. He drove for an hour, then two. At last he heard a siren. Blinking red lights filled his rearview mirror.

Exhausted, he pulled to the edge of the road. A California

highway patrolman loomed at his window. With his domed crash helmet and opaque goggles, the policeman seemed to be from an alien race. For a second Ordway was tempted to slam his foot on the accelerator and blast off into the traffic again, the man was that frightening to see. Yet reflexively, he turned on his famous smile. He said, "I'm sorry, officer, but I was in a hurry to get to the Games Control center. I overslept."

Ordway was unshaven and haggard looking. The patrolman leaned closer and stared at Joe through his blue goggles. The only human feature visible was his mouth set in a tight, thin line. Then it softened in a smile. "Joe Ordway? You're Joe Ordway?"

Ordway nodded. "Yeah. And I'm in a real hurry."

The patrolman's smile became downright enthusiastic. "Awright! It's a pleasure, Joe!" He paused, then said, "You say you're going to the MBC center. You're late? You're going to be one hell of a lot later if you keep going like this. You're going in the dead opposite direction."

Ordway shook his head in feigned bewilderment. "These things always screw me up."

The patrolman's grin cooled. "You drunk, Joe?" His voice was suspicious.

"Hell, no."

The voice coming from the mouth was brisk, authoritative. "You sure were driving like a drunk, Joe."

Ordway said, "Look, I have to go on the air in less than four hours. I've got to get to my hotel room and clean up. The Beverly Hills. Can you let me go?"

The patrolman paused, then reached in through the window and placed a black-gloved hand on Ordway's shoulder. The hand lay there heavily for a moment, then the officer clumsily patted him and said, "My kids think you're the greatest thing since sliced bread. Follow me, Joe."

Back in his room, Ordway dashed cold water on his face.

Suddenly a surprising sense of renewal washed over him. He sighed with relief. He had experienced it hundreds of times in his life. It was the sensation of the second wind, that always surprising, yet oddly inevitable surge of strength that rushed through his system at moments of deepest fatigue. In the past this had almost always occurred during football games—in those last frantic moments when the crowd's roar sounded like an avalanche about to engulf him and each ticking second crushed down on him like a ton of stones. Now it came to rescue him from the exhaustion and shock brought on by Robin Booth's revelations.

The man's capacity for evil was beyond belief—so revolting that Ordway had tried to withdraw from it. He had willed his mind to be empty. He had put himself into something like a trance. He had been like a child, covering his ears and hiding in a closet to avoid an unsavory truth. Now he realized it was not only the shock of this eerie morning that led him to react like a child: he had created an atmosphere of wishful, childlike pretense around his entire life.

The very environment from which he had drawn his identity, his very sense of self, was based on pretense and artificiality. Football was *pretending* to be something real. None of what he seemed to be was true. Certainly not his "heroism." Indeed, given the cheap and dismal secret he had kept for so long, *everything* he had come to be was based on a foundation of deception and pretense. Of course, his "crimes" were pale in comparison to the atrocities committed by Robin Booth. Yet in a way the very pettiness of his misdeeds made his role of American hero all the more absurd, all the more hypocritical.

What could he do about it? He knew that he had no real choice. None at all.

He undressed and stood in the shower for fifteen minutes. The soothing warm water bathed away the last remaining tension. He emerged feeling exhilarated. He shaved and dressed, then phoned Johnny Magnuson. It was nine thirty. He told the director he would be at Games Control in half an hour.

Magnuson's voice was relaxed and easy despite the pressures of the day. "Booth was here when I arrived. He said you were here all night because Scheibl was murdered. You okay?"

Ordway said calmly, "Absolutely. I never felt better. Booth and I were trying to figure out how to get at Ivan Bulov. There's no doubt that he killed Scheibl."

Magnuson said, "That's what Booth said. He also said he tried to call the Soviet delegation and tell them about Bulov. They claimed Bulov wasn't there. In fact, they claimed he was never in Los Angeles at all. What the hell does it all mean?"

Ordway said, "They've probably shipped him out in a box. Where's Booth now?"

"At the hotel. He's one of the VIP's in the President's box at the opening ceremonies. You'll be here in half an hour? I'm going to need you for this little thing called the Olympic Games."

For a moment Ordway debated calling Maggie to tell her what he was about to do. He decided against it. She would see him at his moment of truth—as would about a billion people around the world.

Ivan Bulov felt like he was swimming up from the bottom of a deep brown river, struggling to pull himself out of the murk and turmoil. A low steady rushing sound filled his ears, and he imagined it might be a waterfall and that he was being carried toward its brink. He shouted in panic, fought to open his eyes. He felt a heavy hand on his left arm. It squeezed until the pain was almost unbearable. He opened his eyes. He was lying on his back, gazing up at a low curved ceiling covered in plastic. The roaring sound

continued and he realized he was on a small airplane. He
tried to move and found he was held in a reclining position
by straps bound around his chest, his stomach, his thighs,
and his ankles. His arms were free, however. Now the
painful grip on his left arm loosened and a hulking KGB
man moved back to his seat.

Bulov raised his head. He saw the three agents seated
in front of a small television set. The plane, obviously a
small jet, was carpeted, with leather seats, a parlorlike atmosphere. Bulov was strapped to a stretcher. A dull pain
throbbed at the base of his skull. He felt there gingerly with
his fingers. The sore spot was swollen like a bee sting, and
now he remembered what had happened outside the Coliseum. A wave of fear surged through him. It was as palpable
as pain. He let his head fall back on the stretcher. This was
what he had feared more than anything. He was being sent
back to Russia, a prisoner of the KGB, a victim for Gulinka.
The long years of self-preservation now stood for nothing.
He had sacrificed everything in order to live, and now he
had lost. He had lost all decency, all dignity, all sense of
virtue, in his quest for survival. He had, in a very real way,
killed himself in order to stay alive. He tried to concentrate
on this enigmatic truth. He had willed himself dead—had
he not?—so he could survive?

Was that it? It was confusing, bewildering. He opened
his eyes. If only he had a mirror. Perhaps that would help.
He asked one of the guards for a mirror. The man said,
"You want to admire your death mask, Ivan?" The man
grinned and his teeth, too, showed the ravages of Soviet
dentistry.

Bulov sighed and said softly, "No, I want to look at my
life mask."

The KGB man gave him a small makeup mirror from a
kit in the lavatory.

Bulov lay back and gazed up at the familiar terrain of

scars and stitchings. He saw that, in truth, he did not in any way resemble his admired Agent 007. He could never have, for 007 was a hero, a man of high intelligence and noble instincts. This heavy-featured face reflecting from the mirror belonged to a man who was stupid, selfish, disgusting to behold.

He had been a victim of his own success, Bulov supposed. He had committed himself to survival to such an extent that his life became meaningless—the more he succeeded at staying alive, the less his life was worth living. The intrinsic paranoia of Soviet society had led him to believe that he was in constant danger, whether he actually was or not. Natasha had been only the beginning. Now he possessed a string of victims—dead, crippled, ruined—that few human beings in history would ever want to claim.

Oddly enough, Bulov felt no remorse. He must have sold that, along with everything else. But he *was* still alive, was he not? Possibly there would still be some hope when he got to Moscow. Possibly he could convince K-1 to let him live. His survivor's mind began to click again. He could offer himself for some weird medical experiments! He could volunteer to fight in the combat zones of Afghanistan, to act as official assassin for dissidents and traitors. He wanted to live. He would do anything. He would kill anyone, betray *any* friend, commit any atrocity . . .

Bulov gazed at his face. It dawned on him that he had come to hate it. He closed his eyes and let the rush of the plane's engine fill his mind for the moment. . . .

Ordway knew that the tape existed. The Omni computer system had been recording everything from every Olympic camera—including the one focused on the set where Ordway and Booth had been. The tape was stored somewhere in the computer innards, and all Joe had to do was find it. When he entered Games Control at 10 A.M., the place was crowded with people.

Ordway approached Johnny Magnuson's command chair
at the console. Magnuson looked like the chief pilot of a
spaceship. Gauges and dials were aglow in front of him—
a welter of technology laid out like the lights of a city as
seen from the sky. From time to time Magnuson spoke
gently into the computer-activator microphone at his left
elbow. At other times he snapped crisp directions through
a chin mike to the army of cameramen and technicians
dispatched across the Olympic venues. The focal point of
today's telecast would be the opening ceremonies at the
Coliseum, where ten thousand Olympians would parade en
masse. MBC's worldwide feed would reach something over
a billion people from Red China to Zambia, from Vladi-
vostok to Nicaragua, from Australia to Alaska.

As Ordway watched over Magnuson's shoulder he heard
the man uttering orders to the computer. "Load Tape 155-
06 . . . load Tape 161-91 . . . load Tape 143-10 . . ."
Magnuson was working from a prepared master plan of pre-
cut tapes that would be interspersed with the live ceremonies
and events as the Games proceeded. For today's opening
there were brief snippets of tape showing a few seconds of
scenes from each nation in the parade. As a team of athletes
appeared marching behind their flag, Magnuson could call
up a tape that might, for example, show the humble homes
of some of the athletes in contrast to the crisp and dressy
uniformed appearance they made on parade. Their goal was
to go beyond the Olympic pomp and spectacle and remind
the world that these athletes were people with lives and
backgrounds that went deeper than mere games.

It was all part of Robin Booth's master plan for bringing
a new dimension to the games coverage.

Ordway greeted Magnuson, then said he was going to
get some breakfast in the Games Control cafeteria. He
crossed the set where he would introduce the first Olympic
telecast in less than two hours. Casually he examined the
camera there and saw that it was numbered 189. He strolled

down the corridor of tape editing cubbyholes until he found one that was empty. He picked up the computer-activator microphone and said quietly, "Load Tape 189—7-28-84."

He hunched over the small monitor in the editing table and, like magic, a picture appeared before him. It showed the set as it had been the night before, dimly lit and empty, but he could easily make out the table and chair where he and Booth had been. In the lower right-hand corner of the tape he saw that the date and the time, on a minute-by-minute basis, had been recorded to indicate precisely when the taping had occurred.

The time on the tape indicated that it began at 4:28 A.M., the moment at which Ordway had activated tape on all the cameras to pick up the assault of Ivan Bulov. He punched a fast-forward mechanism and the tape spun forward until it hit 5:00, 5:01, 5:02 . . . Now Ordway saw his own weary figure move across the set and sit down heavily in his chair. He let the tape progress at normal speed.

At 5:15 the tall figure of Robin Booth appeared. His white hair was like a halo in the dim light. Ordway turned the audio dial. The voice of Booth was clear as he sat on the edge of the table and spoke in a smug, professional way: "*Igry* is the Russian word for 'games,' Joe. The conspiracy began in the summer of 1980 when it was decided that a large number of Olympic athletes would have to be killed or somehow incapacitated so that the Soviet Union would be guaranteed at least a hundred and fifty gold medals here in Los Angeles. The conspiracy was originally my idea, but it was developed with the top powers in the Kremlin. The KGB was assigned to carry out the missions. Ivan Bulov was the number one hit man . . ."

Ordway felt a chill at the back of his neck as he again experienced the shock of Booth's revelation. He let the tape run to its conclusion, then rolled it back and racked it in the ready position. He went to talk with Johnny Magnuson.

* * *

Robin Booth entered the presidential box at fifteen minutes before noon. The Vice-President was there, along with the Secretary of State, an old friend of Booth's from Harvard. There were four dozen other people—United Nations officials, International Olympic Committee executive board members, as well as a contingent of California dignitaries; the governor, a senator, the president of the University Board of Regents, the mayor of Los Angeles, members of the local Olympic Organizing Committee. It was a gathering of power in which Booth felt very much at home. The two presidents—of the IOC and the U.S.A.—had not yet arrived.

Comfortably Booth shook hands around the group and wound up talking to the Secretary of State, who said, "Robin, you've got the finest political show since the Watergate hearings. It's the confrontation of the decade, old man, exclusively yours. Congratulations."

Booth was expansive, his face warm, his eyes alight. "Don't forget, Sam, we couldn't have done it without the Russians. Give credit where it's due for a change."

The Secretary of State shook his head in wonder. "They surprised us. We'd heard rumblings that they might come a couple of months earlier but it just didn't make much sense. Frankly, it still doesn't."

"They're a cunning bunch."

"They've always put a lot more stock in the value of gold medals than we have. But they're also lending their prestige to *our* Games."

Booth was about to reply when the two presidents arrived together. Both were beaming—the small Spanish aristocrat who was president of the IOC and the tall, ruddy-cheeked actor who was President of the United States. They shook hands around the group. Booth had met them both many times before and greeted them warmly, embracing the IOC president in the European manner and gripping the U.S. President's elbow as he shook his hand vigorously. There was a palpable air of triumph in the box already.

The program for the day called for the IOC president to open the Games. This would be followed by a pronouncement of welcome by the U.S. President. Although the United States had hosted the Olympic Games three times in the past sixty years, this was the first time an American President had appeared in person. Booth had known that the hambone actor in the U.S. President—plus his lifelong ties to Hollywood and California—wouldn't be able to pass up this chance. Besides that, this President had been openly hostile and outspoken in his dislike of communism.

The prospect of a confrontation between East and West was thus all the more dramatic. Without question these Olympics would be seen as a Cold War battleground of great significance. The stage was perfectly set, Booth thought, for one of the greatest television events ever.

Booth looked at the large TV screens situated about the presidential box. There were a dozen of them, each an oversized thirty-six-inch screen, all tuned to the MBC feed. Booth turned to the President and said, "Mr. President, you're presiding at a moment of tremendous hope in the history of this country."

The President grinned and said in a whisper: "I've never been prouder of this country. We will wipe the bastards out." He winked and said, "Off the record, of course, Robin."

Booth winked back. He took a Scotch from the tray proffered by a white-jacketed waiter and sat back to witness history. It was, of course, his own self-created and personally produced version of history. The feeling of omnipotence was overwhelming. It was a rare and magnificent sensation.

The first notes of the Ninth Symphony sounded in Ordway's ears. His heart was pounding, his throat was dry, and he felt a vast nauseated hole where his stomach should have been. Yet even as Beethoven's strains thundered through his mind, he felt his confidence surging, and suddenly he was basking in the knowledge that he could do no wrong.

He gazed at his monitor and saw MBC's taped opening for the Olympics. A helicopter-carried camera sped low over the terrain of the Games, then rose high into the sky as it flew out over the Pacific Ocean.

The music rose to a crescendo and Ordway heard Magnuson's voice in his earphone: "This is the biggest one you'll ever do, Joe. Go for it."

Ordway's microphone was on and he spoke his scripted lines: "These are the Games of 1984 held in that most American setting of them all—the sprawl of Los Angeles—land of smog and honey—symbolic capital of the United States of America. And this is the twenty-third quadrennial festival of brotherhood and sportsmanship. Here we celebrate the political neutrality of games. Here we celebrate individual humanity. Here we celebrate exquisitely conditioned men and women performing to standards that lie beyond the reach of most mere mortals. . . ."

The music rose again and the MBC cameras now showed the scene in the Coliseum, live. There were 103,000 people in shirtsleeves and summer dresses. The stadium rim was alive with flags snapping in the warm wind. An orchestra struck up the Olympic Hymn, then played "The Star Spangled Banner." The crowd stood with bowed heads.

The ceremonies proceeded smartly. The president of IOC spoke briefly and simply, declaring Los Angeles to be "sacred Olympic territory." The President of the United States spoke next. His silky, practiced baritone sounded as soothing as a cello over the public address system. He said: "These Games will be historic, unforgettable, in that they offer almost all mankind on earth today the opportunity to witness what goes on here." He paused, then spoke sharply: "For that reason, we hope it will be something more than mere games. We hope this Olympiad will prove something about the way men and women live, about the system of government under which they live as well as the stars under which they are born. All men are not created equal. Nor are all political systems. We are convinced that when these Games are done, the world TV audience—a *billion* strong—will see which system is victorious. History will be made here. We are convinced it will be *American* history."

The crowd applauded. The orchestra struck up a smart march and the parade of Olympic teams began.

Magnuson said quietly into Ordway's ear, "Okay, Joe. Go ahead."

Ordway saw the camera light blink on before him. He was on camera, and the whole world saw him now instead of the Coliseum ceremony. He spoke very carefully: "This is an unscheduled emergency break. The ceremonies are continuing in the Los Angeles Coliseum. But there will be no Olympic Games this year." He paused to let those words sink in. Then he went on. "The following incident occurred early this morning. The speaker is Robin Booth, chairman of the board of the Metro Broadcasting Corporation. Please listen closely. Foreign networks, be prepared to translate from English into your national language . . ."

Ordway sat back tensely and watched his monitor as the tape of Robin Booth's confession began: "*Igry* is the Russian word for 'games' . . ."

The KGB men were grouped around the television set at the front of the plane's cabin. Bulov could not see the screen, but he heard the familiar voice of Joe Ordway speaking over the strains of music. He continued to gaze glumly at his face in the mirror. He heard the IOC president and the American President make their speeches. His mind wandered for a moment . . .

Then he heard Ordway's voice sharpen. ". . . an unscheduled emergency break . . . Translate . . . into your national language . . ."

Next came the voice of—could it be?—the voice of the Gamesman! Never had Bulov heard such terrifying words. ". . . *Igry* is the Russian word for 'games,' Joe. The conspiracy began in the summer of 1980 when it was decided that a large number of Olympic athletes would have to be killed or somehow incapacitated . . . Ivan Bulov was the number one hit man . . ."

Bulov became very calm as he listened. He watched in the mirror as his face settled into a mask of Buddha-like resignation. He heard gasps from the KGB man who understood English. He heard his breathless translation into Russian for the others. He heard them suck in their breath in fear and disbelief. He felt them looking at him in horror. Even they—the paid apes and assassins of the Soviet socialist state—were shocked at the things Ivan Bulov had done to those innocent young athletes.

He continued to stare at his face in the mirror. His hatred for that face was now all-consuming. He could do but one thing about it.

He felt an extreme, almost euphoric calm envelop him as he smashed the mirror against the iron pipe of his stretcher. He felt very relaxed as he picked a long pointed shard from the shattered surface. He held his finger against his jugular vein until he felt the spot that lay against the hardness of his trachea. Quite easily and without much discomfort he pressed the sharp bit of mirror glass against the pulsing vein and sliced once across it. A geyser of blood rose high above his face like a ruby fountain. At the top of its arc it lost its momentum and fell, splashing over his face, his neck, his chest. The last image he saw was that of Natasha, and oddly enough her face was happy and peaceful as it had always been after making love. It was a face that forgave him.

* * *

More than a minute passed before anyone in the presidential box noticed that the picture on their television screens had nothing to do with the events underway on the Coliseum track. The parade went on. The music was crisp and martial, and rank after rank of athletes strode in time to it. The team from Greece was the first in the line, Angola was just behind, followed by Argentina, Australia, Belgium. . . . The Greek flag bearer had just reached the point in front of the presidential box where he would dip his flag in deference to the head of state of the host nation when the Secretary of State said sharply, "What the hell?" He reached over and turned up the volume on a TV set. The voice of Robin Booth filled the box. The Secretary of State was staring at Booth in disbelief.

The President of the United States turned to look at his set. Booth was saying now, ". . . So, Joe, it was not hard to put down thirty-five athletes. No one really even noticed. The first one was murdered by Ivan Bulov . . ."

Booth saw himself on the tube. He heard his words. For an instant he was totally disoriented. What was this? How could he be on his own network? The program called for the *parade*. Where had this come from?

It was only a matter of seconds before he realized exactly what was happening. Tapes had been running all during his recital to Ordway. He could not stop them now.

He watched grimly as he unraveled every last thread of *Igry*. The entire presidential box was silent now. Booth's voice, arch and entirely too pleased with its own sound, crackled on and on. Below on the Coliseum track the parade went on. Athletes continued streaming past. Each flag carrier dipped his banner as he passed before the American President. But the President acknowledged none of the salutes. He sat ashen-faced, staring at the set as if hypnotized. Without taking his eyes from the TV set, he beckoned a

Secret Service man to his side and whispered in his ear. The man nodded. He motioned to two other guards in the box, who then quietly stationed themselves at Robin Booth's back.

As Booth's voice went on, smugly listing each of the thirty-five victims of *Igry*, Ordway felt himself slowly unwind. He rose and walked slowly to Johnny Magnuson's chair. He stood there with one hand on the director's slim shoulder.

As Booth neared the end of his revelations Ordway's grip tightened. Magnuson looked up. Ordway said, "John, you haven't seen the whole tape. Don't switch it off. Don't stop anything."

Magnuson said, "What are you talking about? There's *more?*"

Ordway said, "Yeah. A little more."

Games Control was silent as Booth completed his recital of the *Igry* plot. This was as far as Magnuson had watched the tape.

Now the large monitor in front of Magnuson showed Ordway's angry reaction to Booth, his attempt to reach for the telephone, Booth's sharp retort that Ordway could never make anyone believe the *Igry* story. Then came Booth's recital of Ordway's crime—the betrayal of his game by the great Joey O.

Now the shocked faces of the Games Control technicians turned to look at Joe. Ordway stood with bowed head.

When the tape was finished, Johnny Magnuson turned to look at him in dismay. "Joe, for Christ's sake! Why did you let me play it? We didn't need it . . . Joe . . ." His voice faded and he gazed sadly at Joe Ordway.

PART VII

May 1986

MAY 28, 1986
Blooming Prairie, Nebraska

Ordway squinted in the morning sunshine. The ribbon of highway streaked on ahead of him without a wrinkle in it, zooming straight for miles before it vanished in the green dazzle of the wheat fields. The eternal dome of late spring sky stretched unbroken in a full circle around him. It was an openness of a kind no easterner, no mountain man, no woodsman could know. Nebraska. He was home. He spoke quietly to Maggie. "Nothing quite prepares you for this kind of space, does it? I'd really forgotten."

She looked up and said, "How long has it been?"

"Twenty-one years. I never had a reason to come back."

"Well, now you do."

He scowled through the windshield. "I hope I do. I hope

I'm doing the right thing. It all still feels so . . . so. *raw*. They might stone me. Or boo me."

She said gently, "You don't think I'll clear your name with this?" She held up a copy of her book, a slim volume titled *Martyrs & Heroes*. It was, in part, a biography of Ordway as a paradigm of twentieth-century heroism. She had woven into his life story the tales of the thirty-five Olympians who had been put down in the *Igry* conspiracy. Her way of interstitching their fates with the fate of Joe Ordway resulted in a series of mirrorlike parallels that ended up defining the lives and times of modern athletes in a manner never done before.

He laughed. "Christ, Maggie. I don't think anyone in Nebraska will understand what you're up to."

Maggie's book was to be published within the month. Already it had received some advance reviews that labeled it a significant piece of sociological work. One academic critic wrote: "Ms. O'Rourke brings into sharp relief the shadowy yet pervasive sense of paranoia that infects our society. In *Martyrs & Heroes* we can clearly identify the source of that paranoia: it is the ultimate power of technology to control us. In this case it is the technology of mass media as it controlled Joe Ordway—and ultimately dictated the fates of thirty-five helpless, luckless Olympians. Like the subjects of Big Brother in Orwell's *1984*, we are faced with a definitively omnipotent force in this growing technology: Will we lose *all* control over our own destinies? The answer seems to be yes, according to Ms. O'Rourke . . ."

Ordway was right: the book was not intended as bedtime reading in a Nebraska farmhouse. And he really did not know whether the tidal waves of controversy that followed his Olympic telecast had died away. For nearly two years now he had kept almost entirely to himself, with Maggie, at the two-hundred-year-old farm they had purchased in upstate New York. He had spent most of that time tending the orchards and working the vineyard there, insulated from the stormy public reaction produced by his revelations. He had testified in New York at the trial of Robin Booth, heard himself reviled by the defense attorney as "a cheap fixer, a spoiler of sports," and had felt only sadness when Booth was sent to prison. There had been some talk among a few zealous fans and sportswriters that Ordway should stand trial for his "crimes against football." Of course, the statute of limitations had run out, but more to the point, he was considered both a martyr and a hero by a good-sized segment of the American public. Still, he had continued to receive a frighteningly large amount of hate mail, and for a time he had paid to have a sheriff's deputy stand guard at the isolated farmhouse.

"Do you think it's really finished?" he asked.

"Yes, I do, but we'll find out for sure very soon," she said.

At last, far ahead, a shiny speck appeared on the flat green horizon. He could not really see it, but he knew it was the silver barrel of the Blooming Prairie water tower, the highest structure for miles around on its spidery steel legs. As the car sped closer he could make out the slope-shouldered roof of the grain elevator and then some houses, and soon they passed the sign that said they had entered the "city limits" of Blooming Prairie, Nebraska, population 751.

He drove slowly through the hamlet, out the other side, then turned around in a farm driveway and returned. He swallowed drily and said, "Damn, I'm nervous as hell."

She patted his hand. "Don't be."

They pulled up in front of the school, the same red brick pile that Ordway had attended so many years ago. The front steps and lawn were crowded with people, most of them students. A couple of dozen wore caps and gowns. When Ordway and Maggie moved toward the crowd, the people gaped and gazed, then moved aside in silence, opening a path for them. Joe and Maggie climbed the steps and entered

the cool gloom of the school. A man came forward, iden-
tified himself as the principal, and greeted them softly. His
demeanor was as somber as an undertaker's. He ushered
them silently through the empty auditorium to the stage
where they were shown their seats. In moments the auditorium filled with people from outside. Still no one spoke.
Members of the school band, in uniform, filed in and took
their seats below the stage and soon broke into a version
of "Pomp and Circumstance" so sour-sounding that it was
almost comic.

The graduating seniors assembled solemnly on the stage.
A man in black said a prayer and the audience recited the
Pledge of Allegiance. The principal spoke briefly in welcome and then introduced Joe Ordway, the commencement
speaker for the Class of '86.

Ordway had written a speech and began to read from it.
But it seemed all wrong now. It made no reference to his
own fall from grace or to the telecast in Los Angeles. It
seemed too cold, too impersonal, too *devious* to read to
these people who shared his heritage. So Joe looked up and
said, "I have something else to say to you."

He paused, then told the story of his childhood visit to
Jim Thorpe. It took a while to tell and the whole time there
was not so much as a cough heard from the audience. He
concluded the story in total silence. Then he swallowed and
spoke gently, "I have felt at times in the past two years that
I disappointed all of you just as much as Jim Thorpe disappointed me. But, you know, he was only human. And
so am I. Human. Fallible. Weak. Real. I'm not an image
polished up for television consumption. Not anymore. I'm
not a product, packaged and priced and merchandised for
the profits of big business, big technology, big sports. Not
anymore. I don't have to pretend any longer that I am an
idol or a hero or a paragon. I am Joe Ordway, born and
raised in Blooming Prairie. I am a man, nothing more and

nothing less. Being here with you is like being reborn.
Thank you."

The silence continued briefly, then Ordway detected
some odd sounds here and there in the crowd. They resem-
bled gasps, hiccups, whimpers. He realized they were sobs.
Someone in a far back corner began to clap, slowly and
firmly. And someone else stood up and in another minute
everyone was standing and everyone was applauding. Ordway felt a start of surprise as he gazed at the faces of all
those people and saw that many of them, maybe most of
them, were shiny with tears. He felt tears brimming in his
eyes, too, and he turned to Maggie and said, "It's over. It's
all over."